THE
SHADOW
OF
WAR

With Best Wishes

Preface

I have used Lyn Macdonald's 'The Roses of No Man's Land', Olive Dent's 'A VAD in France', and Vera Brittain's excellent autobiography for contextual detail and other details of a VAD's life and conditions of employment during the First World War. For historical reference I have mainly relied on John Keenan's excellent historical narrative, 'The First World War'. The events, people and places within The Shadow of War are fictitious. Any similarity to any person living or dead is merely coincidental. I would like to dedicate this book to Dave Wood, without whose generosity and hard work both my manuscripts would still be lying in a dusty drawer, John Scutt, who kindly read my manuscript encouraged me and kept me focused, and Moggie, who simply listened and advised.

Mel Owen, June 2011

I would like to thank everyone who helped and supported me during the
writing of 'The Shadow of War', especially Fenney Musgrave. However my
particular thanks must go to Dave Wood, without whom none of this would
have been possible.

Matador
9 Priory Business Park
Kibworth Beauchamp
Leicestershire LE8 0RX, UK
Tel: (+44) 116 279 2299
Fax: (+44) 116 279 2277
Email: books@troubador.co.uk
Web: www.troubador.co.uk/matador

The events, people and places within The Shadow of
War are fictitious. Any similarity to any person living or dead is merely
coincidental.

ISBN 978-1780885-148

British Library Cataloguing in Publication Data.
A catalogue record for this book is available from the British Library.

Cover Illustration © Derek Colligan 2012
Book design © Dave Wood 2012
Typeset in Perpetua

Printed and bound in the UK by TJ International, Padstow, Cornwall

Matador is an imprint of Troubador Publishing Ltd

THE
SHADOW
OF
WAR

J. M. Owen

1

She knew that she had to get to The Hall, her very being depended on it, but she didn't know why. It was a cloudy night and the driveway was dark, it was almost pitch black. She could hardly see where she was going and she was terribly afraid, but she soldiered on. She knew that she must. The only sound that she could hear was the sound of her boots crunching on the loose gravel, and each step sounded like a rifle volley. All she knew was that she had to get to The Hall; she knew that it was imperative, but she was beginning to struggle.

It had been a glorious summer's day and the latent heat was trapped in the leaves of the trees and bushes that bordered the driveway. As they swayed in the gently murmuring night breeze, they released warm fragrant memories of the beautiful day, and the heady scents from the newly mown grass and the annuals that bordered the driveway joined with them. They were intoxicating, and acted as an aphrodisiac that seduced Amy and made her want to cease in her quest. She had to fight a strong desire to sink onto the grass verge, and simply succumb to the warmth of the summer evening. However, she knew instinctively that she must resist the temptation, because the seductive night air, whilst it was pervasive, was also threatening. Like a slightly sinister yet extremely tempting lover that you knew you must resist.

Already tired, she was finding it an immense psychological and physical struggle to carry on. Each step involved huge effort. Her feet seemed to stick to the ground as if she were stepping in treacle; branches reached out onto the driveway and their knarled fingers clutched at her clothes, dragging her back; vines and tree roots seemed to have invaded the driveway with the express purpose of tripping her up. Her hair broke loose and strands fell on her face blinding and choking her. Yet still she struggled on. Why did she feel this desperate need to reach The Hall? She didn't understand she just knew she had to get there.

As she laboured on she could just make out a curve in the driveway ahead. Once she turned the bend, she knew that The Hall would come into sight. Then it was only a short walk to the front terrace and safety. Suddenly alarmed, she realised that another smell was mingling with the pleasant aromas of the warm summer's evening; it was the smell of smoke. Why hadn't she noticed it before? It was so strong it began to fill the air. It blotted out the pleasant scents of summer, and it made her gag and choke. She tried to run, but her skirt seemed to have grown longer, and it was wrapping itself around her legs and tripping her up. She became clumsy and kept losing her footing, her heart was racing and her lungs were bursting as she struggled with the obstacles that tried to hold her captive and prevent her reaching her destination.

At last she turned the bend in the driveway and as The Hall came into view, the moon came out from behind the clouds and cast a ghostly hue on the awful scene that greeted her. The Hall had disappeared; it had burned to the ground. All that was left in its place were blackened ruins. They stood outlined against the silver backdrop of moonlight like an open mouth full of rotten, jagged teeth that screamed in agony at the night. All was lost. Only these cruel ruins remained decorated here and there with wisps of dying smoke, which floated to the heavens taking her dreams with them. She felt herself screaming. She was too late, too late. Where was he? She would never find him now; he was lost to her forever.

She was screaming so loudly that she woke herself up. She had been dreaming about the fire again. Sometimes she felt that it would never leave her in peace. She lay still, quietly trying to get her bearings and it took her a few moments to work out where she was. She knew she was in bed, because she was all tangled up in her bedclothes and drenched in perspiration. Her heart was hammering in her chest as she tried to calm her breathing. She was safe, but exactly where was she? Then she remembered. The home, the residential home for the elderly, she had moved in yesterday. Eventually her eyes became accustomed to the dark and she began to recognise the few pieces of furniture that she had been allowed to bring with her, and their familiarity reassured her. Suddenly the door opened and light streamed in through the crack. It made her jump, but it was only one of the carers checking on her. She spoke softly.

'Are you alright Amy? Shall I put the light on, I heard you shout out, were you having a bad dream?' Even in her distress Amy wondered why young people felt that it was alright to call you by your first name when they hardly knew you. It made one feel so old and inconsequential, but this carer was a nice girl and meant no offence. She replied,

'Yes dear, please put the light on and come in, you were right, I had a bad dream and it woke me up.'

The carer came into the room. 'Would you like a cup of tea?'

'Yes I would, thank you very much.'

When she left the room Amy lay there musing for a while. The Hall, so long ago, would it ever stop dominating her dreams? Would she ever be free of the nightmare? It all happened so many years ago and still it haunted her. As soon as she felt calm enough, she climbed out of bed and wrapped herself in her dressing gown. She felt more tranquil now and she set about rearranging the sheets and remaking the bed. Once it was tidy she moved over to the dressing table. During her restless dream her long, grey, hair had escaped from its night time plaiting and looked knotted and unkempt. Deep in thought she unplaited it, brushed it through and then neatly replaited it. She then removed her dressing gown and her damp, dishevelled nightgown, which she discarded before retrieving a fresh one from her chest of drawers. Feeling rejuvenated she climbed back into bed just as the carer returned with two cups of tea. She put both of them on the bedside table and pulled up a chair.

'Oh Amy,' she reproached, 'You've tidied the bed and changed your nightdress, you should have let me help you with that.' As though to make up for not having straightened the bed herself the girl tucked in the sheets and smoothed the bed cover before sitting down. Amy studied her closely. She was quite young, early twenties she thought. A pretty girl, she had luxuriant, thick titian coloured hair, which was waist length and tied back with a white scarf.

'Oh it was no trouble. I'm quite used to looking after myself. You mustn't spoil me you know.' Amy smiled her thanks at the carer who was now handing her the tea.

'Do you mind if I stay and keep you company whilst we drink our tea? She asked, 'It's deadly dull tonight and I'd be glad of the company.'

Amy thought it more likely that she was staying to keep an eye on her and reassure her after her nightmare. Nevertheless, she was really rather grateful for the company and she told the girl she was welcome to stay. The fact was that her dream had rather unnerved her, as it usually did.

'Have you settled in here?' Tanya asked.

'Yes I think so. It's still a bit strange, but I'm sure I will be happy here. I'm grateful to have someone to care for me.' Amy smiled, 'It's early days yet.'

'Of course it is.' Tanya replied, 'What made you cry out? Were you having a bad dream?'

'Yes, I had a nightmare.'

'People often do, you know when they first come in here. It's being in a strange place, leaving their home and knowing that they will never return. It's very unsettling. Were you dreaming about your home?'

'In a way, yes, I was dreaming about The Hall, Leaversham Hall, I used to work there, you know. I dreamt that I was trying to get to The Hall, it was urgent. I had to find someone, but when I arrived The Hall had burned to the ground and all I found were smoking ruins. It's a dream I've had many times before.'

'Leaversham Hall,' Tanya murmured, 'Yes, I remember my mother telling me about a fire there in the 1920s. It was in Cheshire wasn't it?'

'That's right; it was reported in all the national newspapers because it was such an important house architecturally. It was a tremendous fire, a positive inferno which completely gutted the place and destroyed many fine works of art and some beautiful furniture.'

'Did you know The Hall well?'

Amy pondered for a moment before replying, 'Yes indeed, I lived and worked there as a lady's companion for many years. I was working there when it caught fire.'

'Wow!' exclaimed Tanya, 'I bet that was scary. What an experience. Maybe you would tell me about it some time? Not tonight though, I don't think that would be a good idea. You'd probably end up having another nightmare and I would be to blame! I wonder though, would you think I was being nosey if I asked you to tell me a little about your time there? It's a world that doesn't exist anymore and I find it intriguing. I'm a history student at Manchester University, and I'm particularly fascinated with life on those large estates before the First World War. If you hear about it from people who experienced it, it's far more helpful than just reading about it, because people supply the personal details that you never find in books.'

'I would be delighted to tell you about my past, but are you quite sure you want to listen to me reminiscing? You might be bored! Of course I'll tell you anything you want to know. It would be nice to have some company and I don't think I'll go back to sleep now, I'm too afraid of repeating my dream. I agree with you, it would be tempting providence to talk about the actual fire tonight Tanya, but I could tell you a little about my childhood. Is that the sort of thing that you want to hear about?'

Tanya nodded, 'Yes please, any little details you can think of. What is everyday and ordinary to you would be of great interest to me.'

'Right where shall I start? Well, I come from quite humble beginnings. I was born on 14th November 1896 in a little cottage on the Leaversham Hall Estate. It was only small. We had two rooms downstairs, a kitchen with a large black leaded range and there was a little scullery off the kitchen with a cold tap and a slop stone. The copper was in there too, you know the copper that we boiled the clothes in?' Tanya nodded. 'We lived in the kitchen, which was always warm and cosy. The range had to be kept lit summer and winter because we used it for hot water and all our cooking. There were two old rocking chairs and a settle in front of the range and a large pine table stood in the middle of the room. Upstairs there were two bedrooms and an attic room where I slept. How I loved that little cottage, although it never belonged to us. Father was head gardener at Leaversham Hall and the cottage was a tied cottage and went with the job. It was strange really, he loved his job, and had great pride in his work, yet he worked long hours, and didn't earn much money probably the fact he was head gardener gave him great satisfaction, I certainly never heard him complain. Life on the big country estates before the First World War was hard, but it was ordered and secure, and that is how I remember my early years. I lived in the cottage quite happily with my mother and father and my beloved older brother, Tom. There were just the four of us, father, mother, Tom and me. We were quite a small family for those days. It was because mother was very ill when she had me and the doctor told her not to have any more children.

My mother had been in service at The Hall as a young girl, and that's where she met my father, but once they were married she became a housewife and only helped out occasionally at The Hall if they were having a large function. She used to tell me wonderful stories of the parties up there when she was a lady's maid and she would describe all the gorgeous dresses and sparkling jewels that the ladies wore. People really dressed up in the Victorian era and I loved hearing about them. Mother had been quite a beauty in her day and I think she used to dream sometimes of being a lady and having fine clothes, but they were harmless dreams, she was quite happy with my father. I inherited her long blonde hair and large dark eyes and was considered to be a pretty girl. I think she hoped I would marry well and live out her dreams for her.' Amy paused for a moment deep in thought then added, 'Maybe in some ways I did.' Tanya wondered what she meant, but was reluctant to interrupt her flow, so she let her continue without comment.

'Anyway, I enjoyed my life until I was twelve years old, when Mother became pregnant for the third time. As I said, she had been told not to have any more children after me, pregnancy did not suit her, but I suppose my parents loved each other, and the baby was an accident, I don't really know, anyway she was ill during most of the nine months and I had to grow up quickly and take charge of the household. Everything was labour intensive in those days, and it was hard work. Whilst there was a woman in the house, the men expected a meal on the table every night, and their laundry to be done every week, even if she was only twelve. It was a full time job running a house in those days and I had mother to look after as well, so it meant that I had to leave school early and become a housekeeper and carer'.

'That was an awesome responsibility for a girl of twelve,' Tanya interrupted, 'Was there no one else who could take care of your mother while you finished your education?'

'Oh dear, things have changed so much. Girls weren't expected to be educated. They were trained to be good housekeepers. I had learned to read and write and add up and that was considered to be enough. All it meant was that I was going to start my career as a housekeeper a little early, that's all. It wasn't too bad, I only had two men to look after and mother, but she was no trouble. I loved caring for her as she rarely complained and was always grateful. I'm really glad that I spent those last few months with her. Father had carried a bed downstairs for her so she could rest during the day and it meant that we could chat whilst she watched me do my chores, although I think that having to lie there and watch me do her work frustrated her. Anyway went into premature labour when she was seven months pregnant, and it was a complicated birth. Unfortunately, in spite of the doctor's best efforts, the baby was still born and mother was very ill afterwards, she developed a high fever and never really regained consciousness. She died on a beautiful June morning a week after the baby. He was a little boy.' Amy's voice broke slightly, 'Even after all these years it still upsets me to talk about it.'

Tanya held out her hand and clasped Amy's. 'Don't go on if it upsets you.'

'Oh, I don't mind really,' Amy smiled, 'I like to remember him, even if it does upset me. Anyway, after mother died father changed. I think he blamed himself for her death, and he became withdrawn and bad tempered. I carried on looking after him and Tom, but then Tom started courting and one day about a year later, I'd be thirteen, father told me Tom was getting married. His new wife, Lizzie, was going to move into the cottage and take care of them so he had found me a place at The Hall. I was to be trained as a lady's maid. I felt bereft really. I had just lost mother and now I had to leave home. It was hard.'

'Is that what you wanted to do?'

Amy smiled sympathetically, 'I had no choice my dear. In those days you did as you were told. I started at The Hall in October, a month before my fourteenth birthday. Initially they took me on as an upstairs maid and I was to be trained as a lady's maid. The Hall was truly magnificent in those days. There were over forty rooms, just imagine. The first floor was raised above ground level and a terrace ran along the front of the house. Guests approached this terrace by climbing steps which fanned down from the enormous front door. The entrance was framed by four large Corinthian pillars, and it led into a vast entrance hall that reached the full height of the building and culminated in a lofty vaulted ceiling. Imagine two storeys high, it had a black and white floor and two massive fireplaces and a large white, marble staircase swept up to the first floor where an open gallery looked down onto the hall below. Leading off this impressive entrance hall were various smaller rooms, Lord Leaversham's smoking room and study, a card room, a billiard room, a music room for the ladies and a large library. Behind the entrance hall a long corridor ran the length of the first floor, and divided it in two. The entertaining rooms, the salons and the large formal dining room, were situated on the other side of the corridor. There were three salons and they were all decorated in a distinctly English way, but with slightly different themes, there was the Chinese salon, which was full of oriental cabinets and Chinese Chippendale furniture, the Egyptian salon, which had a token mummy, a painting of Cleopatra and some fine Regency pieces, and the French salon, which was full of Louis Quinze furnishings, large cut glass chandeliers and huge oil paintings in gilt frames. This salon was the largest and had double French windows that opened out onto a terrace that ran the full length of the back of The Hall. It was south facing and always sunny. In the summer the family took tea on the terrace if it was fine and had pre-dinner drinks there on warm summer evenings. The family had occupied the house for over two hundred years and in that time had accumulated some fabulous paintings and antique furniture, together with magnificent porcelain and a large collection of Georgian silver. All the salons were sumptuously decorated and were full of valuable 'objets d'art'. They were truly magnificent.

Upstairs another corridor ran the length of the house, mirroring the one on the first floor. Eight bedrooms led off this main corridor, each one had its own dressing room, newly installed bathroom and distinctive colour scheme, and the apartments of Lady Leaversham, and her daughter were also situated on that corridor. Above that were the attics where the servants lived and the ground floor was occupied by the kitchens and housekeeping rooms. They covered the whole of the floor, and a large stone flagged corridor, again like the one on the ground floor, ran the length of the house. Off this corridor ran the housekeeper's, cook's and butler's private quarters and their offices. Then there were the housekeeping rooms, the laundry rooms, the kitchens, the back kitchens, the stores and the cold stores. Below this floor were substantial cellars where the wine was kept. The Hall was an outstanding house and had an indoor and outdoor staff of over a hundred, who were an entire household in themselves.

So it was that I set off for The Hall one Sunday morning after church. I only had a few belongings and I wrapped them in one of mother's shawls. It didn't take me long to walk through the park then I approached The Hall from the driveway, which was fringed with rhododendron bushes and great beech trees. It curved at the end so you couldn't see The Hall until you turned the bend.' Amy went quiet as her dream returned to haunt her.

'Are you alright?' Tanya asked gently, 'You look troubled.'

Amy started, she smiled at Tanya, 'No dear, it's just talking about the driveway brought back my dream. I'm fine.' She continued with her story. 'When I arrived, I went round to the east side of The Hall and into the courtyard where all the estate offices were situated. I had been to The Hall many times with mother so I knew my way around a little. I entered the main corridor and asked for Mrs. Foster, the housekeeper, in the servants' hall then was directed to her room. I was told to knock and wait until she called me in. Mrs Foster was in charge of the household, and she was strict, but fair. I heard her call me to enter and went in. She explained what my duties would be and what my terms of employment were. I was to be paid £12.00 a year, and I was to have one Sunday off a month.'

Tanya gasped with shock, 'You are kidding!'

Amy smiled mischievously, 'I know, it sounds ridiculous now doesn't it? Anyway Mrs. Foster then called to Elsie, one of the kitchen maids, to take me to my room. It was up the back stairs, in the attic. I was to share with another lady's maid, Rose. Elsie showed me to my room and told me to change into my uniform. She pointed to a corner of the chimney breast which had been curtained off for use as a wardrobe and told me it was in there. Then she left me to get changed. I felt so lost and lonely. I just sat on the bed and wept. Then the door flew open and Rose rushed in. She had heard that I had arrived and had come to make sure I was alright and had settled in. She was a bit older than me, and we got on well. I missed my mother very much and Rose was kind to me and comforted me, she also taught me my job as a lady's maid. She became a kind of mother figure to me, but she died you know, of the 'flu after the Great War.' Amy seemed lost in her thoughts for a while then continued.

'My uniform consisted of a long black dress, white pinafore and lace cap. It was very smart. I soon settled in and although the work was very hard and we worked long hours, from six in the morning until bed time, I enjoyed it. The house was owned by Lord Leaversham in those days, and the household consisted of him, his wife Lady Leaversham, his twin sons Sir Guy Le Beauvort Leaversham, the heir, and Sir Garth Le Beauvort Leaversham, the younger twin, together with his only daughter Lady Felicity Leaversham. There were only five bedrooms occupied when the family were in residence, so the work wasn't too hard. For most of the season the family took a London house and spent their time down there. During the hunting and shooting season though, they had great house parties and balls and that was hard work. All the guests brought their servants and the servants' hall bustled with strangers. We all used to sit round the kitchen table and gossip, and I loved it. The valets knew all about the affairs of their masters and mistresses and I used to listen enthralled. I sometimes wondered what the people upstairs would have said if they had known that their affairs were being discussed in such detail.

Rose trained me to be a lady's maid. She showed me how to sew, how to clean and store the dresses and hats, how to launder the underwear, how to clean and store the jewellery, what clothes to pack for the season and weekend house parties. I also had to store furs and winter clothes in the summer and pack away summer clothes when it got cold. It was quite a skilled job. The mistress didn't have to worry about anything except maybe choosing new clothes. Rose and I would spend hours in the winter tucked up in front of the fire in the sewing room gossiping, and laughing while we did the mending and sometimes in the summer we would sneak outside and do it in the sunshine. After a while, I was allowed to help look after Lady Felicity, dress her and do her hair and when we had company I helped the visiting maids. It was better than working below stairs. The kitchen maids worked terribly hard, especially the skivvies. On my one Sunday a month off I would go back to visit Father and Tom. I didn't enjoy it much, it wasn't the same without Mother and Tom's wife was a cold woman. She didn't make me feel very welcome and I didn't feel as though I belonged there any more, although Father and Tom did try to make me feel at home. I still saw them in the gardens though, so we remained close. I always stopped to talk to them if they were working near the house. They were halcyon days for the rich, and Britain presided over a rich Empire that straddled the globe. We all felt quite secure in our dominance, but our ordered way of life was already under threat, and storm clouds were gathering over Europe that were destined to break and change our lives forever.

2

I had been at Leaversham Hall for four years in the autumn of 1913 and had been promoted to lady's maid. Rose had left to get married the year before, and I was given her position as Lady Felicity's personal maid. I got a great deal of satisfaction out of having a position of responsibility, and still enjoyed the life, the camaraderie in the servants' hall and the feeling of security and belonging. I never felt lonely or depressed, although sometimes I got very tired, but I had grown up to expect hard work and never really questioned my conditions of employment. That was the way things were and the way I expected they would always be. I thought that our world would last forever.

I had a memorable encounter that autumn that proved to be of great significance later in my life. The Leaversham's were entertaining a large shooting party at The Hall that October and some of the most important families in the county were invited. The servants' hall was full of strange valets and lady's maids. I was now seventeen years old and was beginning to attract the attentions of the opposite sex. Most of it was unwelcome, although I enjoyed a little harmless flirting with the visiting male valets. However, life could be particularly difficult if one of the sons of the guests made a nuisance of himself. In some houses, though I stress not in ours, the master of the house encouraged his sons to look upon the female staff as fair game, sexually that is. When they came to stay at Leaversham Hall, they often thought that it was their right to have a little flirtation with one of us to while away the weekend. Usually, if you gave them the frosty maiden treatment, they looked elsewhere. There was always someone else in the servants' hall that would oblige, stupidly in my opinion. If you got caught or became pregnant, you were dismissed immediately without a reference. Anyway, there was one young man who was particularly keen on me and he was very persistent. His name was Montague, and he was the eldest son of Lord Friedland. The Friedlands were a very wealthy and influential family, who had large estates in the south of England, Sussex I think it was. Montague was a very impressive looking young man. He was very tall with jet black hair and a rather supercilious manner. Although still very young he was incredibly arrogant and I sensed a cruel streak in him, which combined with his feckless and weak nature made him dangerous. I found him quite sinister and did my best to keep out of his way. Unfortunately he seemed to find me irresistibly attractive, and I kept meeting him in corridors and quiet rooms all over the house. I was sure he was following me about, so whenever I encountered him I avoided eye contact, nodded politely, answered any questions in a monotone and hurried away as fast as I could. He made me feel very uncomfortable.

After dinner on the Saturday night of the shoot I went upstairs, as usual, to prepare Lady Felicity's room. I would go up and lay out her nightclothes and turn down her bed while she was dining. At the end of the evening she would ring for me when she was ready to retire for the night, and I would go back up to her room to help her undress. It seems strange to us to think of having someone to help us dress and undress, but those Edwardian outfits were very complex and awkward to put on and take off. They had layers of undergarments, with corsets that needed lacing up and they usually fastened down the back with tiny buttons or hooks and eyes, which couldn't be reached by the wearer. There were no such things as zips in those days and a lady's maid was a necessity. Once Lady Felicity was in her night clothes I would comb out her hair and braid it for the night, then I was free to retire myself.

I looked forward to that moment in the evening when it was time to go upstairs to turn down Lady Felicity's bed, and I could spend some time alone with my thoughts. It was unlikely that anyone was going to ring for me or call me during dinner, so I used to spend a little time by the fireside and daydream, not for too long though! I would pretend that it was my bedroom and I was a grand lady, silly really. I often just sat and considered my future, although realistically I couldn't see any future for myself other than that as a lady's maid or the wife of an estate worker, but it was lovely to spend a few moments dreaming of something different, but I daren't be too long or Mrs Foster would be after me. This particular evening, however, as I was carrying some towels out of the bathroom into the bedroom I noticed a figure in the shadows. At first I thought that I was imagining it then I thought it must be a ghost, all those big houses were haunted you know Tanya, and I was scared half to death, when suddenly the figure moved into the light and I recognised Montague Friedland. He was smoking a cigar and my first thought was to tell him to put it out. I would get into terrible trouble if her ladyship came to bed and found that her room smelled of cigar smoke. She never allowed smoking in her rooms. He simply leered at me and dropped his cigar into a glass of water which was on a nearby table. I remember hearing the hiss as it hit the cold water and extinguished. He was finding it hard to stand up or focus, and he was obviously very drunk. Once I had recovered from the shock of finding him in her ladyship's bedroom, I found the situation a little ridiculous. What was he doing there? Was it a comical attempt at a seduction? I was fairly sure that he was so drunk that he would be incapable of doing any serious damage, but I couldn't be absolutely sure.

Montague simply stood there swaying and leering at me, and I had to decide how to deal with this awkward situation, without drawing attention to myself. He was so drunk that I didn't think he would cause me too much difficulty, but I was very aware that he could cause an unpleasant scene and get me into a great deal of trouble. I decided that my best approach would be to be brisk and business like and pretend I thought he had lost his way. I felt if I could appease him I might be able to get him out of the bedroom room quickly, and summon help from another servant. So I took command of the situation and said,

'Oh it's you sir, I think you've wandered into the wrong bedroom, your room is down the corridor. Let me direct you.....' I tried to push past him to reach the door, but he put out a hand a grabbed my arm as I passed.

'Just give me a little kish, eh? You're a proper little shweetie,' he slurred. He had my arm in a vice-like grip and was pulling me towards him. I dropped the towels that I was carrying and put my arm out to prevent him drawing me close. He reeked of brandy and cigars. I had no idea what to do next, so I decided to be stern.

'Now sir that will do, I think you've had too much to drink and should go downstairs and join the rest of the party.'

'I will when I've had a little kishy kish.' He was smirking like a child, but his grip was extremely strong. I couldn't shake free of him, and I was tempted for a fleeting moment to give him a sharp kick, but dismissed the idea immediately. He might be an affable drunk now, but it wouldn't take much for him to turn nasty. I was beginning to panic. If I was found in this compromising position I would be sacked on the spot with no reference.

'Please sir, will you go. You have no right to be in this room and you will get me into terrible trouble.'

'Ah you're sho lovely when you're crosh,' he drooled and made another lunge at me and this time I found myself totally enclosed in his strong arms. He started to try and kiss me, but I turned my head away. I was really starting to panic as my struggles were not helping me to escape and he was starting to get annoyed. We struggled, locked together like two hapless dancers for some time, then suddenly I felt him stiffen, drop his arms, let me go and step back. I didn't know what had happened to make him behave like that, but for one awful moment I thought Lady Felicity had walked into the room, and I hardly dared turn round to look. Then I heard a deep masculine voice address him,

'For God's sake Montague, what do you think you are doing? You have been warned and warned about this sort of thing. Your father will not tolerate any more scandals and my father would be furious at the way you've abused his hospitality. Now come on. I saw you watching that maid earlier today and I've been keeping an eye on you. Now come along, before we all get into trouble.'

I turned round and found myself looking at one of the twins. We hadn't seen much of the boys as they were growing up, as they spent most of their time away at boarding school, or staying with friends, and then they went to university. I had seen them around playing cricket or riding, but I had never taken much notice of them until recently and that was because they had grown into extremely good looking young men. They had inherited the unusual ash blond hair and deep blue eyes of their mother. I don't know whether it was the fact that he had saved me from Montague's embraces or just his sheer physical presence, but my heart quite literally stood still. Guy and Garth were not quite identical, but they were very alike, and people often confused them, however I had never had a problem identifying them, and I was sure that my saviour was Guy, the older twin. One fact that consolidated this view was the fact that Garth, his brother, had rather an arrogant streak and it was unlikely that he would have bothered himself with the fate of an upstairs maid. I looked closely at my saviour, Guy had grown into a handsome young man, he had always been tall, but had now filled out and looked very manly, and although his presence was very welcome, it was also rather overpowering. Montague was as meek as a lamb after Guy appeared. He seemed to exude authority, and Montague did exactly what he was told to do, he let me go and left the room, without apologising I might add, and went back downstairs. Left alone with Guy I tried to mumble my sincere thanks, but could hardly find my voice. He didn't seem to notice and as he left the room he turned to me and said,

'I am so sorry about this. Can we just forget it? Montague is very young and very drunk and no real harm has been done has it? He could get into serious trouble,' If I had any doubts before, I knew for certain at that moment that it was surely Guy. His eyes held mine for a moment too long and I felt something pass between us. I still couldn't speak so I just nodded and mumbled my thanks. Then he was gone.

I slumped down in front of the fire because my legs were shaking so much I don't think they could have supported me much longer. I don't think they shook from fear, but as a result of Guy's potent presence. I sat quietly for a moment trying to gather my thoughts together, but I needed to shake myself pretty quickly and get the room in order. I had been gone for a long time and would be missed and it was never advisable to let Mrs Foster miss you. I picked up the towels that I had brought from the bathroom and dropped them into the linen basket then I grabbed the offending cigar butt and glass of water. I wrapped the butt in tissue and put it in my pocket and rinsed and dried the glass. Then I opened the windows to let out the smell. When I had finished I turned down her Ladyship's bed, and when I was quite confident that there was no trace of the cigar smoke lingering in the room, I closed the window. After a cursory glance round the room, I left and closed the door. I felt strange as I walked down the stairs. I hadn't enjoyed the encounter and at one point I was very frightened indeed, but it had ended without incidence, so why was I so troubled? It was the effect that Guy had had on me, it shook me. I tried to dismiss it as a romantic fantasy. After all he had saved me from the clutches of that ridiculous young man who could have caused me no end of trouble, but I knew it was more than that. He was the heir to the estate, and I was a mere lady's maid, but I felt as though I had met my soul mate. In reality that was something that could never be and I knew it was best to put if from my mind, but I couldn't and from that night onwards I watched Guy quietly from the wings with an ache in my heart, as he lived out his life on stage as heir to one of England's greatest estates.

Mrs Foster was waiting for me when I got downstairs. I told her an edited version of the events that took place upstairs, that Mr. Montague was rather drunk and had stumbled into Lady Felicity's room by mistake. I explained that I had tried to guide him back to his own quarters and fortunately had met Sir Guy on the way who took him over. She gave me a sharp look, but she didn't say anything. We all knew the hazards of drunken guests, but we were well trained servants and learned to deal with all eventualities quickly and quietly. Nevertheless, I often wondered whether I could have dealt with Mr. Montague Friedland alone if Guy Leaversham had not been keeping a close eye on him and come to my aid. My dear, I'm beginning to feel sleepy. I think that is enough for tonight, Tanya.'

'Oh I'm sorry Amy. You don't mind me calling you Amy do you? It's just that I was enjoying your story so much that I hadn't realised the time. I will get into trouble for keeping you awake.'

'Not at all Tanya and you may call me Amy I was grateful for your company after that awful dream. But I'm not young anymore and need my sleep.'

'Goodnight then,' Tanya rose from her chair and collected the two cups before walking over to the door. She turned and smiled at Amy just before she left.

'I'll leave you to turn out the light. You will continue tomorrow won't you? I do want to hear the full story and the significance of your young saviour, Guy.'

Amy smiled then leaned over and switched off her lamp.

3

Tanya visited Amy, as promised, the following evening with a cup of cocoa. She waited until she had settled all the residents down and given them their medication before she joined Amy, who found that she was looking forward to seeing her. She found that she was enjoying revisiting the past after all the years of suppressing it. At any rate, it was preferable to nightmares about The Hall. At about ten o'clock Tanya put her head around the door.

'Good evening Amy, I'm just going to make a cup of cocoa. Shall I bring you one? Are you tired or do you feel up to carrying on with your history?'

'Oh I'm fine, thank you. I'd love a cup of cocoa it always helps me to sleep.' Tanya went off the make the cocoa and appeared some minutes later with two mugs. She settled herself down before she spoke. 'I do appreciate this, you know. It is so interesting to me. It's a world I know so little about.'

Amy smiled at her. 'I'm glad it's useful.....'

'Oh and interesting,' Tanya interjected. Amy smiled again.

'Where did we get up to last night before I dozed off?'

'It was 1913 and you had just fended off the unwelcome advances of Montague Friedland.'

'Oh yes, Montague Friedland, the arch villain, and Guy my knight in shining armour, quite the stuff of romances! It was strange that meeting. Although I had watched the twins grow from unruly boys into handsome young men, and we had almost grown up in parallel worlds, they rarely overlapped and I had very little real contact with them. In fact, I hardly knew them at all as I lived in a curiously female world. So the meeting with Sir Guy was quite significant.

Anyway, after the incident with Montague Friedland, life carried on in much the same way at The Hall. It was quiet when the family lived in London and frantically busy when they entertained during the hunting and shooting season. As lady's maid, I now accompanied Lady Felicity to London during the season. I used to really enjoy that. It was nice to have a change of scenery, although I hardly saw anything of the city as we were kept so busy. Nevertheless, when I did get out I made the most of it and visited historical places like the Tower of London and Buckingham Palace. It was quite a change for me after living on a country estate all my life. At first I found it terrifying, but I soon got used to the noise and bustle of the city and became quite an urban girl.

I saw little of Guy, as I now thought of him. He was up at Oxford and only appeared now and then for social occasions. There were no other men in my life as no one could measure up to Guy, although I knew he was unobtainable, but it didn't stop me dreaming. I enjoyed working for Lady Felicity. She was quite a reserved young woman, and although I had been her lady's maid for some years we had a professional relationship with clearly defined boundaries. She never enquired about my private life and she never confided in me. Obviously, I knew more or less what was going on, but she never chatted with me as an equal, and I was glad of that. I preferred to have a working relationship. However, when she fell in love with Bertie, Lord Bertram Ellerswood, a very handsome man and heir to large estates in Cornwall, it affected her so profoundly that she couldn't keep it to herself. She was so much in love with him that she wanted to talk about him day and night and I was a willing listener. I watched their relationship grow with interest. I suppose I lived my life through her at that time, but I liked Lady Felicity and I was delighted that she had met someone she could love. The affair blossomed and Bertie eventually asked Lord Leaversham for her hand in marriage.

The Leavershams were delighted with their daughter's choice of husband. It was an advantageous match, which they wanted to advertise, so they decided to hold a large society ball to celebrate the engagement. It was to be held at The Hall towards the end of July 1914 and was going to be a large affair with invitations going out to all the best society families and even some minor royals. I didn't know it then, of course, but it was going to be the last big ball that was ever held at Leaversham Hall. The events that took place in the autumn of 1914 led to changes in their lives that none of us could ever have foreseen. However, the spring and summer of 1914 was a time of great happiness and enjoyment. We spent most of it preparing for the ball. We were all so excited, Father, as head gardener, was in charge of flower decorations for the public rooms, particularly the French Salon, which was going to be used as a ballroom, and the reception hall. Father had always been in charge of the floral decorations for formal functions, but this ball was somehow different. It was as if we sensed that our way of life at Leaversham Hall was coming to an end. The preparations took place as they normally would for a large function. Father worked the young gardeners until they dropped, Parkes, the butler, had the footmen cleaning the already spotless silver and polishing the crystal, Cook was the scourge of the scullery maids as she tried out different recipes, and Mrs. Foster wore the housemaids out, spring cleaning every room from top to bottom. We smiled as we watched the housemaids beating carpets, taking down curtains, and dusting pictures as though their lives depended on it. Though don't imagine that they thought it was very funny!

My task was to dress Lady Felicity and start to plan her trousseau, and for the first time I came into direct contact with Lady Leaversham. Up until then she had been a rather distant figure. She was very beautiful, and Lady Felicity took after her. They were both quite tall and slim, with the same ash blonde hair and blue eyes, and they both had an aura of calm and tranquillity about them. I never once heard Lady Leaversham raise her voice, but she ruled the household with a rod of iron and knew exactly what was going on. She also commanded great respect and affection from the servants, because she was fair as well as strict. Normally she left Lady Felicity to choose her own outfits, but she took a personal interest in the designing of her dress for the engagement ball, because it was so important. I also think that she was genuinely delighted that her daughter had found happiness and wanted to share in it.

The Leaversham ladies all bought all their clothes from the main French and London couturiers and fashion houses. Sometimes they would visit the fashion houses personally, but more often than not they expected the designers to visit them at The Hall and bring their designs with them. They would come for an initial visit, when the patterns and materials were chosen, then they would go away and make up the garments. They had models made to Lady Leaversham and Lady Felicity's measurements, so they could fit the garments in London. Then they would come back to The Hall for the final fitting, and using the major London fashion houses meant that the ladies were always dressed in the height of fashion. I loved helping Lady Felicity to choose her gowns, and enjoyed taking care of them. Sometimes, when I was alone I would hold them against me and pretend that they were mine! I was such a day dreamer! The engagement ball gown was very special and eventually, between us we decided on a fitted gown made of cream satin, which was covered in cream voile, and embroidered with lilac flowers. The gown was to be off the shoulder with straps made of two diamond necklaces loaned by Lady Leaversham, and each of the embroidered lilac flowers on the bodice was to have a diamond centrepiece. It was an exquisite dress, beautiful, so elegant. I still have it today.' Tanya wondered why Amy would still have the dress, but decided not to interrupt the flow of her story. 'Lady Felicity also had lovely collection of jewels. Many of them were family heirlooms that had been passed down. Some of the pieces were very old and not very fashionable. The main pieces were a small tiara that her grandmother had left her, which was antique, and a beautiful set of amethysts and diamonds that Lady Leaversham had re-set into matching bracelet, necklace and earrings by Cartier as an engagement present. Of course she now had a beautiful diamond engagement ring as well; it consisted of three perfect stones and had belonged to Bertie's grandmother. She wore them all to the ball and they complemented her dress and her deep blue eyes perfectly.

Looking back, the whole atmosphere surrounding the ball was extraordinary and somewhat tense. It was held on the last Saturday in July, which was chosen because it was also the wedding anniversary of Lord and Lady Leaversham. I will never forget that strange heady summer. It was so warm, sunny day followed sunny day, and it seemed as though our way of life would never end. Yet there was an odd imperceptible feeling of unrest and anticipation in the air. The Archduke Franz Ferdinand, heir to the Austro-Hungarian Empire, was murdered in June in Sarajevo, a town in Serbia. The Austro-Hungarians were outraged, the Germans too. The Russians had sworn to defend Serbia from any antagonist and we were acting as mediators. No one took it too seriously as the European powers were always arguing, and we had just enjoyed a hundred years of relative peace. Yet at the same time we held our breaths hoping that the German Kaiser wouldn't do anything stupid, because we all knew he resented our powerful empire. From 1870, when the Germans became one unified nation, they kept creating minor diplomatic incidents which resulted in skirmishes in our colonies all over Africa. Many of our young men were really fed up with the posturing and sabre rattling of the Germans, and wanted to 'give the Hun a bloody nose' to teach him a lesson. Yet in spite of all the talk, I don't think Britain really ever intended to go to war and would certainly have resisted it had we any idea what it would entail. However, talk of war dominated the salons, drawing rooms and servants' halls throughout that curious summer. The last of the peace was dominated by a strange stillness as we prepared for the ball in the shadow of the gathering storm clouds.

It is significant that Lord Leaversham felt so confident about the situation that he didn't even consider cancelling the ball, and he was representative of the country at large. He felt he had done his duty and that was sufficient. He had made preparations in case war broke out, and as a gentleman he had volunteered for Active Service in the local yeomanry. Guy, as heir to the estate, had also joined the local yeomanry, although he was not required to fight as his brother, Garth, was an officer in the regular army. So Lord Leaversham felt that the family had done all that they should under the circumstances and he intended to carry on with his life as usual.

Oh Tanya! The ball was such a glittering, glorious affair. I had witnessed many splendid formal dances at The Hall, but this was special. On the day of the ball we were all nervously dashing around below stairs, but eventually all the work was completed and when everything was in place I went up to prepare Lady Felicity for the ball. I dressed her hair and helped her on with her gown before fitting her jewels, and she did look lovely when I'd finished. I felt quite emotional as I put the finishing touches to her gown and she thanked me sincerely and actually gave me a hug! Then she went downstairs to stand with her parents, Lord Ellerswood and the twins to greet her guests. As she glided down the magnificent marble staircase I caught sight of Bertie's face as he watched her, and it was a picture of love.

The ball was attended by all the prominent county families and everyone had house guests from London and abroad. Fabulous limousines and elegant carriages glided up the drive one after another. A covered walkway had been erected against the front façade of The Hall, and guests gathered under this protective canopy as they waited to be announced by the footmen and be received by the family. The great hall was full of potted palms and ferns and there were huge pink and white flower arrangements above both of the magnificent fireplaces. The grand staircase and the balcony above the great hall were decorated with swatches of vines and leaves all intertwined with exotic flowers. It smelled like a perfumed garden.

As long as they were discreet, the upstairs servants were allowed to look down from the gallery and watch the guests arrive. I felt so proud watching Lady Felicity as she stood in line greeting her guests, but I couldn't take my eyes off Guy, who looked so tall and handsome in his officer's dress uniform. Oh how I wished that I could wear a ball gown and go down and dance with him! But I had to be content with watching from above. Later, when all the guests had arrived, we sneaked out onto the terrace, masquerading as downstairs servants, so we could peek into the ballroom. What a sight it was, like something from a fairy tale. The huge cut glass crystal chandeliers blazed with a hundred lights, the Louis Quinze furnishings gleamed, the vast gilt mirrors shone and Father had really outdone himself. The whole room was festooned with pink carnations, lily of the valley, pink orchids and Madonna lilies. I was so proud of him, to think that he was in charge of gardens that could produce blooms like these, and the perfume made us all feel heady.

The music was provided by Monsieur Nicholas Bassano's Orchestra, who came all the way from London. They were positioned on a small podium at one end of the room. There were twenty five dances on the programme, which were mainly waltzes, but included two steps and single lancers. Lady Leaversham would not permit any tangos as she felt that they were too fast for Cheshire society and we fully agreed with her! The women in their gorgeous gowns swirled round and round with their elegant partners, most of who were already in dress uniform, and their jewels flashed and sparkled in the light of the chandeliers. What a sight they were and how my feet ached to join the dancers! At one point I saw Guy go dancing by with a beautiful blonde woman, who was dressed in a pale green gown, and my mood became rather deflated, but nothing could keep me down for long. I also noticed Lady Felicity and Lord Ellerswood dancing on the far side of the ballroom and they were positively glowing with happiness.

Upstairs, during a break in the dancing, supper was served in the dining room, which was simply decorated with broom and potted plants, but smelt divine. The tables simply groaned with food, whole salmon, and sides of beef, chickens, and mixed salads. The tables were decorated with huge silver and cut glass epergnes, which were overflowing with grapes and every type of fruit you could think of. The library, billiard room, card room and smoking room were made available to the older guests, so that they could sit quietly away from the music. There were four hundred guests, can you imagine that today! The young people waltzed the night away, and when they could escape their chaperones, took romantic promenades in the shadows on the terrace. It was an extraordinarily memorable night and drew comparison with the great ball held in Brussels by the Duchess of Richmond on the eve of the Battle of Waterloo a century earlier. The only difference was that 1815 marked the end of the Napoleonic wars, whereas 1914 signalled the beginning of the Great War.

After spying on the ballroom from the terrace, we maids crept downstairs to the servants' hall and once the food was served upstairs, we had our own party. Lord Leaversham sent down a crate of champagne, and beer for the male servants and we laughed and drank and had such fun. It was an unforgettable night; thank goodness we didn't know it was also a wake.' There she stopped and looked at Tanya, 'Oh Tanya if we had merely a hint of what was to come. But how could we suspect that within months many of the young men who attended that ball would be dead or maimed for life and that hardly any of them would be left alive four years later? It's incredible, but how could we possible suspect that such a thing was possible?'

'Was the change that abrupt?' asked Tanya, 'surely it took a while to adjust and . . . 'Amy interrupted her, 'No, no time at all, it was that abrupt. One minute in heaven the next in hell that is war for you and I pray you never have to experience it. Not one of the families at that ball was left unaffected by the war.'

'I'm not tiring you am I?' Tanya asked.

'No dear, quite the contrary, I'm enjoying re-living the past. I haven't thought about it for so long. Anyway after the ball some of the guests stayed on for the week and I actually remember the day war was announced. It was a hot sunny day and there was a large party for lunch. Lord Leaversham and the twins were both in uniform. Strangely everyone was quite exhilarated by the news of war, mainly because we had no idea what it would mean. Famously we had some naive idea that we would go to France, teach the Germans a short sharp lesson, and would be home by Christmas.

Both Guy and Garth were there that day, resplendent in their uniforms. They looked magnificent, so tall and so alike with their blonde good looks and piercing blue eyes, but I feared for Guy that afternoon. He was only in the yeomanry, but he was still in uniform and could be sent to fight at any time. I had learned that he was not a naturally aggressive man. After the incident in Lady Felicity's bedroom

I followed his career with interest. He had been up at Oxford, with his brother Garth, studying the classics and was a great academic, but from what I could gather Garth had enjoyed the social life more than his studies and only just scraped a third, whereas Guy gained a very respectable first. That afternoon Lord Leaversham asked them to pose together on the terrace and took a couple of photographs of them, with his new camera. Garth threw his arm affectionately around the shoulders of his twin as they squinted at the camera and smiled amicably. The evening sun cast their long shadows across the terrace, prophetically heralding their coming destruction. It was the last time that they were ever together. Lady Leaversham had that photograph in a large silver frame by her bedside until the day that she died, and strangely it was one of the few things that was rescued from her private apartments during the fire. I have it here.' Tanya followed Amy's gaze towards a large silver frame on the chest of drawers.

'Could I have a closer look at it please?' Tanya asked.

'Of course my dear, help yourself.' Amy replied.

Tanya stood up and wandered over to the chest of drawers, picked up the photograph and moved towards the light for closer examination. The silver frame was dented and worn, but the sepia tinted black and white photograph was still clear. It showed two tall, slim, handsome, young men in officer's uniform. They were both wearing their caps and one had his arm laid casually along the balustrade whilst his twin had his arm slung around his brother's shoulder. They appeared to be laughing and looked so alike and so painfully young.

'Which one is Guy?' asked Tanya.

'The one with his arm around Garth,' replied Amy.

'They are so very handsome, no wonder you were slightly in love with Guy and they were so young to die, it doesn't seem right somehow.' Tanya commented.

Amy smiled a knowing smile, 'I know my dear, but war is no respecter of youth, and I am glad I knew him when he was young and handsome like that. Now come back and sit down and let me finish.'

Tanya replaced the photograph, but it continued to haunt her as she returned to her seat.

'Later on that day I saw Father in the gardens, and he told me with great pride that Tom, as a reservist, had been called up and was in uniform and ready to go and 'bash the Bosh,' as father put it. The men had some quaint sayings to express their dislike of the Germans. In the reality of the fighting, the soldiers soon dropped them, but the civilian population clung on to them with odd affectation throughout the war. I saw many a soldier flinch when asked by some fireside soldier if he was 'giving the Hun what for' or some equally banal phrase. To some extent I was swept up with the general feeling of excitement, but it was tempered with foreboding. I was afraid, especially for Guy and Tom. Like him many of the estate workers were reservists and had been required to report for duty. This left my father with a great deal of extra work to do, which was a strain for someone of his age.' Amy became quiet and lost in her thoughts again until Tanya prompted her.

'Did you never have a special boyfriend?'

'No, oddly enough I had no interest in boys, well not the boys I met on the estate. I'd always had a strange feeling that my destiny lay elsewhere and that I would not stay on the estate forever, especially after the war began, and I wasn't wrong.'

Just then one of the patient's buzzers sounded and Tanya said goodnight and went to see to them. Left alone with her thoughts, Amy lay quietly reminiscing for a while then she leaned over to turn out her light, but not before she looked towards the black and white photograph in its dented silver frame on the chest of drawers. She smiled her goodnight to the photograph of the twins, as she did every night, before she turned out her light and prepared for sleep.

4

Although the politicians and statesmen were dismayed at the declaration of war, there was enormous popular enthusiasm for it. The streets of London and all the major British towns and cities thronged with crowds waving Union Jacks and singing 'God Save the King' and 'Onward Christian Soldiers.' Young men, in their Sunday best, marched off to war, cheered on and kissed by young ladies, who often handed them posies of flowers and offered to marry them. It was so exhilarating and exciting! A hundred years of peace had made people forget about the tyranny of war, the bloodshed, the disruption and the deaths. None of the population really took the war seriously, they thought it would just be another Imperial skirmish that would be handled by the professional army and brought to a conclusion by Christmas.

Young men flocked to the recruiting stations to volunteer in case they missed all 'the fun'. Even young cadets at Sandhurst, who were still in training, were afraid it would all be over before they could reach France. It was quite extraordinary, there was almost a feeling of relief as though the pressure put on the British Empire by Germany had been building up and building up and at last was going to be released. Germany had been sabre rattling and daring Great Britain to respond for far too long, and Britain had run out of patience, and was finally going to retaliate. However, she had strongly underestimated the military might of the newly united Germany, and the general public, who were presently clamouring for action, had forgotten during nearly a century of relative peace, that war is like an evil genie that once released from its lamp will cause death and destruction on an unimaginable scale, before it is finally captured and sealed up again, until some other unwitting fool releases it. I pretended to join in with the feeling of excitement, but my heart was heavy. Instinctively I knew that this was going to be a terrible conflict, and unfortunately I was proved right.

The first weeks of the war were very busy. Immediately war was declared, the British sent a force of some 160,000 men to France. They were known as the British Expeditionary Force, the BEF for short, or ironically as the 'Old Contemptibles', apparently The Kaiser referred to them as that contemptible little force or something like that. Anyway the name stuck, but they were anything but contemptible. The British Expeditionary Force consisted mainly of battle hardened regular soldiers or reservists who were well trained and excellent shots. I know all this because Lady Felicity talked to me about the war. She was an intelligent young woman who listened carefully to the conversations at the dinner table and she read the newspapers, consequently she was well informed about what was going on. It was at this time with her encouragement that I started to read and educate myself. Women generally were starting to make a bid for more freedom, the suffragettes were fighting hard to get women the vote, and Lady Felicity fully supported them, much to her mother's distress. She also realised that education was the key to independence, especially for someone from my background so she encouraged me to study and brought me books from the family library. She was a very forward looking young woman and I was very grateful to her for the rest of my life. My education became my greatest treasure.

After the declaration of war and the departure of Sir Garth for France, the household servants were instructed to close up large parts of The Hall. Lady Leaversham and Mrs. Foster realised that until the hostilities were over there wasn't going to be much entertaining done. Only the bedrooms and the downstairs rooms that the family used were kept open. Many male members of both indoor and outdoor staff were reservists and were called up as soon as war was declared. Many more had volunteered and left for training camp, so the number of healthy young men on the staff was severely reduced. Obviously, this meant that there were fewer servants to do the heavy work, so we kept it to a minimum. Father had lost three quarters of his work force and the remaining men were struggling to control the vast gardens. Lord Leaversham had instructed him to leave certain areas fallow and concentrate on the gardens around the house. Both he and Mrs. Foster had a difficult task maintaining their high standards with so few staff available, and it grieved both of them and made them very grumpy.

In the early months of the war, my life didn't change greatly. I was still involved in the domestic world of a lady's maid and the planning of Lady Felicity's wedding was taking up most of our time. In September we had no intention of cancelling the large society wedding that Lady Leaversham had originally planned just because of a small skirmish in France. We had more important things to think about, so we were kept busy with dress designers and caterers. With a reduced staff, Lady Leaversham was concerned that she would not be able to host the wedding breakfast without the help of an outdoor catering firm. Just a few weeks before, when we held the engagement ball, the idea of the Leaversham's hiring caterers would have been unthinkable. This was a small and quite insignificant example of how the war had started to alter people's perceptions. Change was coming, but we couldn't imagine how complete the transformation would be. As the weeks passed even the problem of catering became less and less important to us until eventually our enthusiasm for a large society wedding waned completely. Sir Garth was now in the thick of the fighting on the Western Front and we waited for news with bated breath. As yet Lord Ellerswood, Bertie, Lady Felicity's fiancé, was still in Britain training volunteers, so he was not in any immediate danger, but he too could be sent to France at any time. It was becoming apparent that the Germans had a large, well trained, and well armed army and defeating them was not going to be as easy as everyone had imagined. As winter approached, and we suffered defeat at Mons, people began to be really concerned. This was no Imperial skirmish; it was serious warfare and Britain was struggling.

One lovely, misty, autumn morning, early in October, Lady Felicity and I were meeting with Lady Leaversham to discuss the wedding plans, when she put into words what we were all thinking that this was no time for a large celebration. She said that whilst she didn't want to disappoint Lady Felicity, she felt that the wedding plans should be put on hold until things were more 'settled', as she gently put it. Lady Felicity wasn't at all disappointed her mother was merely echoing what we were all thinking, masters and servants alike. It would have been insensitive to carry on planning a large celebration, when most of the young men on the wedding list were fighting for their lives in France and some had already been wounded or killed. So it was that the wedding was put on hold.

It was just as well that Lady Leaversham had put the wedding plans on hold, because on the 5th November 1914 she and her husband received a telegram from the War Office, which changed everything.

It was almost brutal in its simplicity and read, 'We regret to inform you that 2nd Lieutenant Garth Le Beauvort Leaversham was killed in action on 30th October 1914.'

He was killed during the First Battle of Ypres defending a town called Zandvoorde, in Belgium. Oh Tanya! It was a terrible blow, we just couldn't believe it! I was so upset, I felt as though I had lost a member of my own family. Lord Leaversham had been in the north east training troops, but he came home immediately on compassionate leave to support Lady Leaversham, who was inconsolable. She floated around the house like a ghost, looking pale and wan. I never saw her weep, but my heart broke for her and I don't think I ever saw her smile properly again. Sir Guy was devastated as only a twin can be. He blamed himself and said he felt like half a man. He wanted to join up immediately, and go out to France to avenge his twin's death. Naturally his parents were horrified at the idea of Guy facing the Germans and possible death so soon after the loss of Garth, so they managed to persuade him to wait for a while, but they knew he would go eventually. Lord Ellerswood was still safe in England, for the time being, but Lady Felicity was now terrified that he, too, might be sent on Active Service at any time. Her wedding would have had to be postponed anyway once the family went into mourning and she was relieved that the decision had already been made. It was one less thing to worry about.

Although Lady Felicity was heartbroken at the news of her brother's death, she confided in me that she was also frustrated and tired of inactivity. I understood fully, sitting and waiting for news from the Front was nerve wracking for all of us. She wanted to be out there doing something to help the war effort and she told me that she had suggested to her parents that she join the Queen Alexandra's Imperial Nursing Service. They were horrified and wouldn't hear of it, their beautiful daughter, brought up to a life of luxury, working for a living, even worse nursing strange men! And her brother recently killed! No, it wouldn't do! Never! But as the war progressed that way of thinking soon disappeared as desperately needed women, from all walks of life, flocked to replace the men who had left their jobs to fight in France. By the middle of the war they were working in the offices, in the factories, on the buses, in all kinds of unlikely jobs, and there was an overwhelming need for trained nurses to care for the growing list of wounded men returning from France. However, at this early stage in the war there was strong resistance to sheltered young women leaving home to work, no matter how noble the work was considered to be.

After Garth's death, the house became like a mausoleum. Everything was draped in black and everyone spoke in whispers and crept about trying not to disturb the family, who were clinging together trying to make some sense of what had happened. It seemed worse, somehow, that Garth was a twin who had died and left his brother alone. We servants couldn't relax though, because we still had to run the house and cater for a stream of visitors. One after another those same large motor cars and carriages that had brought their owners to the engagement ball returned to The Hall, however this time the occupants were not in evening dress, but were swathed in black crepe. They, too, were grieving for a son or a grandson, who had been killed in France. They came either to console the Leavershams or to share in their sorrow. Lady Felicity told me that Sir Garth's battalion had been part of the 7th division. They had sailed for Belgium with 400 officers and 12,000 men. By the end of 1914 they had been reduced to 44 officers and 2,336 men. Mr Peake, our butler, also told me that 'Debrett's Peerage and Baronetage' did not appear in the spring of 1915, because the editors did not have sufficient time to make all the necessary revisions. So many heirs to the great estates and houses of Britain had been killed that it took them many months to make the alterations. In four short months the social landscape of Britain had been altered forever.

As the weeks passed, I learned of other deaths when I returned home to visit Father, so many of the outdoor staff, who had gone to France with Garth, had been killed. Many of them were only in their early twenties and had grown up with Tom and I, it was a very depressing time. I once commented to Lady Felicity that Sir Garth's death had been the waste of a young life; she disagreed with me quite strongly. She felt that if the BEF had not held the Germans at Ypres in the fateful autumn of 1914, the war would effectively have been lost and the Germans would have invaded Britain. She explained to me that the BEF and the French combined forces had been surprised then overwhelmed by the superior numbers of German troops. They had fought and been defeated at Mons then retreated via Le Cateau to the Marne. However, this meant that they were so far south of their supply lines in the coastal harbours of Calais and Boulogne that they were in danger of being cut off from them. The German army was also stretched thinly as they had attacked too far south. The British took advantage of the fact that the German army needed reinforcing to strike north again to protect the Channel ports. The Germans tried to stop him and what was known as 'the race to the sea' began. Fortunately, the British held the Germans at Ypres, where Sir Garth was killed, and in so doing they secured their supply lines, but they paid a terrible price in casualties. Lady Felicity seemed to think that was when the Germans missed their only chance of winning the war. After that the two armies, now of equal strength, dug in and began a terrible war of attrition. So she claimed that Sir Garth was killed in the most momentous battle of the war. Somehow that made his death more significant and meaningful. The later slaughter seemed to make no sense at all, when thousands were killed for little or no gain.

I tried to keep busy and cheerful, but it was very difficult. As Christmas approached the world took on a surreal quality, we were all trying to celebrate the birth of Jesus in a house of death. It was dreadful. Compared with previous years it was very subdued, but everyone tried to be jolly. We went through the same rituals as in years past; Lord Leaversham held a party for the staff on Christmas Eve and gave them each a present. We had a huge, carefully decorated pine tree in The Hall, which stood two floors high and had been grown on the estate. As usual, the staff sang carols round the tree, but the poignant hymns were too much for some who were recently bereaved, and they could not hold back their tears. The family maintained control, but looked so strained and unhappy that it wasn't a pleasant affair at all. I was glad when it was all over and I could retreat to bed. I spent Christmas quietly, with Tom's wife and father and couldn't wait to get back to The Hall, and normality. I was glad to celebrate the New Year, as I felt it couldn't possibly be as bad as 1914, and might herald the end of this dreadful war. If I had but known it was only just beginning.

Sir Guy never recovered from the death of Sir Garth and in the New Year, became very quiet and withdrawn. I would watch him prowl around the gardens in the January murk. Up and down the terrace he skulked, with his head sunk into the collar of his great coat. Oh how I longed to go out and take him in my arms, and try to give him some comfort, but there was none to give. At the end of February he joined Queen Alexandra's Own Hussars and left to join his regiment and keep his promise to avenge Garth's death. Thankfully, he didn't sail for France until May, which gave his parents and me some small comfort.

Lord Leaversham never really recovered from the death of his younger son and became a shadow of his former self. He seemed to shrink both physically and mentally and I found that quite shocking.

He had seemed like a god to me, as he managed the household like an invincible, yet paternal despot and here he was a broken man. Lady Leaversham busied herself closing yet more of the house down to help the shrinking indoor staff. Slowly, the junior staff started to drift away to Manchester to work in the burgeoning munitions factories. The wages were much better and they had more independence, but it wasn't respectable and something in the shells made their skin go yellow, so they were called 'canaries'! I felt it was not quite right somehow, not proper to work in a factory, but my duties as a lady's maid had lessened, so as the junior staff left, I began to help those house maids that were left to keep the house up to the required standard. Most of the furniture in the large salons, entertaining rooms and guest's bedrooms were now covered with dust sheets and much of the fine china was packed away with the silver. With almost two thirds closed up, The Hall was virtually reduced to a large family home. I liked to think that it was simply in hibernation waiting to emerge like a butterfly from its chrysalis at the end of the war, which I felt would be soon. Not even the most pessimistic of us thought that it would continue after the end of 1915.'

Tanya spoke for the first time in a while. 'It's strange somehow, although you worked for the Leavershams you talk about them as though they were your family not your employers. Was it really like that?'

'Yes, in a way, because we had no lives of our own and their lives were more interesting. We lived with them and were in their company day and night and a bond formed between servants and good masters, a deep relationship of trust. I was probably closer to the Leavershams than I was to my own family. I hadn't really thought about it before, but that is how it was. They were my family.'

Tanya stood up to leave, 'It's so interesting, a lost world,' Amy slowly nodded her agreement; 'Well I had better go now and let you get some rest. I'm not in tomorrow and then I change my shift. I'll be on days. Perhaps we can go for a walk in the gardens and you can finish your story?'

Amy smiled her agreement, 'Good idea, I'll look forward to it, I need to get out and get some fresh air.'

With that Tanya left the room, taking the empty cocoa cups with her and Amy settled down for the night.

5

Later in life, Lady Leaversham told Amy how hard it was to cope with the loss of Garth. In the early days of November, following the death of her younger son, she had to draw on every resource that she possessed to present an aura of calm and control. His death had taken her by surprise. He was young and fit and seemed invincible to her, it never occurred to her when he left for France that he wouldn't return and she would never see him again. How she regretted the time she had wasted with him. She thought he would be there forever and she had never really talked to him or told him how much she loved him, how proud she was to be his mother. It wasn't done amongst members of her class to show affection, so she remained aloof and dignified, and how she regretted her reserve. Continually she asked herself why had she never held him, hugged him to her whilst he was still alive. She hadn't realised that grief could be so physical; the pain in her heart was real, unbearable, like a wound. She wanted a pain killer to relieve it, but no such palliative existed.

She spent her days walking through the house pretending to check on the storage arrangements for the porcelain and silver. She oversaw the placing of dust sheets on the furnishings in the various parts of the house that were being closed up, and was constantly on the move doing something, anything. The reality was that she daren't sit still. She needed to be occupied and on the move so that she could stop focusing on the pain. She needed time to try to make some sense of her terrible loss, and she knew that the servants were watching her, taking their lead from her, so she spent her days striding from one end of the house to the other, giving out instructions and checking the contents of the various boxes.

She was glad that it was November and not spring. The world was cloaked in a dour, grey mist that signified the onset of winter and suited her mood perfectly. She looked out of the window at the outline of the trees in the park. Stripped of their foliage their branches stood out against the grey rain clouds like so many old knarled hands that were clawing at the sky. She thought of Garth clawing to get out of his grave and back into the young world that he had barely had time to experience, but immediately banished the dreadful thought. She closed her eyes in weariness. She must not think like that. It was not healthy. She looked down across the south terrace to the lawns below and her heart lurched. There was Guy. He spent his days pacing up and down the terrace and wandering around the gardens, whatever the weather. Like her he could not keep still. Every time she saw him she had some mad hope that it was Garth come home and the telegram notifying them of his death was just a terrible hoax after all. But it was always Guy, like her trying to deal with his loss. It was almost worse for him, he'd lost his twin and that was like losing a part of him. They had been almost identical, and even as children seemed to have a telepathic link, each seemed to know what the other was thinking or feeling. She watched him pacing up and down, round and round, hour after hour muffled against the cold in his army great coat and cap. She knew with a sense of inevitability that he would be the next to go to France. He felt such a strong urge to avenge his brother that it almost overwhelmed him. Yet what good would it do? Would it make him feel better? Pacing up and down the terrace and gardens was the only release he had, so maybe going to France, fighting his brother's killers would help. She didn't know, but it seemed such a waste of a young life.

She moved away from the window and continued checking through the list that Mrs. Foster had prepared. Guy paced the terrace, and she floated through the house like a ghost, half dead, half alive. However, her family and the staff were relying on her strength, and she could not afford to collapse. Phillip, her husband, had taken the death of his youngest son very badly, and wanted to stay with her, to give and receive support, but he was required to return to his training post in the north east. There at least he could immerse himself in his work and escape, but for her there was no escape. Now Felicity, who was inconsolable and spent most of her time in her room, wanted to rush off to London and become a nurse, whatever next! But she knew in her heart that her daughter would go and then she would be alone, without a purpose in life, just waiting. Guy in the army, Felicity in London, Philip in the north east, and she alone, here with her memories, she shuddered involuntarily. What had they become in three short months? They were changed irrevocably from sociable, charming, outgoing creatures into introverted, uncommunicative ghosts. Guy paced the grounds in morbid silence, she hid in the dark shuttered remnants of The Hall, her husband fled back to his regiment and her daughter hid herself in her room. It was dreadful. Yet she felt instinctively that this was only the beginning that they were in it for the long haul and before it was over they were going to be bled dry.

She looked up from her list and cast her eye over the Chinese Salon. The elegant Chinese Chippendale furniture was covered in dust sheets. It looked like an army of avenging ghosts in the gloom. The paintings and mirrors were shrouded in dust sheets and all the beautiful ornaments and silverware had been packed away. She closed her eyes for a moment and imagined it as it had looked on the eve of the ball, when the crystal chandeliers glowed with a thousand electric light bulbs, and every surface was covered with beautiful flowers, whose perfume made her dizzy. Round and round the glittering couples had waltzed, beautiful young women dressed in the height of fashion dancing with tall handsome young men, many of them already in uniform. What would become of their generation?...... a sob caught in her chest and she grappled in her sleeve for her handkerchief and dabbed her eyes. She must not give way, she must not. If she started crying she would never stop, she must control herself. She wondered idly if Garth had ever known or loved a woman. Well she would never know now.

She walked across the French Salon into the Chinese Salon. She couldn't bear to stay in that room of ghosts any longer. Her closest friend, May had called the day before. Her only son, heir to a large, neighbouring estate, had been killed the day before Garth. She must be thankful for small mercies at least Garth had not been her only son, at least Leaversham still had an heir. May was devastated; the estate was entailed and on her husband's death would pass to some distant cousin. She had no idea what would become of her. Lady Leaversham looked out again at the forlorn figure pacing up and down the terrace. Maybe the war would be over before he went out to France? Who could say? She had to believe it might end before it took Guy too, and so she continued her wanderings alone with her grief, alone with her thoughts.

That afternoon she and Felicity had arranged to visit the estate workers who had lost their sons in France. She had to show them a good example and try to give them some measure of hope and comfort. She was trying to be useful and had already organised a knitting circle to be held weekly at The Hall. The soldiers would be in dire need of warm socks and sweaters in the coming winter months. The Dower House on the east boundary of the park was being converted so that it could be used as a hospital. She had arranged for members of the Red Cross to come to The Hall to give her, Felicity and the servants basic training in First Aid. When the hospital was established she intended to manage it with the help of the Red Cross and possibly to help out there when needed. That was all she could do besides watch and wait and that was going to be the hardest part of all. She glanced down at her fob watch. It was almost lunch time. She had better go and warn Felicity. She glanced out of the windows once more and was relieved to see that Guy had ceased his pacing. He had always had a healthy appetite and it must have driven him in for luncheon. She sighed and turned towards the door that led to the long corridor. Life must go on she supposed, but she sometimes wondered why.

6

Amy awoke to feel the warm sun filtering through the curtains onto her face. It was a fine spring day, and she had overslept, so she hurriedly showered and dressed and made herself a light lunch, before meeting Tanya in the conservatory. They sat drinking their coffee there before they went for a stroll in the grounds. Amy was both flattered and bewildered that Tanya was interested in hearing about her early life. She had always considered that her life had been rather dull and uneventful; apart from the war years, of course, but it seemed young people were now interested in those years again. It was a far cry from the immediate post war years, when no one wanted to hear anything about war experiences. Then the Second World War had raised its ugly head and started to roar. It followed too quickly on the heels of the First World War as a direct consequence of the vengeful Peace of Versailles, and the war weary generations, which immediately followed 1945, just wanted to forget about both wars with their shortages and brutality. Two global conflicts in less than twenty years had killed their appetite for war completely and they just wanted to be carefree and enjoy life.

This current generation, however, had a completely different attitude towards the wars. They had grown up in a time of peace and prosperity and whilst they had a horror of the waste of both wars, they also had a great admiration for those who fought in them, both on the battle field and in the bombed cities. They were also rather incredulous at the way that the young men of those generations gave up their lives without a murmur, and their admiration gave Amy a sense of satisfaction that the courage of the young men she knew and loved was at last being recognized.

As they walked Tanya asked Amy to continue her story. She couldn't remember where she had finished, but Tanya was as sharp as a knife and remembered that it was New Year 1915. With an inward sigh Amy continued her story.

'That's right, New Year 1915, well the casualty lists were still long, of course, but we hadn't yet experienced the slaughter of the big pushes of 1916. At home, we were starting to come to terms with the fact that our lives had changed forever. Lady Felicity was still trying to persuade her father to allow her to go and train as a nurse, because of course she couldn't go without his permission. Her fiancé, Bertie, was no longer safely training troops in Britain, but was now out in France, and in continual danger. Although women's regiments were formed towards the end of the war, in 1915 the only way women could serve during war time was by nursing the sick and wounded, so that's what Lady Felicity intended to do. She saw the war as an opportunity to gain some independence, as well as help the war effort; however, Lord Leaversham was still resistant to the idea of his daughter working for a living. He couldn't accept the changes that had taken place in the six months since the war began. I think he still thought that it would suddenly end and everything would go back to the way it was. Anyway, Lady Felicity continued to pester him day and night for permission to go and train. She had also suggested that if she went, I should join the Voluntary Aid Detachment, and also train as a nurse. I was doubtful at first, but the more I thought about it the more it seemed an attractive alternative to sitting and waiting for news from the Front.

The spring of 1915 was a fairly quiet time in the war. The casualty lists continued to appear in the Times, but there were no great offences. Then on April 25th 1915, a combined British and Australian Force landed at Gallipoli. It was a total disaster, but the news only filtered back to us slowly that was a black time. Then the Battle of Loos took place on September 15th 1915 and it was the first big offensive to take place in France since the First Battle of Ypres the year before, when Garth was killed. The fighting was fierce and the casualty numbers were very high. We were terribly shocked when we read the long casualty lists that appeared in the British newspapers after the battle. But they were nothing compared with the later losses on the Somme, and we were still rather naïve then and believed the papers when they told us that every offensive was a great victory. Later we realised that they always initially described every battle as a great victory. Eventually we realised that the 'victory' consisted of gaining very little ground at an enormous cost in lives, and actually was relative.

I was feeling terribly restless. I had had more conversations with Lady Felicity about training to be a VAD. I was beginning to feel really useless; the house was no longer the busy, sociable place it had once been, and I was tired of drifting around aimlessly.

'Could you just have gone and nursed? Would you have had to have permission from any one?'

'Oh yes, if Lady Felicity was denied permission, I couldn't really go. I liked working for the family, it was all I knew. If I just walked out I had to consider what would happen after the war ended. I would have no position, no reference and there was the issue of loyalty as well. The family had looked after me, even though I worked hard for them, and I couldn't leave without their blessing and father's permission. Anyway, things were solved for me eventually; in the late autumn of 1915 Lord Leaversham relented and gave Lady Felicity permission to apply to the Queen Alexander's Imperial Nursing Service to train as a nurse. He had begun to accept that the war was not going to be won quickly, it was going to be a long hard struggle and we needed every able bodied man and woman to help.

I was still undecided what to do. It's difficult for you to realise now Tanya, just how hard it was for us women to make an independent decision. We had been under the rule of men all our lives and had never been given the opportunity to make an independent decision. I was also more than a little afraid. I had visited London, but as an employee of the family, and the thought of going to live there alone terrified me. I decided to seek father's advice, and on my day off I went to the cottage to see him. He had changed such a lot since the outbreak of war. I think he was working too hard, trying to maintain his high standards in the garden. He just couldn't do it without the man power and watching his beloved gardens fall into neglect simply ate away at his very being, and he was continually worried about my brother, Tom. He had been home on leave twice, but he was so changed, and distracted that it worried father. Tom wouldn't talk about the war; he was pale and thin and flew into rages over nothing. With Tom in the army father was left in the care of Tom's wife, Lizzie. She was not a warm character and although she took care of father, she was not much company for him. I think he was lonely and disillusioned.

I went to see him on my next day off. I never really felt at home in the cottage after mother died, as I've said before, but I never stopped visiting father. After lunch he suggested that I go and see his vegetable patch. He was always proud of his ability to make things grow and he did seem to have a special touch, green fingers he called it, also we could talk in private there, without Lizzie eavesdropping. It was a warm autumn day and we strolled up and down the beds admiring his vegetables, especially his prize cabbages. Eventually, he suggested we rested on the little bench at the end of his garden. Once we were seated I waited patiently whilst he messed about filling and lighting his pipe. When it was successfully glowing he sat puffing contentedly on it for a while before he spoke and I knew not to disturb the peace. When he finally did speak, he asked about life at The Hall and when I'd given him all the gossip, I asked if he'd heard from Tom. His face seemed to darken. He admitted that he was worried about the lad, he'd heard that things were bad out there, as he put it and Tom had been in the thick of the fighting about Loos. He'd told me that Joe Turner's lad had come back from the front a total wreck. Joe worked for one of the tenant farmers. His son, Harold, got the shakes at the slightest thing and had terrible nightmares, woke the whole household up screaming at night. Joe didn't know what to do for him. I think father was more terrified of Tom coming home like that than if he never came home at all. I knew he'd been worried about his state of mind on his last leave. I wrote to Tom myself and got a few lines back now and again, but he was no correspondent and he never conveyed how he really felt about the war, so we were left to wonder.

I decided that now was my chance and I explained to father that I felt I must do something for the war effort. I explained what the Voluntary Aid Detachment was and suggested that perhaps I might join the VAD. He didn't answer at first, just continued puffing on his pipe. Then he said quietly that he couldn't bear to lose me too. Not after losing mother and Tom being away. I felt strangely touched. He'd never expressed his feelings towards me, not since I was a small child. I thought he saw me as part of the furniture, someone to help with the housework or earn some extra money. I just patted his hand to reassure him that I wouldn't do anything without his blessing then we continued to sit there quietly in companionable silence until he finished his pipe and it started to go chilly, when we went indoors. I was due back at The Hall at eight, so I bid Lizzie and father farewell and strolled back through the Park. I didn't feel I could apply to become a VAD just then, but things were to change very quickly.

Two days after I had spent my day off at father's cottage he arrived at the door of the servants' hall. We had closed off most of the servants' area and just kept the kitchen and the servants' hall heated. He looked terrible. He was dressed in his outdoor clothes and held his hat in his hand. He asked if I could be excused, so I got up and went outside with him. He walked behind the wall that sheltered the estate offices and put his head in his hands. His shoulders were shaking, I watched him with dread as I knew what was coming. Then he suddenly seemed to take control of himself, rifled though his pockets and pulled out a telegram. I could hardly bear to read it. I already knew what it would say. My worst fears were confirmed. Tom was dead. He had been wounded at Loos and died of his wounds at a casualty clearing station. I just put my arms round father and we clung together. I think he wept, though I couldn't be sure. I had never seen him exhibit emotion before, and it scared me to see it. He always seemed to be so solid, nothing ever worried him, but the death of his only son was a terrible blow and there were no grandchildren to comfort him. I think he felt that his life had been for nothing, and there was nothing to show for his hard work, no one to follow in his footsteps. Eventually we pulled ourselves together and prepared to return to our work. Him to the gardens and his memories and me back to the servants' hall, but I was too upset to do much work that day.

Work had no meaning for either of us anymore. The satisfaction that was to be gained from partaking in the smooth running of a successful estate had gone. Leaversham Hall was looking tired, run down, and shabby. Father looked at me fiercely before he went back to the gardens. He told me to join my nursing group and get out there to France. Maybe if I'd been there our Tom wouldn't have died from his wounds. Flawed logic I know, but I understood what he meant. I walked back to the servants' hall with a heavy heart. Tom, dear dependable Tom, dead. I could hardly believe it. We had never been terribly close, but I loved him just the same, and I cursed the damn war with its insatiable appetite for young men, I cursed it to the heavens. One little thought comforted me though, that was the thought that Tom would be with mother again. They would have each other.'

'How did you bear it? All those deaths, all that misery?'

'We were all in it together that's how; everyone was suffering the same so it made it bearable somehow.'

'Did you want to join up? Did Tom's death make you keener?'

'Oh yes, as soon as I got the opportunity I asked Lady Felicity for information about becoming a VAD. I could see that my position as a lady's maid was about to become redundant. Once Lady Felicity left to train in London there would be no place for me, Lady Leaversham had her own maid. I think I mentioned before that Lady Felicity had encouraged me to read and educate myself. She helped me by guiding me to suitable books in the library and I enjoyed reading them. She also took the time to show me how to write a letter correctly then we would discuss the books that I had read. We had a far more informal relationship during the war than we had before the fighting started. Lady Felicity thoroughly approved of my ambition to help the war effort.

She gave me the address of the Red Cross at Devonshire House in London and helped me to draft a letter. Full of trepidation I wrote to them to enquire about the possibility of training to be a VAD. Whilst I was never going to be an intellectual, I had learned a lot whilst working for the Leaversham family. Lady Felicity had helped me to improve my education, but I had also grown up and learned to speak properly and conduct myself in a lady-like manner. I was at home with people of any class and these attributes were useful when applying to the Red Cross.

The letter inviting me to go for interview came in November 1915. I had some money saved up, but the Leavershams, or rather Lady Felicity, paid for my rail fare to London. I don't think I have ever been so terrified in my entire life. I got a taxi cab from the station to Devonshire House and arrived in good time. I was interviewed by the matron. She reminded me a little of Lady Leaversham and I tried to answer her questions as truthfully as I could. I lied about my age, of course, I told her that I was twenty three, when I was, in fact, only nineteen, but I wanted to work in the Army Hospitals and that was the required age. I didn't think that they would take me, but I received a letter in December instructing me to report for duty at the beginning of January. I was numb with shock. Me, a lady's maid, being accepted to nurse soldiers! I was overwhelmed. I didn't think that I'd be good enough.

I asked leave to visit father to tell him the news. He looked sad and old. He had lost his only son and now his daughter was going away. Oh he didn't try to stop me, but I could see what an effort it was to hide his feelings. I admired the fact that he wasn't at all selfish about it; he knew I wanted to go, and he knew I was needed. He always put the feelings of others before his own. So I said my goodbyes to him and prepared for my new life as a nurse.

7

I felt like a real woman of the world travelling down to London on the train. I was to be attached to a military extension of one of the large London Hospitals, which was situated in the East End. It was in a rundown working class area that seemed to consist of slum housing and public houses. I wasn't very impressed at all. I was billeted in a house some two miles away from the hospital, which I thought was ridiculous. I had always lived in the house where I worked and I disliked the trek to work every morning and the same trudge home at night. It also seemed inefficient to me, by the time we got to the hospital in a morning, we were already tired. There were trams that ran from the nurses' home to the hospital, but at that time in the morning they were full of workmen and there was rarely a space on them for us. Most mornings we walked all the way there and all the way home at night. If it rained, we got soaked, which meant that nurses caught cold and went off sick. It seemed such a waste of man power, or woman power,' Amy twinkled at Tanya who smiled back, 'but they didn't seem to care, we were young, enthusiastic, easily manipulated, females, and quite simply they knew we would tolerate any kind of accommodation they allocated us and they were right. They took advantage of us. They could easily have built temporary accommodation in the hospital grounds or found somewhere that was nearer.

The powers that be had adapted an old school as a nurses' home for the VADs. The rooms had been divided into cubicles using curtains to separate each living area, but no attempt had been made to make it cheerful or welcoming. The curtains were second hand, miserable, and washed out. They did nothing to cheer up an already depressing room. We each had a bed, a chest of drawers and a wash stand. They were adequate, but no more. Even the servants' quarters at Leaversham Hall had been more cheerful than this, and some of the girls had come from privileged backgrounds, so it was very hard on them. The house was freezing cold, but there was no heating in the attics at Leaversham so I adapted quite well, but many of the girls came from warm homes and immediately went down with chills and fevers. So having no heating seemed counterproductive to me. When I arrived, I kept a very low profile, as we were a mixed group of girls. Some were from aristocratic families, some from wealthy homes; others had fathers who were in the professions or business. Most were upper or middle class and fairly well educated. There were few working girls like me, but most of the girls were friendly. I didn't tell them I had been in service, I passed myself off as the daughter of a Cheshire farmer, which wasn't far from the truth and I got away with it, because I spoke without an accent and knew how to behave. I was afraid that some of the girls would look down on me, but no one did apart from the odd one who was a bit snooty, but they didn't seem to stay long. Most of the girls worked as a team, and we all suffered the same shortages and discomforts.

Our job was hard and it was especially difficult for the girls who were used to living in upper class comfort with servants. They had never done any domestic work in their lives, and it was a terrible hardship for them at first, but I never heard anyone really complain. We all grumbled a little as our day was long and unrelentingly tough. We rose at 5.45 am, had a quick wash in icy water then walked to the hospital. We ate breakfast in the nurses' dining room, then changed our shoes, put on clean aprons in the cloakroom, (which was at the back of the hospital, miles from where we worked!) and had to be on the wards and ready for duty by 7.30 am. We were then on duty until 8.00 pm. They were shorter days than I had worked at The Hall, but there were no breaks. We were never allowed to sit down on the wards or disappear for a chat around the nursery fire. We were on duty the whole time and it was tough. The other girls, who weren't as used to physical work as I was, found it particularly exhausting, but they rarely complained. After work we had supper at the hospital then walked home. The workmen's trams were nearly always full at night too!

When we got back to the nurses' home all we wanted was a hot bath to ease our aching bones and sore feet, but there was only one bathroom between twenty young women, which made no sense. We had all been dealing with septic wounds and infectious diseases all day, and apart from the fact that a warm bath would have been comforting, we needed to keep clean to avoid infection. However, we hardly ever got one. The bathroom was like something out of a museum. It had an old, useless geyser, which took an age to fill the bath with tepid water, it was never actually hot. Of course, the senior nurses always bagged it first, so the VADs rarely got a bath in the nurses' home. I used to sneak off to the public baths on my day off and have a good soak. They weren't the pleasantest of places, as you had to queue up with all the working girls and your bath had probably been used by thirty other girls that day, but they were clean and it was bliss to soak in hot water after spending a week strip washing in cold water! Once we'd had a strip wash we only had a short time to chat and get into bed. At 10.00 pm prompt the lights went out. Usually, we were so exhausted we fell fast asleep, but it didn't matter if you wanted to read, the lights went out and that was that.'

Tanya laughed, 'Oh and I can imagine today's young women putting up with those conditions! The unions would have something to say, even in wartime! You were being treated like children! I can't believe it, being put to bed at 10 o'clock!'

'We had no choice, my dear, and we were used to being told what to do, but in spite of the discomfort we had one enormous advantage, freedom and independence! I had worked in a large house and was on duty twenty four hours a day; even on my day off I was expected to go no further than my father's house. The girls I was living and working with had lived with their parents and been chaperoned all their lives, like Lady Felicity. To be able to come and go as we liked, walk to and from the hospital alone, and go where we pleased on our half day off without being accountable to any one was heaven. These were great freedoms to us, as parents and employers felt that they had to keep young women on a short leash in case they broke free and started living loose lives! Men had been in charge for centuries and suddenly women were working, earning their own money, and able to do what they liked in their spare time. Men were confused and afraid of the changes, but it was wartime and they needed our help, so they controlled us as best as they could, but they couldn't watch us all the time. Our working lives were strictly segregated though. We weren't allowed to talk to or mix with any of the male doctors, and we had to be professional and distant with the male patients. Any hint of a relationship would have resulted in instant dismissal. The doctors weren't much of a temptation, all the young medics were at the front and we were left with the older doctors, some who had come out of retirement. However, as the patients started to recover they flirted shamelessly with us and it was impossible to be cross with them. You had to be careful that sister didn't see though. She was a tartar.'

Tanya was still laughing, 'It's barely believable that they treated you like that and in a war situation. Did any of the nurses have affairs with the doctors or patients?' Amy laughed too, 'Some took the risk, but we worked so hard we didn't have the energy for men.'

'Did you meet anyone Amy?'

Amy went quiet. 'Not really, my time came later. There was one patient I nursed; he was an officer with a dreadful stomach wound. He recovered and went back to the Front. He wrote to me for a while then the letters stopped abruptly, because he'd been killed in action, so I avoided getting too involved after that,' she smiled ruefully at Tanya. 'That was how it was. I had little flirtations with the patients, but I saw what the war was doing to men. They were dying like flies. I saw my fellow VADs walking around like living ghosts, their hearts broken in two because their fiancée or boyfriend had been killed or wounded or worse gassed or blinded so I tried to avoid any serious commitment. I think it was instinctive, not planned, but it was wise. Men just didn't last long in France, or if they did, they came back broken in spirit and health. It was a terrible crime that war, as it devastated a whole generation, my generation, and it was unforgivable that the government allowed it to go on for so long.'

'But the authorities must have been so grateful to you, working as volunteers. You must have been so necessary, with the growing number of casualties.'

'On the contrary my dear, we were treated with contempt. The sisters on the wards seemed to resent the VADs. They saw us as untrained nuisances and gave us all the unpleasant chores to do. We emptied bed pans, cleared up soiled dressings and took them to be incinerated, scrubbed bed mackintoshes, scrubbed floors, cleaned and dusted the ward. It was unrelentingly hard and unpleasant and much harder than being a lady's maid, but I was paid £20.00 a year, £8.00 more than in my previous job, and I got my laundry done, and had a small uniform allowance. I also got one half day off a week, which was better than one day off a month, and although we had to fit in supper and walk back to the nurses' home, my evenings after 8.00 pm were my own. If I could stay awake that is! There were quite a few advantages to nursing, but I found the physical labour hard, very hard indeed.'

'It's ridiculous Amy, to expect you to do the cleaning as well as the nursing. That would never happen now. It was a different world. Aren't we lucky?' Amy smiled at her.

'Indeed it is, a totally different world, but it's a fairer world. Mind you we only had to clean the wards. There were cleaners who did the really heavy stuff.'

'Did you do any real nursing?'

'Oh yes, as far as the nursing was concerned we were thrown in at the deep end, because the wounds inflicted by shrapnel were appalling, and we had to help with the dressings every day. Sometimes I wondered how men could be so seriously wounded and survive, and there was little in the way of pain relief, with morphine at one end of the spectrum and aspirin at the other, there were no analgesics. The worse time on the ward was after a big push when we had to assist with the dressings of recently injured men, and there were so many of them. Some of the wounds were, oh I don't think I can describe them, they were obscene. There were no antibiotics then and gangrene meant amputation or death, so we had to keep them scrupulously clean because of the risk of infection. I remember the first amputation dressing that I had to assist with. I had to stand and hold the stump of an amputated arm whilst it was being cleaned and re-dressed. I nearly fainted, but the nursing sister, who was doing the dressing, would have treated me with such contempt, her worst fear was that we were silly, untrained and hysterical. If I'd fainted I would have proved her right, so I controlled myself and managed to remain upright. Also, the patient, who was almost green with the pain, didn't faint or scream, so how could I insult him by letting him know that his raw bleeding stump repulsed me? I couldn't, but sometimes after the dressing was finished I had to rush off to vomit in the sluice, but that was in the early days, I soon got used to it. The bullet wounds were bad, but as I said the shrapnel wounds were the worst. It was hard, almost pitiful, to see healthy, strong, young bodies disfigured in this way. I eventually became hardened to it or I wouldn't have been any good to anyone, but it still angered me. The men were wonderful, so brave, so uncomplaining, I used to marvel at their capacity to endure pain. So we had to stay cheerful and bright. We owed it to their courage.'

Amy and Tanya walked along in silence for a while.

'There was one young man I remember in particular' Amy's

voice suddenly broke into Tanya's thoughts, 'He was only eighteen and he had been hit in his lower abdomen. He had been completely castrated. I can't start to imagine what went through his mind. He was a lovely looking chap, with blonde curly hair and a cherubic face. We had to dress his wound every day and I hated it. It was agony for him and us. As soon as he heard the dressing trolley squeaking down the corridor he blanched with fear, and watched it, with large, dark, terrified eyes as it travelled down the ward until it stopped at his bed. His wounds were terrible and in such a delicate place. We all dreaded the dressing, but never once did he scream out or cause a fuss. Throughout the dressing he lay there biting his lips, with perspiration standing out on his forehead, but he never uttered a sound. He was so brave. Nevertheless, in spite of our best efforts he died. He had been left too long in the clearing station, and the wound had become infected before he reached us. I heard he was an only child with an elderly widowed mother.' Amy's voice broke and she stopped. Suddenly a leaf on a nearby rhododendron bush needed her close attention. Tanya respected her privacy and walked on a little feigning interest in the spring flowers. Once she had gained control, Amy joined her and took her arm.

'Sorry about that. He was a bit special.' Tanya patted her arm and they walked on. 'Once the patients started to get better, life on the wards could be quite good fun, as long as you kept out of the way of sister. The men all had gramophones and they played all the latest records and flirted with us nurses, it was good fun, but once they were better they were discharged. Then the empty ward was scrubbed and disinfected, and the beds prepared for the wounded of the next push. I hated that, looking at row after row of clean, freshly made beds waiting for the next consignment of wounded. We knew we had to face stretcher after stretcher of injured men. If the casualty stations and hospitals in France were overwhelmed we sometimes received the wounded straight from the battlefield. They were in such a state when they came in; they were caked with foul smelling mud and crawling with lice. Often their wounds still had a filthy field dressing on, and were encrusted with blood. It was no wonder they became infected. We had to cut the clothes off most of the men and burn them. We then had to clean them up and de-louse them, before we could see to their wounds. Sister had a horror of lice and scattered lice powder everywhere. We had to be very careful not to catch any, but it did happen. I've thought about it so much Tanya, what kind of conditions were they fighting in to get into that state, and how did they get such terrible wounds?' Amy shook her head. Tanya guided her to a garden seat and they sat in silence for some time.

'I suppose it was the advance in technology that caught them out,' Amy said eventually breaking the silence, 'You know, they went off to war in 1914 expecting cavalry charges and muskets and they got massive battery guns, machine guns and gas. The defences didn't catch up with the weapons until the tank arrived, and the generals didn't have the imagination to alter their strategies. They just kept on sending waves of men, mere flesh and blood, against molten steel. It's easy for us to criticise, but I don't suppose they knew how to deal with the new weapons, the new mechanised warfare. Still it was hard to take, and they were dark days, four years of darkness and misery for a lot of people. I mean people made the best of it. They laughed and joked and put on a good face, but underneath there was this terrible feeling of tragedy. I never knew how to cope with white faced nurses who had lost their fiancées and sweethearts in the fighting. Men they had been deeply in love with, who they were unlikely to replace. I felt for them, but there was nothing I could say that would really comfort them, and they knew and I knew that they were unlikely to find love again, because there were so few marriageable men left, so they probably faced a life alone without a husband and children. I felt so sorry for them. Then there were mothers who lost their sons, like the mother of my blonde soldier. Terrible, just terrible, unimaginable in 1913, but there it was.

Anyway this won't do. I'm getting a bit maudlin. Why don't you tell me about your life? Are you enjoying university?'

Tanya smiled, 'My life is extremely boring compared to yours. I am an only child; my parents still live together happily in a Cheshire village. I had a wonderful childhood; we were not rich, but comfortable. I had an old pony and spent most of my time on it. I worked hard, did well at school, always wanted to read History and I got a place at Manchester University and work here part time. Eventually I want to work as an archivist or writer or something. I have a very boring life when you compare it to your young life.'

'It sounds a lovely life. There's a lot to be said for being bored. Haven't you got a young man? You're a very pretty girl?'

'No, just haven't met anyone, like you during the war. Do you regret those years?'

'I don't know. In a lot of ways the war was the making of me. I began to think of myself as a whole person, not just belonging to a family and being in service all my life. I matured, mixed with people I'd never have met on an equal footing in my previous life, I travelled and I gained my independence. But I missed my brother and although I didn't have a particular loved one to worry about, I felt the loss of others, and the waste. However, throughout the heartbreak that surrounded us daily, we lived life in a state of heightened emotion that was never quite as dramatic again. I didn't realise, at this stage, that the real part of my life was just about to begin, and I was about to fall deeply in love.

8

The two women continued to sit in silence on the bench in the spring weather, but after a short discussion about her life, Tanya wanted to hear more about Amy's life as a VAD and she pressed her to talk some more.

'How long did you nurse in London?'

'Oh, about eighteen months in total, some on night duty. That was easier because we were billeted in the grounds of the hospital in army huts, so we didn't have that long trek to and from the nurses' home. It was a really rough area you know, we often had to pass fights outside pubs on our way home at night and sometimes it could be quite alarming, although we coped. Drunkenness was a big problem during the war that's why the government introduced licensing laws, to stop the workers turning up to work drunk and causing accidents, or worse still not turning up at all because of a hangover.'

'Nothing changes then!' Tanya quipped and they both laughed.

'Well a strange thing happened when I was on night duty. We had prepared the wards for the 'Big Push', as The Battle of the Somme was known then. It was the evening of July 1st and we nurses had cleaned and sterilised the wards and were standing looking at the rows of clean beds waiting to be occupied by yet another wave of seriously wounded men to arrive. There were so many wounded on the first day of the Somme, over 60,000 dead or wounded that the medics in France were overwhelmed. It was inconceivable, 60,000! Many were brought over straight from France by boat then transported to Waterloo Station where they were sorted out and sent to the appropriate hospitals by ambulance.

As the first ambulances started to arrive it was pandemonium. The stretcher bearers were just bringing the wounded in, one after another, and putting them on the floor, eventually we had to stop them, because we were full to capacity. No one, but no one had expected casualties on that scale! As well as the huts that had been equipped for use as wards, they had to erect marquees in the grounds to house the injured. We worked non-stop, cutting off the filthy uniforms, cleaning the men, getting them into bed and then starting to dress their wounds and give them some pain relief. Stretcher after stretcher we processed in this way, working against the clock. The longer a wound was left with a field dressing on, the more likely it was that infection would set in and amputation or death could occur. On and on we worked, oblivious to sore feet, aching backs or even hunger. The men were what was important then, we had to get them cleaned up, in bed and comfortable as quickly as we could. It's an awful thing to reveal, but when you are dealing with as many wounded men as that, whilst of course each man is important, and you give them all the care you can, they cease to be individuals. They are just khaki clad soldiers who are being processed, and need to be made comfortable as quickly as possible.

Anyway, I was in the process of undressing one officer when I heard him utter, 'Amy.' I was so tired that I thought that I was hearing things, but no, the officer repeated my name again in a rasping whisper. I was in the process of removing his uniform prior to washing him, so I gently wiped his face clean, and I could hardly believe my eyes when I revealed the face under the grime. It was Bertie Ellerswood, well still Lord Ellerswood to me. He looked completely different from the smart gentleman who used to visit The Hall. He was dirty and unkempt like all the soldiers, and his eyes were full off tears with the emotion of seeing someone from home. I, too, was choking then he whispered 'Felicity' I understood and told him not to worry, I would get word to her. I took his hand, but he must have passed out, as he was badly wounded, and in terrible pain; his leg was badly smashed up and he was on the list of emergency operations for the next day. I think we were both equally overcome from seeing someone from home, someone who remembered life before the war. Once I knew who he was I passed him over to another VAD for washing. In all modesty, even with my training I couldn't wash a former employer.

Once he was washed, and was safely in bed I was sent with the dressing party to clean and dress his wound. I was horrified when I saw his leg. The femur had been completely smashed by shrapnel and the surrounding flesh was just keeping the leg intact. His foot was hanging at a peculiar angle and infection had already set in. I had seen wounds like that before, and I felt quite heartsick. He was very ill indeed. I kept checking on him all through the night, even in the ongoing chaos of admissions, but I had to be careful that sister didn't become suspicious. Mercifully he was unconscious most of the night, and probably full of morphine. All I could do was pray as hard as I could that he would live, at least until he saw Lady Felicity. I knew that he was seriously ill and I had doubts that he would survive the operation.

After what seemed like the longest night of my life we were eventually relieved by the day nurses at 7.30 am. Exhausted as I was, the first thing I did when I got off duty was use the public telephone to contact Lady Felicity's hospital to tell her that Lord Ellerswood was alive, and on my ward. I had no trouble getting through and they promised to get a message to her. I then went along to the dining hall for breakfast. I was so exhausted the night before that I hadn't really absorbed the enormity of the coincidence that he should land on my ward. Oh Tanya, I was so glad that morning that I was staying in one of the huts whilst I was on night duty and didn't have to walk to the nurses' home. I think that I would have fallen asleep on the way. As it was it took a great effort to stagger over to my hut after breakfast and I collapsed on my bed fully clothed. I was so exhausted that I slept in that position unit late afternoon when I awoke; it was about 4.30 pm and almost immediately I remembered Bertie Ellerswood, he would have had his operation by then and I needed to find out if he had survived the likely amputation. I decided to get dressed then go back to the ward before I was due to go on duty to find out how he was.

Making a great effort, I pulled myself off my bed, collected a fresh set of underclothes and uniform and walked over to the hospital to have a much needed bath. The availability of the hospital bathrooms was another advantage of being on night duty, but the plumbing in them was hardly any better than that in the nurses' home. It was ancient and you had to share the bathroom with a variety of cockroaches and beetles. However, the water was hot and the soap was fresh and it was delicious to feel clean. My uniform, which I'd dropped on the floor, was covered in mud and blood and other unrecognisable substances. It looked as though I had fought on the Somme myself. I just gathered it up and stuffed it in the laundry bag. It was strange Tanya. Maybe it was a subconscious mechanism to protect myself or maybe I simply became brutalised, but I never allowed myself to become sentimental about the fighting men. However, in the intervening years I have not been so successful at chasing away the ghosts of the many men that I nursed. It's strange, but they seem to be clearer and closer the older I get, and I seem to suffer far more acutely now than I ever did at the time.' Amy smiled ruefully at Tanya who grasped her hand and gave it a reassuring squeeze.

'Well once I was clean and respectable I made my way to the surgical ward where I was working. I didn't want sister to know that I was enquiring about a patient. She disapproved of any kind of emotional involvement, so I intended to intercept one of the VADs. Our ward was full to overflowing at this stage, so the chaos of admitting new patients had subsided. I turned off the corridor into the ward and nearly fell over Lady Felicity. I was so pleased to see her, but was amazed at the way she greeted me. She gathered me up into her arms her whole frame shuddering with sobs, 'Oh Amy,' was all she could say. I just held her until her sobbing had subsided, then I asked her how Lord Ellerswood was.

'He's alive, just, but he's very ill.' She paused, biting her lips and looking at the floor as she tried to keep control of her emotions. 'They've amputated,' was all that she could manage, 'just above the knee, gangrene, you know.'

I certainly did know. I persuaded her to take a walk in the hospital gardens. It was a beautiful July day, the sun was shining, the birds were singing, and it was impossible to imagine that just across the Channel the battle was still raging. It became known as the blackest day in the history of the British Army, but thankfully we had no idea how bad things were at that point. We sat holding hands for some time. I had to be back on duty, and although she had been relieved of her shift for the day so she could visit Bertie, Lady Felicity or Felicity as I now knew her, and would continue to call her after the intimacy of the day, would have to return to her hospital. If he survived the operation, and he was very ill, Bertie, as I now referred to him, would be invalided out of the army. She realised that he would then be safe, but he had to survive the operation and survive the mental damage that a year at the Front and an amputation would have inflicted. We didn't talk about death. We talked about the future, when he was discharged. She intended that they should go down to his place in Cornwall and marry quietly. She was going to leave nursing and devote her time to him. She invited me to stay, and I was very touched. We talked like old friends and I thought what a curious transition this war had wrought on everyone.

We parted cordially and I promised to let her know if there was any news about Bettie's condition, then I went to the dining hall for my supper before I went back on duty.

9

Bertie was very ill after the operation to amputate his leg and for the first few days he ran a high temperature and was quite delirious. The doctors were worried that during the amputation they may not have removed all the infected tissue and that gangrene had set in further up the leg. However, on the third day his temperature dropped, he regained consciousness and started to improve. Felicity came to see him whenever her nursing commitments allowed her to. It was difficult for her to get leave to see him as often as she would have liked, as the sister in charge of her ward wouldn't radically alter her shifts for one wounded fiancée, when so many men were ill and wounded and needed caring for. Felicity also had the added problem of having to travel across London in wartime to try to get to the hospital for official visiting hours. She was quite lucky though, although our Sister was a tyrant on the ward with her own nurses and VADs, she was very kind to relations who had travelled long distances to visit seriously ill husbands and fiancées. She was particularly kind to nurses from other hospitals, perhaps she felt that they already knew the routine of a ward and wouldn't interfere with its smooth running. Also the visiting nurses would sit by the bedside of their loved ones during the dangerous hours after surgery and could observe the patient with a trained eye. It meant that our own nurses didn't have to spend precious hours on one patient when there were fifty others who required their services.

The professionally trained sisters were efficiency itself, they drove their nurses and VADs very hard, yet their love and devotion to their patients, whilst never sentimental, was without question total. They always put their patient's needs before anything else. Their wards ran like clockwork, were spotlessly clean and their patients were nursed to the highest possible standards. I had, and still do have, the highest regard for them all. So it was that Sister allowed Felicity unlimited access to the ward as long as she sat quietly by Bettie's bed and didn't disrupt our strict routine. This only lasted as long as he was seriously ill; once he started to improve Felicity had to revert to normal visiting hours like everyone else. I don't know how she managed to keep going during those weeks. Her own hospital would have been as busy as ours was and the work on the wards was relentless and I certainly needed all the rest I could get. When I finished working, I usually fell straight into bed, but as soon as Felicity came off duty, she travelled straight across wartime London to my hospital in order to see Bertie at all. She then stayed with him until it was almost time for her to go back on duty. She can't have been having more than a few hours of sleep a night and she was under intense emotional pressure during the first few days after the operation as there was a very real chance that he may die.

As I went about my ward duties, I watched her sitting by his bed, holding his hand, lovingly wiping his face with a cool, damp cloth, and willing him better. The shock of seeing him so desperately ill would also have taken a toll on her emotions. She was being stretched to the limit both mentally and physically, and I wondered how long she could go on. I couldn't help but compare this pale, thin, exhausted woman in her nurse's uniform, with the beautiful society heiress who was the envy of the county at her engagement party less than two years ago. Then she was leading the life she had been born to, a life of privilege and wealth, and the most important thing she had to worry about was the design of her wedding dress. Now she was in a life or death situation watching over her once tall and handsome fiancée who was now a shattered man, an amputee who may not survive the intensive surgery he had undergone. Nevertheless, I don't think she ever thought about the past or regretted the loss of her privileged life. Her relationship with Bertie was based on a deep abiding love and all she wanted was his recovery and survival. She didn't care that he was ill and disabled; she just wanted him fit and well so that they could marry and live as normal a life as possible. I think that she was secretly relieved that he was permanently disabled because it meant that he couldn't be sent back to the Front and that meant that the war was effectively over for both of them. Most of her childhood friends, her brothers, distant cousins and most of the young men of her acquaintance were in constant danger and many had already been killed or wounded, now, even if he had lost a leg, the man she loved was safe.

Occasionally she caught my eye as I rushed past his bed with a bedpan or kidney bowl and we exchanged a wan smile. If she was leaving the ward as I was coming off duty she would wait for me and we would walk to the dining hall and talk about her future life with Bertie. He had been taken off the 'at risk' list after the first few weeks, so she was able to relax a little and start to anticipate a future life with him. It was so strange the way that our roles in life had changed so dramatically; we were no longer mistress and servant, but two nurses doing the same job; two nurses who had a deep concern for all the young, wounded men in our care and a particular interest in her fiancée, who was lying on my ward recovering from a radical amputation. The problem was that although he was recovering quite well physically, he couldn't adjust mentally to the idea of having lost a leg and it was having a terrible psychological effect on him. He sank into a deep depression, which was not at all unusual with amputees as they started to improve. As young men it was a terrible blow to all of them to realise that they could no longer move about freely; no longer run and jump and join in the rough and tumble of a rugby game or swim in a lake. Bertie had enjoyed all types of sport and been an expert horseman and polo player, and although he would be fitted with a prosthetic leg and have reasonable freedom of movement, he would never again be able to compete in those sporting activities that had so defined his life. He would, with time, achieve a fairly high level of mobility, but nothing would be quite the same. He was also concerned that Felicity was standing by him merely out of pity; he felt that he was a burden to her now and at one stage he was so depressed that he tried to break off the engagement so that she would be free to marry 'a whole man', as he put it. He seemed to have forgotten that he was the man that she loved, and that with or without his leg, he was the man that she wanted to marry.

Felicity was having to deal with all these life changing problems more or less alone, and during those dark days I was the only person she had to talk to. I was her link with the past, and as a nurse I understood how difficult and complex Bertie's physical and mental recovery was going to be. I was able to give her support and encouragement in those dark days after the amputation, and talk with her about the past and the future that they would now have together. Over that time our relationship changed slowly, yet subtly, we became friends. She was totally dependent on me to sustain her during that difficult time, and I gave her all the support that I could. We became very close and remained close for the rest of our lives. Those terrible months bound us together in some, and the servant and mistress days were gone forever.

Lady Leaversham came down to visit Felicity and Bertie several times. She recognised me and was always gracious and kind, but I was still Amy, her daughter's maid, to her. She was finding it very difficult to adjust to the quickly changing world that had emerged during the war, and it was easy to see why. Life had changed out of all recognition in two short years and a lady of her age, used to a comfortable and settled existence within a prescribed social hierarchy, couldn't be expected adjust to this new and terrible life. So we remained mistress and servant, although she was very complimentary about my nursing and my work for the war effort. I think she admired all of us and I know that she worked hard in the hospital that she had founded in the Dower House on the estate. Nevertheless, she couldn't quite extend friendship to a former servant and I didn't expect her to. However, I was terribly shocked the first time she came to visit the ward. Her hair had turned quite white; she had lost a tremendous amount of weight and was no longer the statuesque Edwardian beauty that I remembered. But she was still a force to be reckoned with and had lost none of her indomitable spirit.

When we spoke she told me that Guy had been fighting out in France for eighteen months. He had been wounded, like so many others, on the first day of the Battle of the Somme, and was living at home while he convalesced. She told me that his time in France had changed him. Felicity confided in me that he was much altered and damaged both physically and mentally. He had never really recovered from the death of his twin brother and a year at the front had ravaged his nerves. The family felt that with rest and care he would recover, but Felicity had her doubts. They were also very afraid that once his physical wounds had healed, he would insist on returning to the Front, but were aware that he was not really strong enough to cope. For Lady Leaversham, the grief of losing her youngest son and the unremitting worry about Guy, were slowly wearing her out.

Eventually the strain of nursing and visiting Bertie affected Felicity too, and she collapsed whilst on duty on the ward at her hospital. She was diagnosed as suffering from extreme neurasthenia, stress and exhaustion to you and me, and sent on immediate sick leave. About this time Bertie was considered sufficiently recovered to travel and was discharged into the care of the Leaversham family, as his own parents had died when he was still quite young. Lady Leaverhsam came down from Cheshire to accompany them both back to Cheshire, but I daren't imagine what life was like at The Hall during the following months. The two women were already worn out, and near to collapse and yet still had to support their shattered men, while they tried to piece together some kind of life.

Men at that stage of convalescence were not easy to deal with and were prone to long fits of depression and feelings of uselessness. Illogically, they seemed to feel that they were letting their comrades down that they were shirking in Britain and leaving the fighting to others. It didn't seem to matter that they were physically and mentally unfit to return, but it demonstrated the strong camaraderie and emotional bond that had developed between the fighting men. It was sad, but probably inevitable, that as the war progressed a great chasm emerged between the soldiers and the civilian population. The general public just couldn't comprehend the appalling conditions the troops were enduring at the Front. How could they? So the soldiers found it difficult to talk about their experiences to civilians, who couldn't start to understand the effects of mechanized warfare.

I missed Felicity when she returned to Cheshire she was a link with my former life and a reminder that there was life beyond the war. I felt so sorry for the whole family, and wondered how they were coping. I did ask father for information, but all I got was the usual monosyllabic responses. Felicity, however, did not forget me and wrote regularly, but as to be expected, her letters were full of brave and cheery news, so it was difficult to assess the true situation. I felt curiously flat in the months that followed. I carried out my work efficiently and got a certain satisfaction from that, but I felt that I could do more somehow. I was tired of life in a London hospital and wanted to be nearer the action, at the Front, in France. I think in some curious way I wanted to share the soldier's experience as well as I could. I was a strange little thing in those days. I lived an isolated, detached sort of life, as though I were in hibernation until it was time for me to emerge and my real life to begin. I had plenty of friends, but never became too emotionally involved with anyone; I think it was probably a defence mechanism to help me survive during the war. Miraculously at the end of 1916 I was among the lucky few to be given Christmas leave. I had been working for over twelve months, and was due to a week of my two weeks annual leave. It was the first leave I'd had since I started nursing so I decided to go home to see father. He was getting old and I was concerned about him.

One day early in December I came off duty to find a large white envelope waiting for me. I rarely got post and if I did it was usually a rumpled brown envelope from father or one of the girls that I had worked with at The Hall. I certainly never received correspondence on good quality stationery, so I was intrigued. I opened it carefully with great anticipation, and was overwhelmed when I found it contained an invitation to the wedding of Bertie and Felicity. They were getting married at Leaversham Hall on Christmas Eve in the family chapel. Felicity had included a note to tell me that it was going to be a quiet informal affair, just family and close friends. I was delighted to be considered as one of the family or a close friend, I could hardly believe that they would invite me as a guest and I was so pleased that they were going to be together at last. Nevertheless, it was a far cry from the society wedding we were planning in the summer of 1914. But what did all that matter, he was alive, they were happy and suddenly I longed to be at home with the people I loved, the people who had meant so much to me as a child.

The thought of spending Christmas at The Hall breathed new life into me and lifted me out of my lethargy. I set about my work with new enthusiasm, and the days flew by until it was time for me to prepare for my leave. I had earned more money whilst in London, than I had ever had before in my life and I had had very little opportunity to spend any of it. I sent money home to father every week so that he could enjoy small luxuries such as tobacco and a drop of whisky, but the rest went into my savings account at the Post Office. I had saved quite a tidy sum, so on my half day I decided to go into London and buy myself a new outfit for the wedding. I had a wonderful outing; it was the first time that I had ever been shopping for my own clothes. The other girls gave me advice on where to go so I took a tram to Victoria and went to Gorringe's on Buckingham Palace Road. There I bought the first new, fashionable clothes that I had ever owned. I chose a beautiful white lace frilled blouse and a violet velvet coat and skirt for the wedding. The skirt was so short that it showed my boots, so I bought a new pair shoes with a heel and strap that fastened over the top. I'd never worn shoes before, only boots. Then I chose a black hat trimmed with green, and violet to match the velvet suit. I was so thrilled! As an afterthought I treated myself to a bright red Tam O'Shanter with a matching scarf. I decided to travel up to Cheshire in my uniform coat as it was the only good coat I owned, but I intended to wear my bright new scarf and hat to brighten it up, and keep me warm. It was strictly against the rules, but I was a little tired of uniform. Whilst I was in the city I bought some material and silks to make and embroider a tray cloth for the happy couple as a wedding present. It was such a wonderful, heady feeling to be able to spend money that I had earned myself, and to spend it as I pleased.

Christmas on the ward was a lovely time, the worst cases that had been brought in from the Somme had sadly passed away, but those who had survived their wounds were now feeling quite perky, and I had to put up with quite a bit of teasing, mild flirting (when sister was out of earshot) and innuendoes about my love life. They all assumed that I had a 'young man' at the Front and it was easier to let them believe that than to protest. For the first time in my life I began to see myself through the eyes of men and I realised that I was considered to be quite pretty. I had always considered myself to be a poor thing, thin and unattractive, but I had filled out and had a nice figure. I had a good skin, smooth and milky with dark thick lashed eyes and hair of a most unusual colour, a sort of auburn blonde. I think they call it strawberry blonde now, and it was thick with a tendency to curl and escape from under my cap, much to sister's annoyance. I was proud of my hair you know and even after the war when everyone else cut their hair to be fashionable I wouldn't part with mine.

The one abiding memory of the wards I think all VADs and nurses will have was the gramophones, and the men loved to play them. The old wind up ones, you know? They played all the old wartime favourites, 'If You Were the Only Girl in the World,' 'When Irish Eyes are Smiling' and Harry Lauder choruses – he wasn't a favourite of mine, but the men loved his records, and they played them over and over again. At times they nearly drove me mad, but now I can't hear them without feeling very nostalgic. They remind me of those wonderful, brave, cheerful men. Anyway, with convalescing patients and constantly playing gramophones, the weeks before Christmas were a lovely time on the wards. We decorated the ceiling and walls with coloured paper chains and put together bags for the men containing Red Cross gifts, small home-made presents, sweets, nuts, and paper hats. I really enjoyed myself, and for the first time in my life, in spite of the war, and the unremittingly hard work, I felt young and attractive, something of a miracle with swollen feet, chapped hands and aching bones!

Many of the nurses and VADs had lost lovers and fiancées in the past year and they found it hard to join in the festivities. I felt so sorry for them. The sister on night duty with me during the nights leading up to Christmas had been married to a young doctor who had died of wounds on the Somme in the late autumn. I could almost feel the pain that she endured, it was terrible. I just sat each evening and listened patiently while she talked about him. It was cathartic for her and to keep talking about him somehow kept him alive to her. She had been so much in love it was such a terrible shame.

Night duty in the huts at that time was very strange and rather eerie. When the men were settled we nurses sat around the stove in the centre of the ward, and just had one lamp lit which was shaded by red screens so as not to disturb the men. Often when I was alone, if sister had to leave the ward for any reason, I felt an almost ghostly presence. I felt, or imagined, cold, unseen fingers brushing my cheek, or stroking my hair, and I heard footsteps, which walked down the ward then simply stopped in the middle, but there was never anyone there. The men also spoke of strange happenings they had experienced at night, sudden cold draughts and white ladies gliding down the ward. I don't know how much was the product of our over wrought nervous systems and the daily nearness of death, but night time on the ward was strange, not frightening, just strange, but the young and healthy were dying unnaturally early and in enormous numbers, I felt that perhaps they couldn't quite let go of their short lives, and wandered about the hospital until they could find peace, I don't know, maybe it was just our imagination. The men said it was the same at the Front. When they went over the top they spoke of seeing dead colleagues running beside them towards the German trenches, friends who had been dead for months, who seemed to have come back to protect them. It was part of the mystique of that strange time, but my time alone on night duty was quite daunting at times. I was not alone though, all the nurses reported similar experiences.

10

Soon it was time to take my leave of the men and start my journey home for Christmas. I was so excited. I went back to my hut and carefully packed my new clothes, put on my coat and my new Tam O'Shanter hat and scarf and went to wait for the tram to take me to Euston Station. The journey was long and cold, but I felt all aglow in my new red hat and scarf, and I had two soldiers, who were on Christmas leave, for company on the journey to Manchester Piccadilly. There I caught the branch line to Knutsford and started to walk to The Hall. However, half way there I was overtaken by one of the farm hands driving a cart back to the estate. He had been to market, and he recognised me and stopped and offered me a lift to the cottage, which I gratefully accepted.

I was really looking forward to seeing father again, but wondered if working in London would have altered our relationship. I had seen so much devastation and misery and had to grow up very quickly. I had also learned to be independent and had gained in confidence. As I had matured and grown stronger; he had become older and weaker. His role in life had changed completely, his position as head gardener, in charge of a small army of under gardeners, had all but disappeared. He had been a respected figure on the estate, but now he was just a gardener. The war had aged him, as it had most of the civilian population since the beginning of the hostilities. He had always been so tall and strong and physically capable, but I had noticed before I went to London that he was beginning to look stooped and careworn. His eyesight was failing and he could no longer work the long hours that he was used to. He still went to work every day, but he was finding the physical effort hard. Would these changes have altered our relationship, I wondered.

When I arrived he was sitting in front of the range, which

contained a roaring fire, smoking his pipe, waiting for me. When he turned and saw me as I entered, he looked so pleased to see me that I was really touched. He stood up and silently took my valise. I don't think he trusted himself to speak. While he took it up to my room I took off my coat and put on my old apron and made us a pot of tea and some cheese on toast, which we sat and ate in front of the range in the kitchen while we talked about the war. I was so pleased to be home basking in the warmth and security of the fire and the oil lamps. It made me think of my childhood and forget about hospital and all its horrors. The only regret I had was that Mother was not there. It was very depressing to hear stories of so many childhood friends who had been wounded, maimed or killed; there was hardly a family in the village that hadn't been affected by the war. He spoke fondly of Tom, and I don't think that I had realised just how much he grieved for his son, especially as he was getting older, Tom would have been such a help to him.

I asked about the family at The Hall and told him about Felicity and Bertie. He looked shocked at my use of their first names, but didn't comment. He admired Bertie and had seen quite a lot of him on the various shoots that had been held on the estate before the war. It grieved him to see him reduced to a shambling wreck, who struggled to walk and ride, when he had been a strapping, healthy young man just two years ago. He told me that Sir Guy was home for the wedding, which I knew would be a bonus for Felicity. He was still recovering from the wounds he received on the Somme. Father had seen him wandering about the estate and said he didn't look a well man. Apart from his shoulder wound he seemed to be suffering with his nerves and looked grey and haunted. That was something that I could identify with after nursing so many soldiers, often we could repair the physical wounds, but were powerless to heal their broken spirit. The gossips had told father that Bertie had been fitted with a special prosthetic leg for his wedding. I thought it was a bit early, but no doubt he had insisted as he would want to walk down the aisle at his own wedding rather than hop and hobble down on crutches. Father said he had seen him practising on the terrace, trying to get used to his new leg and balance without his crutches, and he found it hard to watch him struggle and fall. He wondered aloud just what kind of a war was going on 'out there' that was capable of breaking good, solid men like them. I didn't comment, but I could have told him worse stories. They were among the lucky ones.

Father asked me about my work, but I sketched over it. How could I explain what I saw every day? My father found it difficult to accept that his little girl was doing such important work and living on her own in London, but like most of the older generation he had accepted that the old ways had gone forever and the war had forced changes that could never have imagined only two years earlier. However, he was very proud that I was no longer just a servant and had been invited to the wedding as a family guest. We sat and talked for a long time in front of that fire. I don't think I'd ever felt so close to him as I did that evening. He told me that Tom's widow had remarried and I think he objected to that. Somehow she had betrayed his memory by marrying 'with indecent haste' as Father put it. Tom had not really had time to start a family before he went to war and Father sometimes felt that it was almost as if Tom had never existed. I think he enjoyed talking to me because I had known and loved Tom. It brought him back in some peculiar way. We went to bed about 9 o'clock as was the custom in the country, early to bed and early to rise. He banked up the fire and I washed the pots then we made our own way to our rooms. It had been a lovely warm night, and I had appreciated that closeness with my father in a world that was becoming more and more alien with each passing day and I think he felt the same.

The following day was the wedding. Father had told me about the preparations. The small gardening staff had decorated the chapel with holly and ivy and white Christmas roses. As the wedding was to take place at three o'clock, it would be dark, so the service was going to be conducted by candlelight. I thought that was so romantic, and I said a prayer for the happy couple before I went to sleep. At least they were safe, the war couldn't touch them anymore and for that I was grateful.

I must have been more exhausted than I realised as I slept quite late the next morning. It was a wonderful luxury. Margaret, the widow of an old estate worker, came in every day to see to father. She cooked his breakfast and then brought him an evening meal, which she sometimes shared with him. I think they had an 'understanding', though he never spoke of it, and I wouldn't have dared question him about it, but I was pleased that he had some comfort in his life and someone to care for him. By the time I got up and dressed, Margaret had been in and revived the fire before giving father his breakfast and tidying round. He always rose with the sun. When I got downstairs I decided to decorate the cottage. I went outside and picked some holly, bits of mistletoe and strands of ivy. I used them to decorate the kitchen, where we would be eating our Christmas dinner, although what on earth it would consist of I had no idea. However, when I looked in the larder I found a small Christmas cake and a pudding. Obviously Margaret's handiwork, though how she had managed on war time rations I'd never know. When I'd finished, I made some toast and a pot of tea and sat roasting in front of the fire until it was time to go upstairs and get ready for the wedding.

I took my time dressing, and when I came down father was standing in the kitchen clothed in his Sunday best. All the workers had been given a half day holiday to watch the wedding and then there was to be a party afterwards in the servants' hall, all courtesy of Bertie and Lord Leaversham. I could tell by his face that he liked my outfit, but he didn't say anything just took my arm and patted my hand while beaming down at me. It was a rare happy day. Father had arranged for a cart to take us to the chapel and it discreetly dropped us at the back. We walked round to the front, where he escorted me into the church, but sat at the back with the servants, whilst I was ushered to the front to join the family and guests. I felt slightly uncomfortable with this arrangement, but he was quite happy and rather proud that his daughter was an invited guest.

The chapel looked beautiful. There were holly wreaths bound with scarlet ribbons on all the stone window sills, and wooden posts had been attached to all the pews, which were wreathed with ivy and Christmas roses and mounted with lighted altar candles, which gave a warm glow. There were still some exotic flowers surviving in the greenhouses and father had put them in pots and arranged them around the chapel. It made me rather nostalgic for the sumptuous bouquets that he had used to decorate The Hall for the engagement party, but he had done a wonderful job with his now limited resources. The whole chapel was bathed in gentle candlelight, and the family crib stood where it always had done by the altar. It was decked with Christmas roses and lit from within by tiny oil lamps held by the three wise men. I felt so peaceful, and the war seemed a million miles away.

Out of a sense of humility I sat at the back of the area reserved for guests, and tried to identify the other people in the chapel. I recognised Lady Leaversham; she was sitting with a young man in uniform, who I assumed was Sir Guy. Bertie, dressed in his dress uniform, and looking terribly nervous, was sitting on the other side of the aisle with his best man, a fellow officer who I vaguely recognised from the engagement party. There were only about twenty other couples; many had an officer on leave with them. They were mainly county families, who I knew by sight, but there couldn't have been more than fifty guests altogether, another sign of the changes wrought by the war.

Suddenly the organist struck up Mendelssohn's Wedding March and Felicity entered the chapel, I turned to watch as she seemed to float slowly up the aisle on the arm of her father, looking positively ethereal in the candlelight. She wore the long, white satin dress, that we had designed together before the war, but she had simplified it by dispensing with the train and all the trimmings, and adding a plain white lace veil of her mother's, which was secured by her engagement tiara, she also wore the set of Cartier amethysts and diamonds that her mother had given her and her jewels flashed a million hopeful messages in the candlelight.

The vicar conducted the traditional wedding service from the Book of Common Prayer, and Bertie stood unaided all the way through it. I was probably the only member of the congregation who knew how painful and difficult that would have been for him. However, I think that he was so happy that he barely noticed. Once again I thanked God that he was safely invalided out of the army. After the service, the wedding party retired to the vestry to sign the register, then the organ struck up Widor's Toccata, and the new Lord and Lady Ellerswood emerged from the gloom of the vestry into the warm candlelight of their new life together. Bertie was starting to look a little strained, but he walked unaided down the aisle, beaming his welcome greeting at everyone until he reached the carriage that was waiting outside. What few members of the estate staff that the war had spared, were waiting outside the little chapel to throw rice, and offer their congratulations to the happy couple, before leaving for their party in the servants' hall. I felt a bit strange going to the family reception in The Hall, but everyone seemed to accept it as normal. I was now a nurse in London with Lady Felicity, not just a lady's maid, and so it was considered right that I went to the reception in The Hall

As I entered the hall alone I felt rather overwhelmed, and I was so glad that I had been in a position to buy a new outfit. At least I felt as well dressed as any of the other guests. The reception hall looked glorious. There were roaring log fires in both the huge fireplaces, and a massive Christmas tree, which would have been grown on the estate, stood in its customary corner. It nearly reached the hall ceiling, and was decked with white and silver baubles, white satin ribbon, and plain white tree lights. Father had decked the hall with winter roses, holly, ivy, and mistletoe and placed small tubs and jardinières full of winter flowers in strategic positions on the marble floor. Small bouquets of hothouse flowers adorned every surface and it looked beautiful. The menservants greeted us at the door with trays containing steaming glasses of mulled wine to warm us after the short walk from the chapel, and the pungent smell of cinnamon, orange and cloves greeted me as I entered The Hall, I almost caught my breath as it all looked so elegant and luxurious. It was such a contrast to the wartime austerity that I had become accustomed to. Fleetingly I was transported back to 1913 and managed for a brief moment to forget about the war and all the unhappiness and deprivation that was causing so much upheaval.

Felicity and Bertie greeted their guests at the entrance to the inner hall and as I stood in line waiting to be received, I felt a little nervous and out of place. I expected to be exposed as a fraud at any moment and be ordered down to the servants' hall, but I needn't have worried. I was a welcome guest, the bride and groom both greeted me like a treasured friend, Felicity took my hand in hers and actually kissed my cheek, and when Bertie took my hand he gave me a special smile, our shared experience had brought us close together and it was a bond that would not be easily broken. All the guests were kind and polite to me, I don't think any of them realised that I was a former domestic, but assumed I was a nursing friend of Lady Felicity's from London. If Lord and Lady Leaversham found the situation a little irregular, they did not show it and were very gracious in their manner towards me.

Once the guests had entered The Hall they were supplied with a crystal flute of champagne, which was permanently refilled by the army of servants hired for the occasion. I couldn't help thinking that there was a time when they would all have been members of the household staff. I had to keep putting my hand over my glass to dissuade them from refilling it. I wasn't used to strong drink and had no intention of making a fool of myself by getting drunk! I spent the first few minutes standing by one of the fireplaces talking to a neighbouring land owner and his wife, who had lost their only son on the Somme on 1st July that year. They were still in deep mourning and wanted to question me about conditions in the military hospitals. He had died in a casualty clearing station of his wounds, and they just wanted to be reassured that everything had been done to save him.

I did reassure them, it would have been cruel to have done anything else, but like all the other VADs and nurses, I knew that the medical preparations for the aftermath of the first day of the Battle of the Somme were woefully inadequate. Sixty thousand men were killed or wounded and there was only one train allocated to take the wounded from the battle field and casualty clearing stations to the Channel ports and home. There were insufficient numbers of casualty clearing stations, and they were inadequately staffed and poorly stocked with medical supplies, there was even a lack of coffins, but I felt sorry for the elderly couple and did not want to add to their distress, so I reassured them that everything possible would have been done to save their son. As I was standing by the fire side sipping my champagne and chatting with the couple, Guy walked in, and the effect he had on me took me by completely by surprise. The sight of his young, old, ravaged face made me feel quite weak. I was having difficulty breathing, and I felt as though I had been winded. What on earth was the matter with me? It took all my self control to concentrate on what the old couple were saying to me and I was sure that my face was flushed, but thankfully, the couple I was talking to didn't appear to have noticed that anything was wrong with me. I fought hard to regain my self control and took a long drink of my champagne to steady my nerves. I recovered slightly and eventually raised the courage to steal another look at him. He still had a powerful effect on me, but this time I was more prepared. He was still a handsome man, but his face was lined and grey and his hair was silver at the temples. Although he couldn't have been more than twenty five years old, he looked at least forty and my heart went out to him. At that precise moment he looked up and our eyes met; my heart simply stopped. In that instant I knew for certain that I would never know another moment's peace as long as this war lasted, and he was fighting in it. I had done the very thing that I had been determined to avoid. I had fallen in love with a serving officer on the Western Front who had a life span that could be measured in months, and I would now begin to suffer like all the other women who had loved ones in France. It was that sudden, and that certain. I felt the colour rise in my cheeks again, and had to pinch my arm and tell myself not to be so stupid. He held my eye for a split second, and he seemed to look straight to the heart of me then as suddenly he looked away. My heart was hammering so loudly that I was sure everyone in the room could hear it, but no one seemed to notice. I muttered my apologies to the elderly couple, and fled to the ladies cloakroom, where I tried to get a grip of myself. This was stupid, he was the heir to the Leaversham Estate and I had been a lady's maid for his sister. He had never even noticed I existed and never would and I had allowed him to have this affect on me. It was ridiculous; no it was worse that ridiculous it was pathetic, but it was real. It had happened and I could no more control it than redirect a fired bullet with the flicker of my eyelash. I splashed my face with cold water, patted it dry and tidied my hair. Once I retained control of myself I returned to the hall and the guests.

I moved around the room and chatted politely to the other guests. I had regained control of myself, but I was continually aware of his presence in the room. I sneaked a look once or twice, and invariably caught him looking at me as though he recognised me, but couldn't quite place me. Eventually it was inevitable that I found myself talking to him in a group. It was excruciating, I felt as if my cheeks were burning, and my hand was shaking. I thought everyone must have noticed, including him, but no one seemed to. We spoke of the war and he asked me where I was nursing, and if I was the young lady who had nursed Bertie back to health. I laughed and said it had taken more than my meagre ministrations. I asked him which hospital he had been in and he told me and spoke very highly of the nursing staff. Whilst he was talking I was drinking in every plane and hollow of his face. He and Garth, his twin brother, always had piercing blue eyes, but his were now a dull blue, dead and lifeless. I also noticed that he had a slight nervous tick in his left cheek and a slight flickering under his right eye. They were imperceptible, but obvious to a trained eye like mine. He was still suffering from shell shock, nerves, the war, whatever you wanted to call it, but he was not a well man. Eventually other people drifted into our group and he moved away. He was polite to everyone, but seemed to be merely going through the motions. His heart was in a different place altogether, and I thought about his twin brother, Garth, he must still have felt his death most keenly.

As he moved away it was announced that the wedding breakfast was being served in one of the smaller rooms off the hall. It was significant that the large formal dining room had not been opened up for the occasion. However the room looked stunning. There were four tables leading from the top table and each one was laid out with the family silver and crystal. The candelabra were all lit and the tables were decorated, like the hall, with winter greens and white winter roses. Large epergnes were loaded with grapes from the greenhouses and all manner of fruit, and the main meal was game from the estate. It was a wonderful spread for wartime, and I thoroughly enjoyed the meal and the speeches, but I still had to keep pinching myself to believe I was really there. I was positioned so that I could observe Guy without being seen. I still couldn't believe that I was behaving in such an immature manner, but I simply couldn't take my eyes off him. He was out of my reach, of another world, and it was more than likely that he would not survive the war, but I couldn't help myself. Against all my better judgement, I had fallen in love. After the speeches the party broke up, and I was sent home in a carriage. Father was still up when I got in and wanted to know all about the reception. He also wanted to know how his floral decorations were received. I reassured him that they were beautiful, and admired by all. Satisfied he retired to bed and I followed him. I was exhausted and fell into a deep sleep, but dreamed about the war and Guy.

11

Christmas Day dawned crisp and bright. I awoke late again to the delicious smell of roasting goose drifting up the small staircase. I stretched luxuriously. It was wonderful to be back in my old room, and not to have to leap out of bed at the crack of dawn into a cold inhospitable dormitory full of chattering nurses. There was never a chance of privacy there, with everyone struggling to get ready on time to leave for the hospital. Enjoying the peace, I turned over and allowed myself a few more minutes of luxury whilst I mulled over the events of the previous day. As so often happens, events filtered through my brain slowly, in stages, until I was fully awake. I remembered the lovely candlelit chapel, the warm welcoming hall with its roaring fires, Felicity looking so beautiful and then the dramatic impact of seeing Guy. Guy as he entered The Hall looking so distinguished yet so haunted. My heart contracted again, and I was aware that foolish or not, I had lost it forever.

The previous evening I thought that I must have imagined the impact he had on me. I put it down to the effect of the champagne or maybe it was the excitement of the day. However, in the clear light of morning, when I remembered his entrance into The Hall, I experienced the same overwhelming feeling. I gave myself a stern talking to. I was a serious, hard working nursing VAD who knew full well that people from my background did not waste their time having fantasies about people from his world. I also knew that if they were stupid enough to entertain such foolish ideas, they ended up in trouble of some kind. The two worlds simply didn't mix and that was that. Even a war wasn't going to break down the rigid class barriers that had been in place for centuries. Nevertheless, with all my logical reasoning, I couldn't deny the fact that the impossible had happened to me. The encounter that you read about in cheap novels, eyes meeting across the room, love at first sight, whatever you wanted to call it. I had experienced it last night and it was real to me. I could deny it to myself, but it would be futile. Foolish or not I had fallen in love with the eldest son of my employers and it was a love that was doomed before it had time to struggle into life.

Although my thoughts were bitter sweet, I was warm and cosy luxuriating in my comfortable bed and had no inclination to move. However, I knew that I must get up and dressed and at least make an attempt to help Margaret in the kitchen. I could hear her moving about. I knew full well that she wouldn't allow me to do anything. However, with reverse login, she would expect me to make an early appearance and offer to help. I forced myself out of bed, put on my day dress ready for work and went downstairs. I could always slip up to my room later and change into my 'wedding outfit', which is how I thought of my new clothes, ready for lunch. As I descended the stairs and entered the kitchen I walked into a welcoming place full of warmth and delicious smells of roasting goose and sage and onion. Margaret was standing stirring something over the range. She was red in the face, and her hair was escaping from under her cap, but she was obviously quite happy and had everything under control. She smiled at me as I entered and pointed to the hob where she had left some cooked bacon for my breakfast. I made us a pot of tea, fried myself an egg to accompany the bacon and sat down at the kitchen table to eat. I was starving, in spite of having eaten everything in sight at the wedding. Whilst I was eating Margaret demanded to hear every little detail of the wedding. She wanted to know how father's flowers had looked, what the guests wore, how I was treated, and what we ate. She had an endless list of questions and I was only too happy to re-live my wonderful experience.

Once I had finished my breakfast, I cleared away the dishes and laid the table for Christmas dinner. Father came in and we had a glass of the wine that The Hall had sent as a present then we both had a wash in the back kitchen and went upstairs to change into our best clothes. Margaret left everything simmering and darted back to her cottage to put on her Sunday dress. We all assembled about two o'clock. Father carved the goose, Margaret served the vegetables and roast potatoes and I put the cranberry jelly and bread sauce on the table. Then we sat down to eat. Father said grace and a prayer for absent friends and we all spent some silent moments thinking of those who were spending Christmas in the freezing trenches.

It was an unforgettable meal. We rarely ate so well during the war years and it was mainly because of the generosity of Lord and Lady Leaversham that we were so blessed. There was a great sense of peace as we ate our meal and thought of our loved ones. Margaret had been widowed the year before and she had lost her only son at Ypres in the early days of the war. Father and I thought about Tom and his absence cast a long shadow over the day. There were few families that grim Christmas of 1916 who had not lost someone dear to the voracious appetite of the war.

After we had eaten, cleared the dishes and washed up, father got the cards out and we spent a happy few hours playing the few games of our limited repertoire. I was so pleased that he and Margaret had each other for comfort in their declining years. I worried about him being on his own when I was in London, so it was a great relief to me that he was being cared for. They asked me about my work in the hospital.

I gave them edited details. The effects of the wine, good food and roaring fire, together with the accumulative effects of months of over working made me very sleepy. I made my apologies and left father and Margaret to enjoy the rest of the evening and went gratefully to bed. I slept well and woke to a cold, but bright sunny day. Frost was sprinkled all over the fields and hedgerows and twinkled like so many diamonds in the bright sunshine. I looked at my watch and was horrified to see that it was mid morning. I scrambled out of bed and into my clothes and went downstairs ready to be accused of being a 'lie a bed', but the kitchen was empty. Margaret had cleared away dinner the day before and she had been in to see to father. The range was glowing and there was some bacon in the pantry so I cooked myself a full breakfast, then decided to explore our old haunts, Tom's and mine. He was on my mind that morning and I wanted to revisit the childhood playgrounds where we had spent so many happy hours as children.

I put on my new red 'Tam O'Shanter' and scarf and my uniform coat and went out into the cold frosty morning. Father would have been hard at work in his greenhouses for hours now he only ever took Christmas day off. I felt guilty for being so lazy, but I did deserve a rest, I never stopped in the hospital. I wandered the lanes randomly, remembering the trees that Tom and I climbed as children; the hedges where we had special dens and the fields where we fought the battles of old. I remembered all the young boys of my childhood who were no longer alive, most especially Tom. I loved the Cheshire countryside with its old oaks, flat plains, and gentle rolling hills. I decided that this was where I belonged and this was where I would return at the end of the war, if I survived.

I had roamed at will, without a plan, lost in my thoughts and memories and I found myself near The Hall and the chapel. My mood was pensive, so I slipped quietly into the deserted chapel. The family had always left the chapel unlocked and available to the estate workers and they had always respected the privilege. The flowers were still in place, and the whole chapel was filled with their perfume. I slipped into a pew near the front. The candles weren't lit so even on this bright morning it was gloomy. I knelt and said a few prayers, for Tom and for other lost childhood friends, and patients who I had cared for. Then I slipped into my pew and just sat and thought. I'm not sure what of exactly, the war, it was never far from our minds, my life, things in general, Guy. It was so peaceful in the little chapel, that you could forget the outside world.

Suddenly I heard the door creak open and someone walked down the aisle and slipped into the pew behind me. I didn't look round as I had been taught that it was bad manners to stare in church and disturb the peace of others. However, the person spoke, and at the sound of that voice the world seemed to stop:

'Hello, I'm sorry to disturb your peace, but it is my custom to slip in here each morning to remember.'

I didn't need to turn round to know who was speaking, but I did. It was Guy. I turned and looked into his young, old, face, dominated by his dead, blue, eyes, which were as lined as a middle aged man's then he smiled and the chapel seemed to light up. I didn't have to ask who he was remembering, I instinctively knew. I smiled at him and he smiled back and suddenly we were talking like old friends. He asked me about my work, where I was based, and the men I had nursed. We talked for what seemed like hours, drawn together by a common cause, drawn together by a mutual understanding. We both knew, and he was able to speak of his experiences, his lost friends. However, he never once mentioned his dead twin. I wondered if he noticed the high colour in my cheeks, my trembling hands, and my quavering voice, but he seemed oblivious. He just wanted to talk. He thanked me for my help in nursing Bertie, it was as if the whole family credited with me carrying him from the battlefield, and single handedly saving his life, and I had to protest, it was hardly just me! But he just smiled and ignored my protests. He seemed like a thirsty man who needed to drink, he talked, and talked, and talked, and I listened, ecstatic that I had this chance, an undreamed of chance, to be with him on my own, face to face in such intimacy. We were oblivious of the time, but it became so dark in the chapel that we couldn't avoid realising that it was getting late. I looked at my watch, and realised it was long after lunch. We would both be missed. He told me he was leaving that day going to a friend's estate in Cheltenham for a shoot, and my heart sank, because it meant that I wouldn't see him again before I left for London. Then we said our goodbyes and stood to go. I left my pew and waited for him, because he was still stiff from his wounds, and it took him a while to rise. He shuffled to the end of the pew, and smiled down at me then quite unexpectedly he crushed me in his arms, and kissed me passionately, and I returned his kiss with joy. Then he pushed past me, limped down the aisle, and was gone. After I heard the chapel door slam, I stood alone in the cold, dark, chapel surrounded by the perfume of the wedding flowers knowing that my life would never be the same again, yet thanking God for those few unexpected precious moments with him.

When I left the chapel it was colder, and the sun was starting to go down. There was no sign of Guy so I started home. My heart was in turmoil, why had he kissed me? Was it for comfort, a reflex action, did he care about me? Oh so many questions, but I was overjoyed, and I flew home as if my feet had wings. All I could see was his handsome, ravaged face, and I could feel him all around me. I had experienced something wonderful, and there was no point in questioning why it had happened, so I just savoured the moment.

The fire had nearly gone out when I returned to the cottage, and I felt very guilty that I had allowed Margaret to look after me while I was on leave, even though I knew it pleased her to do so. I banked up the fire, and started the evening meal; Margaret had left a game stew in the larder, and some baking potatoes. While I prepared it I could think of nothing but my meeting with Guy in the chapel. They were bittersweet thoughts though, as I knew that although he was far from well, either physically or mentally, he was doomed to return to the Front.

Margaret popped in to see if everything was alright, and I thanked her for all she had done for me, and invited her to stay to tea, but she declined. I think she wanted to give father and myself some time together. However, she handed me an envelope, which had been delivered to the cottage. She had taken it home for safekeeping.

I recognised the stationery at once. It was from The Hall. I had to stop myself from tearing it open, although I knew that it couldn't possibly be from Guy. It was, in fact, from Felicity asking me to join her for tea at The Hall the following day. Margaret was obviously very impressed by my close friendship with the family, or as she saw it, with the gentry. Felicity had said there was no need to reply if I was going, and I did feel touched that she wanted to see me. Because of the war she and Bertie were not going on a honeymoon, but they intended to return to live on Bertie's Cornish estate as soon as he felt strong enough to run it.

Father returned whilst Margaret was still there, and he repeated my invitation, but again she declined. I made a pot of tea for father and I, which we drank in front of the fire. I told him about my note from Felicity, and he frowned slightly. He told me to be careful, gentry made fickle friends, and when this war was over things would return to normal, and I would be discarded and hurt. I knew there was a certain truth in what he told me, but I didn't agree with him that things would return to normal. I felt that they had changed irrevocably. I also knew that I must always hold that in mind where Guy was concerned. Felicity's friendship was dear to me, but if our ways parted, and I never heard from her again, I would be merely sad. However, the thought of never seeing Guy again, filled me with a hopeless despair. Yet I knew that if he survived the war he would most likely marry one of his own class.

Once the meal was ready, father and I sat at the kitchen table to eat. We were both aware that tomorrow was my last day at home and that I must start back for London. I felt sad to leave him. He was now an old man, and I had come to know him better in the last few years than I ever had as a child. I was pleased that he had Margaret to keep him company, and look after him, and that he was fairly well fed from the estate gardens. I was aware that he didn't eat goose and game every day, but he had more to eat than those of us in the cities. We shared a pleasant meal, and didn't say a lot. We were happy simply to be together.

12

After lunch on my last day, or dinner as father still called it, I went upstairs to prepare for my visit to The Hall. I had spent the morning visiting old neighbours, especially those who had sons fighting. Many families had already lost a son, sometimes more than one son, and it had been a chastening experience, but I was glad that I'd had the opportunity to provide some comfort to my old friends. One visit in particular had been memorable. I called to see Charlie Dutton, who was an old school friend of my brother Tom's. He had lost a leg at the first battle of Ypres in 1914, right at the beginning of the war. He had gone out with the same company as Guy's younger twin brother Garth in 1914. He was wounded in that early major battle when Garth had been killed. Although he felt that fate had not dealt kindly with him, he really didn't realise how lucky he was to have missed the miserable and treacherous war of attrition that followed.

I knew from soldiers that I nursed in London that the First Battle of Ypres was a pivotal battle in what came to be known as 'the race to the sea'. The old soldiers agreed with Felicity's earlier assertion that was the only chance that the Germans really ever had of winning the war decisively. If they had reached the Channel ports before us and cut off our supply lines we couldn't have continued fighting, but our small army of regular soldiers stopped them at Ypres. They were heavily outnumbered and fought bravely, but the casualties were terrible and Charlie was lucky to be alive. He didn't think so though. He was terribly bitter about the loss of his leg, and as I approached the cottage where he lived his mother came out of the cottage, and met me at the gate. She looked worn out and obviously wanted to warn me about Charlie's state of mind before I went in. His behaviour was obviously upsetting, and confusing her. She told me in a hushed whisper that he was terribly depressed and irritable and she didn't know how to help him. Apparently he had dreams, terrible dreams when he screamed and cried out in the night and she had to wake him. I knew what she was talking about; I had seen it many times in the hospital, so I just held her hand and explained that it was not unusual. It was the same for most soldiers who had experienced action, especially a blood bath like the one Charlie had experienced. The soldiers often re-lived their battles in their dreams. I told her not to worry, given time it would pass. It was so hard for civilians to understand the effects that battle had on men, and when they were sent home wounded, mothers and wives were left to look after a severely traumatised man with no prior knowledge or nursing experience to help them, and there was no support or advice from anyone. Often the only help they had was from a local country doctor, who was left to care for the wounded man, and he probably had as little experience as the relative.

When we entered the cottage, his mother left me alone with Charlie. He wanted to talk, to tell me all about the battle and I, who had heard many stories of battles from sick and dying men, was quite happy to sit and listen. He was frustrated that he had been so badly wounded in his first battle and had to sit at home whilst others were fighting for their country. I secretly thought he was very lucky, but I didn't say so. I just reassured him that he had done his bit. I asked him about his dreams, and I think he was a bit embarrassed, and denied that they were still bad. When he was in hospital with other wounded men he could compare his reactions with theirs. Most of them had nightmares, but I think he felt that he should have them under control now. I didn't reveal that his mother had told me about them, but just discussed the reaction of the men on my ward to battle, and the dreams that they had. He seemed reassured when he realised that he was not the only one who suffered in that way. All the men were so terrified of being thought afraid or cowardly, it would have been touching if it had not been so tragic.

Charlie had been given a prosthetic leg. It was fairly basic, but he could get about on crutches. Later in the war the prosthetic limbs improved. I told him he may not think so now, but he was lucky, at least he would be able to do light work and Lord Leaversham had apprenticed him to the estate carpenter so he would have a trade. Those who lost an arm found it more difficult and those who had lost more than one limb found it impossible. I also pointed out that he had avoided the gas attacks that had so cruelly blinded so many men, and left many with such severe breathing problems that they were like old men. He listened carefully to what I said and in later years he told me that my visit had turned him around. He said that I had stopped him feeling sorry for himself and made him realise that most men who had fought in the war suffered in some way and that he was relatively lucky. Charlie lived until he was eighty nine, and whenever I returned to the estate, after the war, I called in to see him. He married and had a lovely family, but he never forgot the war, and his time on the Western Front. Our shared experience created a bond that cemented our friendship for life. I was only twenty at the time, but I was turning into an old soul, a young girl with a wise head on her shoulders. It was sad in a way. The pity of it was that I wasn't using my hard won wisdom to protect myself.

My thoughts were full of Charlie and the other boys that I had visited that morning as I dressed for my visit to The Hall. Tea at The Hall was served about four o'clock, and I knew it would take me about thirty minutes to walk there, but I didn't want to rush so I left the house about quarter past three. I felt rather nervous. I had spent many hours talking with Felicity as a lady's maid, or as a nursing colleague, but this was different. I was visiting by invitation, as a friend or acquaintance and I wasn't quite sure how to behave. The day was bright and frosty and I enjoyed my walk across the park to Leaversham Hall. I took a bridle path across the fields which came out on the main drive which had been cleverly constructed so that it appeared to run straight, but it was fringed with flowering bushes and tall beeches so you couldn't see The Hall as you approached it. Then suddenly, right at the end there was a gentle bend, and as you came out of the bend The Hall was revealed directly in front of you. Leaversham Hall really was a beautifully proportioned building constructed in mellow Cheshire stone with a Palladian front porch, which was approached by a descent of gradually widening steps.

As I reached the steps I faltered. As a guest I should use the front door, but I was accustomed to entering the house through the servants' quarters. I took a deep breath and climbed the steps. I rang the bell and Parkes, the butler, answered. I had worked under him as a lady's maid, but ever the consummate professional he gave no indication that he knew me at all. He asked my name and said I was expected. He took my coat and hat and told me to follow him. If he disapproved of a former lady's maid visiting The Hall as a guest, he gave no sign of it. I entered the hallway, which was still decorated with the flowers from the wedding, and scuttled after him like a frightened child.

He took me up the staircase to Felicity's private drawing room in the East Wing. She and Bertie had taken over a part of this wing as their private quarters when they returned from London. I don't know why I felt so nervous, but once I entered the room it dissipated. Parkes introduced me quite formally, and then retired. Felicity was sitting in a window seat overlooking the park; she rose to greet me and indicated that I should join her there.

She looked very happy, but I noticed the dark rings under her eyes that told me that she was still under a great strain. She took my hands asked me how I was, and how the nursing was progressing. In turn I asked about her and Bertie. She told me that he was recovering well, his black moods were beginning to pass and she was so happy to be married at last. She completely put me at my ease and we chatted like two old friends.

I asked how he was adjusting to his false leg, and she admitted that it was hard for him, as he was still young and active, and wanted to go out hunting and shooting like he did before the war. Maybe he would be able to again in a limited capacity, but at the moment, she admitted, it took him all his time to walk up the aisle unaided at his own wedding, let alone ride a horse and go shooting. I smiled at her ruefully and said, 'He did well though, didn't he?' She smiled back appreciatively. I think we were probably the only two people in the chapel who realised how difficult it had been for him to walk unaided down the aisle.

'At least I've got him, and he's out of it now, Thank God. But he feels it, you know, being here while his men are out there. He feels as though he's shirking, although he knows it's ridiculous. Oh but Amy, Bertie's lost a leg, dear Garth is dead, and Guy is a physical and mental wreck. Could you imagine this happening only two years ago? Oh I know I shouldn't complain, everyone is suffering, but all the men I love most have been affected by this dreadful war. Amy did you see Guy at the wedding?'

Did I see him? That was ironic, I was sure she must have noticed my discomfort at the mention of his name, but she didn't appear to, and carried on, 'He's a sick man Amy, and in no fit state to fight, but he still has this feeling that he must finish what Garth started. Nothing will stop him. We've all tried to persuade him to stay at home, but he won't listen. I suppose it is difficult for us to understand the bond between twins, but he feels compelled somehow to carry on until the war ends or he too is killed. If he doesn't he'll feel he's let Garth down in some way I can't fathom. The army won't make him go back yet, he's still not well, but he's determined.' I knew how Felicity felt, and I could see how weary and battle scarred Guy was, but after our talk in the chapel I knew nothing would have prevented him from going back. I couldn't tell her about that so I just nodded silently, and agreed. However, I couldn't stop myself asking if he'd had any orders to rejoin his regiment.

'No, not yet, Father is trying to pull strings to delay his return for as long as possible, but I don't know. They are getting desperate out there aren't they? So many casualties, so many dead they need every man just to hold on. Father thinks that eventually Americans will have come in, but when? Surely the Germans are getting tired? Can you see an end to it?'

I shook my head, 'I've almost come to accept that the war will never end and we'll suffer like this forever.'

She nodded her agreement, 'It's good to talk to you like this Amy. You and I know what's going on at the Front. We've spoken to the soldiers. But my parents have no idea and I don't want them to, so we keep up this jolly pretence that it's all alright and it isn't. I feel though that I have to protect them from it. They haven't even started to recover from the death of Garth; heaven alone knows what will become of them if Guy is killed too. My father would have no heir, and he would feel his life's work had been for nothing and it would literally break his heart. He's always been so proud of his twin sons.'

Just then there was a knock at the door and Parkes announced that tea was served. A young maid brought in the tea. I didn't recognise her so didn't feel uncomfortable. Once tea was served our conversation dwelt on happier subjects. Felicity invited me to visit them once they were settled in Cornwall, and I was touched. She said that she felt she had more in common with me now than anyone. We both remembered the good days at The Hall, slightly better for her she admitted wryly, but I was happy too, and we had both shared the years of nursing. We had also witnessed the dark days after Bertie returned from the Somme badly wounded, and she said she would never have got through it without my support. We had been through a lot, war is like that, it forges bonds that can never be broken. People have to rely on each other in extreme circumstances and they never forget. I think I helped her because I was familiar, someone she could relate to in a hostile environment, where her loved one was in mortal danger.

I stayed at The Hall for over two hours, and the time flew by as we talked about our nursing experiences and life before the war. Felicity admitted that she missed nursing, and felt guilty about not doing her bit, but she had the sense to realise that Bertie needed her most. He was the most important thing in her life now, and everything else had to take second place. However, she was still helping out in her mother's hospital on the estate, so was not completely redundant. Eventually it was time for me to leave. I had really enjoyed our time together and was reluctant to leave Felicity, but she promised to write. We said our goodbyes, and she handed me a parcel, a late Christmas present she said. I protested, but she wouldn't listen and smilingly rang for Parkes. He led me silently to the front door, and I was convinced he hadn't recognised me then as he was handing me into my coat he told me that he admired what I had done, and wished me well in my war work. I was astonished, because Parkes ran the household when I worked there so his compliment meant a lot to me. I turned and smiled and thanked him. I had forgotten that he had a son, John. I asked how he was and a shadow passed over Parkes's face. He told me that he had been killed on the Somme.

As I walked down the steps in the gathering gloom I reflected that there was no one in this blessed war that had not been touched by tragedy. Everyone was suffering, but it had to end and then what? How would we all recover and get on with our lives after living at such a fever pitch. I didn't have any answers, only questions and the realisation that it was going to last for some considerable time yet. I walked smartly down the drive until I came to the bridle path and then branched off across the park to the cottage. I had come back from London as a professional nurse who had all her emotions in check. A nurse who had the good sense not to get involved emotionally with anyone until this was all over. I was immune. Yet I in one short visit home I had broken all my own rules. I was now emotionally involved with someone who was going to be fighting on the Western Front, and I could no longer be emotionally detached from the war, which was going to make life even more difficult for me.

I returned to the cottage for my last night with father. I sat in front of the fire, and opened my present from Felicity; it was a lovely warm dressing gown, which would be most useful in our cold dormitory at the nurses' home. I put it on, and sat looking into the embers, deep in thought. Tomorrow I was returning to London, and the war, and suddenly I felt terribly exhausted. I wanted to stay here and go back to my job as a lady's maid, back to a world where everyone was secure, to a simple world untouched by tragedy. But I could not go back and I had to find the strength somehow to go forward.

13

Father had arranged for one of the estate labourers to take me to the station the next morning. I awoke to another bright frosty December day. I really didn't want to leave him and return to London, and felt very gloomy as I packed my things. Unusually Father came back to the cottage from the gardens to see me off, I think he was more affected by my leaving than I had realised. Normally we were never demonstrative, but as I left I threw my arms around him, and hugged him tight. I think he was rather surprised, but he hugged me back. Then I clambered aboard the cart and set off for the station, with tears stinging my eyes. I turned to wave goodbye and father stood waving back until the cart turned a corner, and he was out of sight, and I experienced a sudden and intense sense of loss.

The journey back to London was slow, the train was unheated, and I had none of the anticipation I felt on the homeward journey to keep me warm. The journey seemed to be interminable, and I was relieved when we eventually reached London. I managed to hail a taxi, but it was early evening before I finally struggled up the stairs into my dormitory at the nurses' home. Most of the other girls were still on duty, so I took the opportunity to have a bath and wash the journey out of my hair. After my bath I climbed into my pyjamas, and the beautiful warm dressing gown that Felicity and Bertie had kindly given me for Christmas, and sat in front of the fire in the tiny sitting room drying my hair. As I sat there in the firelight, I started to consider my future, and realised that I desperately needed a change. I felt a kind of impatience with London now, a desire to be more involved in Active Service and I started to think about perhaps applying for an overseas posting. After my visit home I felt more than ever that my heart was with the men serving on the Western Front, and most especially with Guy. There was a conundrum, Guy, well I realised that he was lost to me before he was found. He would eventually get his wish and return to the Front, of that I was certain, and men who were as battle weary as he was rarely survived for long out there. They simply didn't have the stamina, but even if he did survive what would that mean for me? One passionate kiss in a darkened chapel was not going to persuade the heir to one of England's finest estates to marry a former lady's maid. I was a fool and no one knew it better than me, but every time I thought of his grey and weary face, my heart contracted. Life had played a cruel trick on me, and I had fallen in love with a man who was not only out of my reach socially, but until the war ended, his life would be in constant danger every day he spent at the Front. I had very little choice, but to live with the consequences.

Eventually as day duty finished, the other girls started to filter back to the nurses' home, and everyone who came in asked about my leave and wanted to hear all about the wedding. As I described what had happened, I was shaken out of my melancholy mood; they in turn relayed all that had happened at the hospital whilst I was on leave in Cheshire, and it seemed as if I had never been away. When I lay in bed that night, I felt as if the events of the last few days had been experienced by someone else, not me, as though I had dreamed them. Weddings in great houses, love affairs with aristocrats, and kisses in darkened chapels, these were the things of romantic fiction. They didn't happen to ordinary people like me, but they had, and I realised that I was growing into a woman and developing a distinct sense of self, of my own worth, and was fast leaving that lady's maid behind.

I really found it difficult to settle back into hospital life in London after Christmas. I was restless and the weather was cold and miserable. I had now returned to day duty, which involved the miserable trek through the grey slums in the cold and dark to and from the hospital every morning and evening. Somehow I just couldn't regain the peace of mind that I had felt before I went home for Christmas. After the carnage of 1916, the beginning of 1917 was quieter on the wards. There was no big 'push' until Arras in April, so our patients were mainly those who had been shot at by snipers or hit by flying shrapnel whilst in the trenches. The soldiers still had appalling injuries, but the flow of patients was not on the scale of the previous year.

New Year's Eve 1916 was miserable and one that I will not easily forget. I had been on duty all day, and had no desire whatsoever to celebrate the coming of the New Year. Just what was there to celebrate? More killings? More Battles? The only thing that I would have celebrated was the end of the war. I could think of nothing to feel cheerful about, and was at the lowest ebb that I reached during those four long years. It was a bitter cold, grey day, which faded into a bitterly cold evening, and as I walked to catch the tram flurries of snow drove into my face. I felt I just could not take any more of the cold weather, the miserable diet, the unremitting hard work, death, injury and the war, the interminable war. Two and a half years had passed since it started, when we were told it was going to end before Christmas 1914 and here we were at the beginning of 1917 and the end seemed no closer. What would happen? Would we go on fighting until all the young men in Europe were dead? It seemed that way. I was war weary, exhausted and very, very depressed. I think it was the contrast between the lovely wedding, falling in love with Guy so unexpectedly and the semblance of happiness and normality at home that made the contrast with war work too hard to bear. As usual I told myself that if it was bad for me in the safety and warmth of the nurses' home in London; how much worse was it for soldiers who had to return to the trenches after spending Christmas at home with their families? But nothing worked to cheer me that evening.

I wearily clambered off the tram, and trudged into the cold, cheerless nurses' home in the depths of despair. I felt so exhausted that I wondered if I could carry on, as I didn't seem to have anything left to give. I couldn't find any reserves to draw on. I needed to do something, change something, but I wasn't sure what. As I passed through the hallway, I glanced into my pigeon hole, as I did every day in the vain hope that there was something for me. Apart from father and Margaret's scribbled notes I rarely received any letters, so I was pleasantly surprised to see a white envelope poking out. I reached in to retrieve it and knew immediately by the stationery that it was from Felicity. I clutched it to my chest and ran up the stairs to my cubicle. Still dressed in my coat I flung myself on my bed and carefully opened it. She couldn't have written at a more apposite time; primarily she was writing to thank me for my wedding present and to wish me a Happy New Year, but it was full of news from The Hall. She was pleased to tell me that Bertie was still making steady progress, and then went on to give me news of the family. Her parents were well and she had seen my father working in the gardens as usual. But, and here my heart almost stopped, Guy had been recalled to Active Service. He was not going back until the end of January, and was not going straight out to France, but was going to train men in a camp in the north for a few months.

I felt physically sick. He may be safe for now, but he would not be kept safe in England for long. They desperately needed trained, experienced officers in France. They were being slaughtered almost as soon as they were commissioned, and in spite of the lift that Felicity's letter had given me, I was still weary and cold. As I lay huddled in my coat alone in my cheerless cubicle, I felt the tears start, and I let them flow unchecked. I knew that my problem was more mental exhaustion than physical tiredness, and it was the first and last time that I ever yielded to that level of despair during the war. It was probably triggered by the contrast between my situation at the hospital, and my wonderful leave. It had been such a morale booster to attend a joyful celebration, where everyone was smartly dressed, and made an effort to be happy. Most people I saw nowadays in London were dressed in a uniform of some kind, or were invariably swathed in black mourning. There didn't seem to be any colour in life any more. That evening my resigned acceptance of the war turned into a cold rage against the old politicians who were sending our young men out there to die in their millions. I lay there huddled in my coat, tears streaming down my face, drenched in self pity until I finally drifted into sleep. When I awoke it was morning and the beginning of a new year 1917, and I didn't dare wonder what it would bring.

I carried on nursing as usual for the next few months and never again did I plunge into the depths of despair that I had experienced on New Year's Eve, but I was not content or fulfilled, I was simply going through the motions. Felicity continued to write to me and our correspondence was all that I had to cheer me. I was relieved to hear that Guy had remained in England training other officers and would do for the foreseeable future. As the cold miserable winter passed, and spring emerged, one could not help but feel lighter and more optimistic. I had made several close friends amongst the nurses during my time in London, and generally spent my days off with one or other of them. Sophie was a special friend, she was a farmer's daughter from Shropshire and her fiancée, whom she had known since she was a child, was out in France. He had somehow survived the mass slaughters of 1916 and was at present stationed in a quiet zone. Faye, another close friend, was from Portsmouth and her fiancée was in the Royal Navy. He had survived the Battle of Jutland the previous year, so the three of us considered ourselves fortunate indeed. I had told them about my meeting with Guy at the wedding, and the effect that he had had on me, and they didn't trivialise it, but welcomed me into the club of abandoned lovers. However, I never confided in them that I had once been a lady's maid in his family home. It wasn't that I was ashamed of being in service, it was just that I had changed so much since then that it didn't really seem relevant.

The spring of 1917 was a quiet time. The army hierarchy had not recovered from the slaughter on the Somme. We had no idea at the time just what a massacre it had been 60,000 dead or wounded on the first day, but we knew it had been bad. We now dreaded any talk of a 'push', as we knew it would mean hundreds of badly wounded men being shipped into the hospital, and thousands of dead being left on the battle field. During that strange spring our days off were spent in wandering around the city. We spent numerous hours in a Kensington tea shop, where all the smart people went. We often wandered through Kensington Park gardens on fine days into Hyde Park and sat drinking tea overlooking the Serpentine. London was full of men in uniform newly arrived from the Front, or about to return, and we enjoyed the mild flirting that often took place when we went out. Remember it was still a novelty for us to be allowed out and about without chaperones. It would have been unheard of before the war. The three of us, however, were devoted to our men on the Front line and there was never any question of the flirting going any further. Sometimes Faye's brother came up from Portsmouth when he was on leave. He took us to several shows. Chu Chin Chow was a great hit and we went to see Romance, with Doris Keane and Owen Nares, now all long forgotten, but they cheered our spirits.

One gorgeous early summer day, June 13th to be precise, it was a date I was unlikely ever to forget, I was alone on my half day off as all my close friends were on duty, and I spent a pensive day wandering around Hyde Park. The borders were full of beautiful, colourful English perennials interspersed with busy lizzies, alysum, lobelia and a wealth of colourful bedding plants, but most of the park gardeners had been called up and the park was littered with army huts and bell tents. You couldn't escape the military wherever you went. However, it was a day when it was good to be alive and young and in love. The mother ducks were still walking proudly along the side of the Serpentine with their young trailing behind them in a shambolic crocodile. The cherry blossom was beginning to fade, but the rhododendrons that framed the Serpentine were in full bloom. It just felt good to be young and alive. I went to one of the mobile cafes and ordered a pot of tea. I had a decision to make. The day before when I went to have my lunch there were a group of nurses clustered around the notice board in the dining hall. It was asking for volunteers for Active Service. Was that the change I was looking for I wondered? The terrible despondency that I felt in January had eventually lifted. Sophie and Faye were happy and their fiancées were, for now, safe. Felicity and Bertie seemed to be enjoying married life, and Guy was still in England so for wartime things were quite peaceful. But I was restless. I was under no illusion that this peaceful time would last much longer. The government was running out of money and men and needed a speedy end to this war that was such a drain on the country and its resources. Now that I had recovered my spirits somewhat the relative inactivity in London was making me edgy and impatient. We had been run off our feet in April after the Battle of Arras, but things had calmed down again. I knew Guy would be going out to France again and I wanted to be out there with him in the thick of it. However, I have to be honest, if I was sent to France I would be nursing in the Front Line, and I was afraid. I told myself that I was only going to be working behind the lines in relative safety and the men sent out there were fighting, facing death on a daily basis, so I was being pathetic. However, the fact remained that I was scared of what I might have to face and I wondered if I would have the courage to cope with it. I sipped my tea and watched the ducks on the water as I struggled to make a decision.

When I had finished my tea I made my way back through Kensington Park Gardens to Kensington High Street. As I strolled along, I noticed a little church in a side street as you so often do in London. I suddenly had a strong urge to sit in the quiet of the church and pray. As I entered the cool dimness of the interior after the warmth of the early summer day, I felt a calmness come over me. I had always loved the peace of churches and as I knelt to pray I remembered the little chapel at Leaversham Hall on that cold December day less than six months ago, when Guy followed me in and we sat and talked. Sometimes I wondered if I had imagined my feelings for him. They were almost surreal, but I knew deep inside me that they were real enough. I sat for a long time praying and thinking and absorbing the calm around me. It cheered me to think that that church had been there for several centuries. We were involved in a horrifying struggle at present, but we had been in many bloody struggles during the preceding centuries and we had emerged victorious. I came out of the church feeling that there was always hope. It was still early so I decided to do some window shopping, as I badly needed some summer clothes. My wedding outfit had served me well, but it was getting warmer and I needed some linen skirts and blouses. The few summer clothes I had brought with me from Cheshire, when I first started nursing, now looked rather dated and I had again managed to save a little money so set off to see if I could find some suitable items.

Even in London we were never far from the war. If the wind was in the right direction you could hear the great guns thumping away across the Channel, and Germany had begun to attack London from the air in 1917 by launching Zeppelin raids. They usually came over at night and dropped bombs and then returned to Germany. It was very frightening when you heard the drone of their engines approaching because at that time we had no effective anti aircraft defences and were totally at their mercy. They had inflicted some terrible damage and succeeded in terrifying the civilian population, who had never experienced aerial bombing before. As I came out of the church that fateful afternoon into the warm sunshine I heard an ominous sound, but it was not a Zeppelin, the sound was a roar of engines that seemed to come from above. I looked up and saw a sinister group of Mosquitoes, which were German planes, flying in close formation. It sounds ridiculous now, but for several minutes I didn't realise what was happening and wondered what they were doing there, then suddenly there was a huge banging and crashing, and I immediately grasped that it was an aerial bombing raid, and in broad daylight too, it was unheard of! Crowds were surging around the High Street in a blind panic trying to find shelter. I turned sharply on my heels and ran back into the church, which I thought was bound to have a crypt. Thankfully it did, a few other people had the same idea and the vicar emerged from somewhere and guided us all down to the crypt where he led us in quiet prayer.

We could hear the bombs falling all around outside. It was quite terrifying. We could hear a huge crashing and banging and the sound of breaking glass and splintering wood. People outside were screaming and shouting and then suddenly an eerie silence fell. We waited for a while to make sure that it was safe and then we slowly struggled to our feet and filed out of the church. The sight that greeted us was quite dreadful, and there was chaos wherever we looked. Everything was covered in brick dust, and everywhere shattered glass littered the pavements. Some bodies were lying under splintered wooden beams and bricks, and ambulances and fire engines together with the police and army were soon on the scene and there was much rushing about. As a nurse I offered my help and did what little I could, which was not a great deal without any equipment, but I was angry, so angry. How dare the Germans attack innocent women and children in daylight? Fighting on the battle field was one thing, but attacking unarmed civilians was another. It helped me to make up my mind. I decided to volunteer for Active Service as soon as I returned to the hospital. I was no longer afraid, I was furious.

14

Later that evening I arrived back at the nurses' home dusty and a little battered and bruised, but none the worse for my experience. The other nurses who were coming off duty had heard about the raid and were outraged at the audacity of the Germans. I was quite a celebrity and had to recount my story several times. Everyone agreed that I had been very lucky indeed, but they were quite dismayed that the Germans had started to attack London in daylight. It made everyone feel very vulnerable.

My resolve to volunteer for Active Service had only been strengthened by the attack, I was furious that the Germans had dared to come and attack London in daylight and bomb innocent shoppers! The following day I added my name to the list in the dining hall that was asking for volunteers for Active Service. Sophie and Faye were very supportive about my decision. I think that they felt a little guilty that they were leaving me to go on Active Service alone, but they wanted to be in London, or at least Britain, in case their respective fiancées came home on leave. I fully understood. I had no one to wait for so didn't have any reason to be in London. I had been nursing for nearly two years now and had earned a red efficiency stripe of which I was very proud. I had probably learned more and had more experience than most qualified nurses would ever have done in their entire careers before the war, but they still looked down on VADs. The stripe just gave me a little more confidence and they showed me a little more respect.

Apart from the daylight raid, something else happened, which stiffened my resolve to apply for Active Service. Felicity wrote to tell me that that Guy had been home to Leaversham Hall for embarkation leave and stayed for a week. She observed him very closely, and she didn't feel that his health had improved at all during the months he had spent in the north training officers. She wrote that he was very 'twitchy' and looked simply terrible. We both knew that officers who were sent back to the trenches in ill health and suffering with their 'nerves' had a bad time of it and their survival rate was reduced. In some cases they found it so nerve racking to be back in the trenches and under fire that death was a welcome relief. The family had tried to talk him out of it and Lord Leaversham had tried to persuade him to apply for sick leave, which he was sure he would get, but he insisted in going back. Felicity said that when he was home on leave he had terrible nightmares still, and one night as she was passing his door she heard him shout out in his sleep. He was shouting to Garth, telling him he was coming for him. A shiver ran down her spine as she wondered if that he meant he was going to join Garth in death. When she got to her own room and Bertie, she just collapsed in a heap of tears. The thought of losing her only surviving brother was more than she could bear.

The news cast me into another trough of despair. Guy couldn't last long in France in that state. Even men in the peak of health were finding the day to day life in the trenches hard to take. More and more of them were dying of pneumonia and other diseases commonly known as 'trench fever', than were being killed by the enemy. It made me more determined to be out there where the action was. Guy was always on my mind, and although we had had no contact since Christmas, I always felt close to him in some indefinable way, as though I was in his thoughts as much as he was in mine. I dismissed this as silliness, but deep in my subconscious I definitely felt a closeness to him that had not been there before our meeting in the church. He opened up to me that day and told me exactly how he felt about life in the trenches. I don't think he had ever opened up in that way to anyone before, what he told me drew us together. He found the life hard, and to go back to it in a poor state of health, both mental and physical, must have taken all his courage.

Towards the middle of June I was summoned to Matron's office. She told me that I had been accepted for Active Service and would be embarking for France on 4th July. She congratulated me on the standard of my hard work and efficiency whilst I was working at the hospital. She explained that I was to be granted a weeks embarkation leave starting on 22nd June, but I was to report back to the hospital on the 1st July to prepare for my crossing to France. I thanked her and then left her office. I didn't know whether to laugh or cry. The thought

101

of that Channel crossing with German destroyers and submarines patrolling the waters made me feel physically sick, but it meant an end to this strange period when I had been quite directionless, almost in a state of limbo.

I enjoyed the last few weeks in London. I had made some good friends and I regretted leaving them, but I was also glad to be moving on. I spent as much time as I could on my days off with Sophie and Faye in the tea rooms, and we spent our time reminiscing. The week before I was due to leave for embarkation leave, they organised for us to have dinner at a restaurant, which was a rare treat and they presented me a gold cross and chain as a leaving present. It was the first jewellery that I had ever possessed and I treasured it for the rest of my life. It became a kind of talisman whilst I was in France and I never took it off. Obviously I was not the only VAD from the hospital to be going to France; however none of my closest friends were going with me. Still at least I would get some letters in future! Felicity and father were my only correspondents and father's hurriedly scribbled notes hardly counted as letters at all.

Although my shopping trip to Kensington High Street had been interrupted by the raid, I had managed to go back into London and buy some new summer clothes. I'd purchased a lovely cream linen skirt and a plain white cotton blouse for day wear and I treated myself to a cream lace blouse for evening wear. I couldn't store any of my belongings in the nurses' home, and I knew that I would not be needing mufti in France so I packed up my few belongings to take back to Cheshire. I didn't really have a great deal, so it wasn't a problem. The summer was cool and damp so rather than carry it, I travelled in my 'wedding outfit' and wore my cotton blouse underneath.

The journey to Cheshire seemed to take forever as usual, but at least it was summertime and I wasn't cold. Father arranged to have me met at the station and in no time at all I was at the cottage. However, I got a terrible shock when I saw him. He had aged considerably since Christmas and had lost a lot of weight. Margaret could see I was visibly shaken. He didn't get up to greet me when I entered the cottage; he just smiled at me weakly. I went over and kissed him, and then Margaret beckoned me to follow her into the back kitchen and out into the garden.

'I didn't know whether to write and tell you,' she whispered, 'did you get a terrible shock when you saw your father? He's very ill, my dear, it's cancer, the doctors don't think he's got long to live.

I'm just relieved that you managed to get leave to see him before you go to France and you can say your goodbyes.' I couldn't speak I was so shocked. I did ask if he knew and Margaret shook her head. She thought he may have guessed, but he never asked. I hugged Margaret and thanked her for looking after him so well and she just smiled and said it was a pleasure. I had to compose myself before I went back into the kitchen, but father hadn't noticed I'd been gone for a while. I asked Margaret to stay for a meal and she agreed. It was hard to see him like that after having known him as a fit, healthy man, but I was so glad that I had that time to say goodbye to him.

Felicity knew I was home and sent word and invited me up to The Hall for tea. This time I felt more confident and Lady Leaversham joined us for a few minutes. She had aged terribly in the last three years. It was no wonder, but she was a strong woman and would never let life defeat her. Felicity told me that now Guy had left for France she and Bertie had decided that they should finally leave Leaversham Hall and go down to Cornwall and open up the house. Bertie was much improved and was coping well with his prosthetic leg. She felt that it was time they had a home of their own, but she felt guilty because it meant leaving her mother. But Lady Leaversham intended to go down to stay with them regularly and although nothing was actually said I think that Felicity expected her to go and live with them eventually, especially if anything happened to Lord Leaversham. Of course it all depended on whether or not Guy survived the war and inherited the estate. How awful to think like that. However, the estate wasn't entailed and Lord Leaversham could leave it to whoever he wanted to, so Lady Leaversham could live there until she died if she chose to. It felt sad to think of the old Hall shut up and empty, but it was huge and if there was no one to run it, it made financial sense. Soon it was time for me to leave. Felicity gave me her new address and asked me to write. She also repeated her invitation to go and stay with her in Cornwall and I said I would certainly try. I told her that father was dying and she was very sympathetic and pointed out that now there was now nothing to bring me back to The Hall. No one, I thought, but Guy.

It was soon time for me to leave. Margaret had agreed to store my clothes and my few belongings, because father's cottage was tied, and as soon as he passed away and ceased to work on the estate it would be given to a new family. I also arranged for her to take all of the furniture and ornaments that belonged to father and use them or store them as she felt fit. It was hard to say goodbye to him, because it was unlikely that I would get leave to come home from France for his funeral. It was a beautiful summer morning when I left. He hardly left his fireside chair now, so did not come out to see me off. I kissed him goodbye, and rushed out of the cottage. Margaret had come to say goodbye, so I hugged her fiercely then clambered up onto the cart and left for the station. As we started off I turned and took one last look at the cottage that had been my home for more than twenty years and then staunchly looked forward, both literally and metaphorically.

Once I was back in London, the time flew. I told Sophie and Faye about father's illness and they were very sympathetic. It was good to share my sad news. However, once back I had so much to do that the time flew. I had to replace items of my uniform that were worn out, and I had to attend a few talks about what to expect in France. We also had to have inoculations against typhoid.

15

Before I knew what was happening I found myself on a ship in the English Channel en route for Boulogne. The crossing was very rough and many of the nurses were sick, but I was lucky, it had little effect on me, and I felt a great sense of relief as we left England. I was naturally afraid, as many boats had been sunk in the Channel during the course of the war, but I was also excited at the prospect of nursing in France. I stood and watched the coast of Britain disappear, then walked to the other end of the boat to look towards France and my new life. I had the curious feeling that the Channel crossing marked the end of life as I had known it and the beginning of a new life, and it was both thrilling and frightening at the same time.

When we landed in Boulogne, we were taken to a small faded hotel called the Hotel du Louvre. There we had to go through all the administrative procedures and fill in a mountain of forms. A sister from Headquarters was there to meet us and give us our orders. She gave us a short talk on what we might expect of nursing in France, and was very honest and straightforward. She told us that the coast around Etaples had not been shelled or bombed because of the hospitals, but we were still in the front line and it was potentially dangerous. She informed us that our train would be leaving the Gare Maritime shortly after 2.00 the following afternoon and until then we could spend the early part of the day as we pleased. So it was that we spent our first night in France in the stuffy, old fashioned hotel.

The following morning, left to our own devices, Frances and I decided to go exploring. Frances was billeted in the same room as me at the hotel and we had known each other vaguely in London and so it was that we chummed up together and wandered into town. We were window shopping, when I spotted a beautiful blouse in cream crepe de chine with tiny lapis lazuli buttons in the window of a drapery shop.

I was not going to be spending much money in the coming months and I loved it so we went in to have a closer look, and I decided to buy it. Frances thought I was mad, as it was a complete impulse buy and just where I thought I'd get the opportunity to wear it I had no idea, but she understood why I wanted it. I'd only brought a day skirt and blouse with me as we had been told not to bring too much luggage as there was no space in our accommodation at the hospital, so one extra pretty blouse wasn't going to cause a problem. It seemed to be a good omen, so after my purchase Frances and I found a little bistro where we had a reasonable meal by wartime standards and half a bottle of red wine, and swopped tales of nursing in London. After lunch we made our way back to the hotel where we were collected and taken to the Gare Maritime.

The train journey was a leisurely one with many stops and starts, and lasted some twelve hours. The main Boulogne – Paris rail link ran between the hospital and the sand dunes that fringed the beach at Etaples. The town was also linked to Camiers by road. As the nursing sister had told us in Boulogne the line, due to the proximity of the hospitals, had not been shelled for the duration of the war so far, so although close to the front line, we were reasonably safe. When we arrived in Etaples we got off the train and left our kit at the station to be collected. By a stroke of luck Frances and I had been allocated to the same hospital. Apparently it was situated on a racecourse some three or four miles out of town, so we were directed to a waiting ambulance that was designated to take us there. We scrambled in, the mackintosh flap was dropped and we drove off into the darkness of wartime France ready to begin our Active Service.

We drove through Etaples, which appeared to be very muddy and the narrow street was full of rubbish. On the far side of the town we entered open countryside, and we could see through the darkness that it was covered with huts and tents as far as the eye could see. Etaples was the main troop transit camp in France and most British soldiers would have passed through it at some time or another. It also contained the main transit hospitals where the wounded were taken prior to being shipped to Britain, those who were well enough that is. The seriously wounded were nursed or died at Etaples. We drove through rows and rows of hospital huts interspersed with sand dunes covered with tufts of grass. Everything was a uniform brown colour and there was no colour anywhere except the bright red of Red Cross signs. Eventually we found ourselves on a clear road and in no time at all we arrived at our hospital, where we were taken to the night duty room, which was filled with scrubbed trestle tables. Here we were given a meal, and we realised at once that we were to get better rations than we had been used to at home. There were unlimited amounts of butter and sugar available. After we had eaten we were given a talk by the Matron who seemed to be far too young for such a responsible position, she was in charge of all the General Hospitals in the Etaples area. She was beautiful in a statuesque way and I noticed that she had South African medals and had obviously nursed there during the Boer War.

After the talk we were taken to a wooden hut which was to be our billet. It contained six bunk beds and each bunk bed had a soap box by it with a washbowl and a candle and there were three nails in the wall above on which to hang our clothes, I hung up my uniform and other clothes and kept my underwear in my kit bag. I was so glad I had only brought what was necessary, apart from my new blouse of course! During my time in France I found that the private areas of the VADs was far more respected in France than in it had been in London, supervision in 'quarters' was slight and therefore the VADs responded by exercising self discipline. It was such a relief to be given some privacy at last and it improved everyone's state of mind and we all got on well. In spite of the hard work, morale was high there.

I was rather horrified initially to be assigned to a marquee ward. In fact, the hospital was nothing more than a series of marquees linked together in a line and each one was named by a letter of the alphabet, but they served well. Each one contained twenty four patients and the work at first was much the same as it was in London, a round of bed making, dusting, temperature taking and bed baths. We then had a snack lunch, changed our aprons and proceeded to feed the patients. However, improvisation was the name of the game on Active Service. There was never quite enough equipment and we were forever borrowing or pinching from other marquees. There was no water on tap and all the water and fuel had to be carried in, but the orderlies did the heavy work. The summer of 1917 turned out to be one of the wettest in history, and one of the main battles we had was against the mud. The paths between the marquees, trampled by a hundred feet during that wet summer, turned to slushy mud of the kind that signified wartime France. It stuck to everything and it didn't have that lovely earthy fresh smell of normal mud. It smelled of death and decay. For us in our ankle length uniforms it was a nightmare.

We had to keep our uniform fresh and clean in the most difficult of circumstances and the mud only added to the pressure. It was also slimy and slithery and more than one VAD fell flat on her face, which resulted in a few broken or sprained limbs.

The time I spent at the marquee hospital was a kind introduction to France and gave me time to acclimatise. I was there less than a month, and although we were busy with convoys coming in, it was far calmer than the nursing I was to experience in August, but Etaples was a strange place as it had a spiritual feeling of intransience about it. A never ending flow of patients were stretchered in day after day, and they were either badly wounded, suffering from some acute infectious disease, or at the end of their ability to tolerate hell any longer and suffering from severe 'shell shock'. They either died, recovered sufficiently well to return to the Front, or were shipped home to Britain. For some very badly wounded soldiers it was the end of their war and they would obtain a discharge on medical grounds, but some merely went home to convalesce and then were sent back to the Front. Many men were wounded two or three times, recovered and went back to the Front. I have wondered since at their courage and resilience and at the madness that took young, fit men, smashed them to pieces, put them back together again and then sent them back to be smashed to pieces again. It was really a refined form of torture for them, but at the time I accepted it as normality as we needed the soldiers, and I just did whatever I could to relieve their extreme suffering.

As well as the vast hospitals at Etaples, its convenient road and rail links made it an ideal place for a transit camp. Most soldiers came back to Etaples after a spell of leave or convalescence to receive their new orders, before they went back to join their regiment, if it still existed, or transfer to a new one. Many soldiers passed through on their way to a new posting or home leave. There was a permanent presence of troop movements. They were not all British. Many of them were colonial troops, or allied troops. It also was a camp for German prisoners. If they were wounded, they were nursed there until they either died or recovered sufficiently to be shipped to a prisoner of war camp. Many of my colleagues worked on the German wards nursing 'Huns'. They were naturally rather dismayed when they initially received their orders, but they gave the German prisoners the same care and attention that they gave their own men and comforted them in their last days on earth.

The crump, crump, crump, of the guns was nearly always with us at Etaples, a constant reminder that the Front was only a few miles away. You couldn't actually hear the guns, but you could almost feel their rhythmic thump. It was continually with you, like the beating of your own heart. The ground constantly quivered and shook with the reverberation, like the gentle after-shocks of an earthquake. I just thanked God that I was not at the epicentre. The noise and effect of the big guns became a part of our daily life, but I'm sure that the constant reminder of their proximity wore away at our inner calm, even though we were unaware of it. In later life I would hear those guns in my dreams and wake to a feeling that my bed was vibrating; it was so ingrained in my subconscious. No wonder the men became shell shocked. The noise at the front must have been terrific.

In June 1917 General Pershing arrived in France, he was the commander of the American troops who had entered the war in 1917. On July 4th, which of course is American Independence Day, elements of the 1st Division paraded through Paris. In the following months more and more Americans, 'dough boys' as they were nicknamed, began to arrive, much to the relief of the exhausted allied troops. But our marquee hospital became a casualty of the American occupation. It was to be taken over by them, and we were to be moved to General Hospital 24 just outside Etaples. I was sad to say goodbye to our marquee city as I had only just settled in, but that was wartime for you! We were driven by hospital car to General Hospital 24 and taken to the mess hut. Here we were given our orders and happily Frances and I discovered that we were to be billeted together in an Alwyn Hut, which was a curious canvas and wood affair that housed two VADs. I was relieved that I was still with her as we'd become close friends, and I would have felt quite lost if she'd been posted elsewhere. I was assigned to a surgical ward which was housed in a wooden hut. It was more convenient than the marquee, but the mud was just as much a problem here as it was there.

It had already been a terrible summer. Even in the late spring when the allies attacked Arras on the 9th April it was pouring with rain and sleeting and it had continued to rain throughout those chilly summer months. Then just a few weeks after my arrival in France, on July 31st the British had begun the offensive that became known as the Third Battle of Ypres. There had been a terrific bombardment for fifteen days before the attack and nearly four million shells had been discharged. That was four times as many as during the big bombardment that preceded the attack on the Somme. The ground was already churned up by the bombardment and then it started to rain and continued to rain throughout August and the whole battlefield was turned into a swamp. Men who had fought there said that the slimy mud was ten feet deep and had the consistency of porridge. It was impossible to move guns and equipment, horses sank into it and motor vehicles got stuck. Men could only walk on the duck boards and if they fell off them into the mud, there was every chance it would suck them under, it was like quick sand. Equally, wounded men who sheltered in shell holes found that the mud at the bottom was so soft that they simply sank into it and drowned. It was hell on earth and that was where Guy had been sent to fight. Haig didn't need to launch an offensive in July 1917, the Americans had entered the war and he just had to wait for their support. I'm no historian, but I think he wanted one last offensive to end the war without their help and to his own glory. But it was the worst battle of the war and became known rather emotively as Passchaendale

Life on my surgical ward here was quite different from my marquee ward, which I think was being wound down before being handed over to the Americans. From my first day on duty a ceaseless stream of Tommies from the Salient (the Ypres Salient) passed through my hut. It was a perpetual round of convoys and every soldier was covered from head to foot in the foulest mud. For the first time at Etaples I encountered serious gas cases from 'Wipers, which is what the men called the Ypres Salient. They were truly awful. I have never witnessed anything as unholy as men in the early stages of mustard gas inhalation. The poor souls were almost burnt alive and were covered with great, oozing, mustardy yellow blisters, which covered most of their bodies. If they had been unfortunate enough to inhale the noxious stuff it blistered their insides and melted their oesophagus and lungs, so they couldn't breathe. They were always fighting for breath; their voices a mere whisper; urgently trying to tell you that their throats were closing and they felt that they were going to choke to death. The gas attacked their eyes so that they were nearly all blind. Sometimes it resolved itself, but more often it led to permanent blindness. I prayed, when bathing their poor eyes all sticky and glued together that they would see again. These poor wretched gas cases either died quickly, which was most usual, or they recovered, but generally died young after suffering with appalling health problems. The galling thing was that there was so little that we could do for them. They followed us round the ward with their mournful eyes begging for help and we had none to give them. What made me so angry is that the gas cases that we nursed in France were never seen in England. I think if they had been the civilian population would have revolted. It was a sin against humanity, and not surprisingly gas warfare was outlawed in the Second World War.

Apart from the wounds inflicted by mustard gas that I witnessed on my surgical ward during the Third Battle of Ypres were those inflicted by shrapnel and they defied imagination. During all my years of nursing I dreaded lifting the blanket covering a wounded man; it never left me, but it reached new heights in that wet, bloody autumn. I didn't think man could receive wounds of that severity and live. The surgeon, sister and I would stand in the operating theatre for hours at a time surrounded by wads of soiled dressing, limbs and body parts. The surgeons became very swift and skilled, but often had to take the easiest option. There just wasn't time to undertake complicated repair work and the wounds that they were faced with were often badly infected. They would often have to amputate a limb that in peacetime could have been saved with complex surgery, but there was no time. One of the major problems was that there was no effective way to move men quickly from the battlefield to the hospital and they were so filthy that the wounds became gangrenous before they got to us. There were no antibiotics then and gangrene was a very real danger so it was often safer to completely sever or cut out any area of possible infection. Gangrene, if it spread meant death.

If I wasn't required to assist at an operation and sister was tied up in the operating theatre, I ran the ward single handed and I was very grateful for my training and experience in London. Morning routine was the same as at it was in all hospitals, beds were made, temperatures and pulses taken, patients were washed and given their medication and dressings had to be changed. Each hut held up to seventeen patients and the work was unremittingly hard. Sometimes we were lucky and had an additional VAD to help, but all the hospitals at Etaples were overstretched and nurses were so exhausted that they kept going off sick. Although nobody took time off unless they literally could no longer stand.

The ward was disciplined chaos, with noisy patients coming round from anaesthetic shouting out, those with delirium caused by infection muttering and raving and the orderlies continually gossiping. A hut is not the most convenient building to house a hospital ward.

It is hot in the summer and so cold in the winter that it has to be heated and all we had were ineffective coal stoves, which had to be constantly fed with fuel to keep them going and permanently poked about to make them emanate more heat. There was no plumbing so we had to carry in cold water then heat it for bathing patients, cleaning wounds, washing our hands, and making feeds and hot drinks. All we had to boil the kettles on were paraffin stoves, horrible black things called 'Beatrice' stoves. I often wondered who Beatrice was and just how flattered she would have been to have these ugly constructions named after her. They were also voraciously greedy and needed constantly feeding with smelly paraffin. I felt like something between a coal merchant and a chemical worker most of the time, and was permanently filthy. With unremitting hard work, though we kept the wards spotless and the men were well looked after and kept warm and comfortable, their well being came before anything else.

We also had a major problem of disposing of the piles of soiled and bloodstained gauze and bandages after we had done the dressings, which had to be burned as they were a source of infection. It was so important to keep everything sterile and clean, but even so the summer of 1917 was notoriously wet and the hot humid atmosphere, together with the prevalence of infected wounds, caused a serious outbreak of diarrhoea and vomiting. It raced through the hospital like a plague and no one escaped, but you couldn't go off sick or someone else would have to do your work and their own. It was a dreadful time, but somehow we struggled through it.

All the casualties from Ypres were heroes. They were sane, courageous and fatalistic. They always kept their sense of humour, but the men from Wipers told us that the conditions in the Salient were atrocious. The casualties were enormous, it took all their effort not to simply drown in the mud and fighting was barely possible. No one knew how many men had drowned in shell holes. Once soldier told me that after the initial battle they had to sit and listen to the cries of badly wounded men who had sheltered in shell holes. The soldiers couldn't reach them to affect a rescue as they were pinned down by enemy fire. The wounded were too weak to climb out and were slowly drowning in the mud and there was nothing the soldiers could do to save them. The Germans held the high ground and if they tried, they simply picked them off one by one. Then Felicity wrote to me that Guy was fighting at Passchendaele and my blood ran cold. My poor Guy, how was he coping in such a place in his condition?

On 3rd August I attended morning service, which was held for the nurses, VADs and those patients well enough to attend. It was held in a large marquee to commemorate the third anniversary of the war. The senior army chaplain to the forces led the service. It was very emotive. The whole marquee was a patchwork of different uniforms, grey, khaki, blue, red and the white of the nurse's caps. The filtered light of the marquee embraced this diverse congregation in spectral warmth. There were representatives of all the fighting forces in France there that morning, and the service had an almost mystical quality. I am sure we were all wondering if this was the last anniversary of the outbreak of war, or was there, in fact could there, be worse to come? I'm sure we all prayed as one that it was the last. When the bugler played the Last Post I had to fumble for my handkerchief and furiously scrub at my eyes, but I wasn't alone. We all stood there thinking of loved ones who were already dead and those who were in danger and there were several moist eyes, although all kept a stiff upper lip. I pensively stepped out of the marquee into the dull rainy French afternoon and asked myself how many more could we realistically withstand?

16

After six weeks of high casualties from the Third Battle of Ypres, or Passchendaele as it came to be known, and no leave, we were all absolutely exhausted. In September, in spite of the pressures on all the staff, Matron insisted on the re-establishment of 'days off'. We were all very relieved as we were running out of energy. I had had a few days off when I first arrived in Etaples, but with the high level of casualties arriving from the Salient, all leave had been cancelled since then as every pair of hands was needed.

The atmosphere in General Hospital 24 was so different from that in London. There we were VADs, amateurs who were resented and treated with some contempt by the professionally trained sisters. However, here in France we carried out our work as professionals and they treated us as equals consequently we mixed socially with the sisters, and some firm friendships were established, which led to a wonderful feeling of camaraderie amongst all the nursing staff, and I never felt alone or ostracized as I had in London.

When our first 'day off' came around, Frances and I were both given leave so we decided to walk into Hardelot. Looking back we must have been mad, it was a sixteen mile walk, but I was now so hardened to living on my feet that it didn't faze me at all. Also, both of us desperately needed a change of scenery, and we enjoyed being out in the open air away from the hospital so much that we didn't notice the distance. The beauty of the warm, sunlit, early autumn day lifted our spirits and it was such a joy to be away from all that death and decay. There was that wonderful autumnal smell in the air that day that made me yearn for something, but I could not quite identify what it was. When we began our walk we chatted joyously, but eventually lapsed into companionable silence, lost in our own thoughts and enjoying the feeling of putting ourselves first after thinking of others for so long. Frances, I imagine, was thinking about her lover, who was fighting at Ypres, and I wanted consider the recent letter that I had received from Felicity. She had written last week to tell me that father had died in his sleep at the beginning of September. She said he had not suffered, and Lady Leaversham had visited him just before the end when he seemed quite comfortable and content. He also asked her to let me know, and tell me that he was quite alright. Bless him. Once she heard that father was seriously ill Lady Leaversham liaised with the doctor to make sure he was receiving the best possible treatment. I was very grateful. I felt very sad that I had not been there at the end, and felt rather guilty. He was my last living relative and I had loved him dearly. I was quite alone in the world now and it felt strange. I had been so busy when I received the news that I hadn't had time to reflect on it properly. Obviously I wrote back immediately and I also wrote to Margaret to thank her for nursing him. She sent me her usual short reply, but she had been very fond of him, and would be lonely without him. She also invited me to stay when I had leave, which was kind, so I didn't feel quite homeless now that father had gone.

Felicity also wrote about Guy. He had been in the thick of the fighting in and around the Salient, so his letters were few and far between. She was still very worried about him, but he seemed cheerful enough when he did write, but then all the soldiers maintained a conspiracy of silence in the trenches to prevent their loved ones from worrying, so that wasn't as reassuring as it seemed. Although he said nothing about his health, the fierceness of the fighting had been reported in the newspapers. She begged me to tell her what I knew about the conditions in the Salient, and asked if Guy was in a great deal of danger. How could I tell her how dreadful it was? She couldn't even start to imagine what was going on over here and it was better that she couldn't. She was worried to distraction as it was. So I wrote back reassuring her that things weren't too bad. Although she was frantic with worry about Guy, she loved her new life with Bertie in Cornwall, and in spite of wartime shortages and lack of man power they were managing to restore the house after years of neglect and create a comfortable, and habitable home. She had fallen in love with the wild Cornish coast and was sure that I too would love it. She continually pressed me to go and stay and I intended to go as soon as I got leave. However, we were so over stretched that I couldn't foresee that in the near future.

Lost in thoughts of our loved ones, Frances and I ambled along peacefully in the warm, September sun. The road was straight and bordered in parts by dark pine woods. The fresh smell of the pines mixed with the salty sea air put a bounce in our step. We were young and fit and the miles seemed to just melt away together with the exhaustion of the last few weeks, which I think was as much psychological as physical. After the pine woods we wandered through sand dunes and then walked out into meadowland. It's hard for you to understand, my dear, in this more liberal age, but there was a strict code of segregation at Etaples and any female found 'fraternising' with an officer was instantly dismissed. He of course, got off with nothing more than a reprimand. Looking back now it was a ludicrous rule. Freedom to mix would have reduced the pressure on doctors, nurses, officers and men alike, and small social functions would have been so welcome and relieved the tension and lifted morale for everyone. I could never understand why they enforced such a harsh and counter-productive rule. It was terribly unfair and very hard on the women, who had to live like nuns, but we abided by the rules because we cared about our work and didn't want to lose our positions.

There was an old chateau at Hardelot called the Pre Catalan, which had been converted into an expensive restaurant 'for officers and nurses'. We arrived there just before lunch, but after consideration decided to move on to a cheaper hotel at Hardelot-Plage. It was a mile down the road, but we didn't mind as we were enjoying the sunshine. It was a small isolated hotel much favoured by the VADs as you could enjoy lunch in privacy without being observed by your seniors and it was cheaper than the big chateau. However, just as we were about to order a meal in the hotel salon, an officer came in with a nursing sister. We heard him enquire about a room for the night before he caught sight of us. We didn't want to embarrass them and respected their privacy so we tactfully abandoned our plans and left. It was none of our business what they wanted to do in their own time. We didn't know them and we disliked the ridiculous rules about non fraternisation, but our presence there made it embarrassing for them so we walked back to Hardelot and enjoyed a delicious, if somewhat expensive meal at the Pre Catalan. My tactfulness that day was rewarded in full some months later when I myself required a quiet place to fraternise.

After our meal we meandered slowly back to the hospital. Frances was good company and over lunch we shared gossip and memories of London and generally enjoyed each other's company. When we got back to the hospital, Charlotte, another VAD, had organised a supper party in the mess. We may not have been able to fraternise with the officers, but we had a far more sociable time with the other VADs than we had ever had in London. Frances and I joined the supper party and shared our bit of scandal, which the others enjoyed with relish. We didn't know who the couple were so it was harmless enough gossip and it brightened our dull lives. Whilst I thought the nursing sister a little foolish to risk her career, I think I felt a small pang of envy. We were never allowed any time with men alone and a life of enforced chastity was quite hard, when you were only in your twenties. Even when women and soldiers had leave and wanted to spend time with their fiancées, they weren't left alone, although as the war progressed things became more relaxed. I don't think the young women in the nineteen twenties realised how much our sacrifice had contributed to the freedom of movement they enjoyed after the war. There was a far more relaxed attitude towards men and women mixing together informally without chaperones.

After that lovely trip to Hardelot we were again confined to quarters due to unrest in the military section of the camp. It became known as the 'Battle of Eetapps' and was, in fact, a rebellion. I wasn't surprised. As I have already told you Etaples was a base camp for those on their way to the front. There, under atrocious conditions, both raw recruits and war weary veterans were subjected to intensive training in chemical warfare, bayonet drill and long sessions of marching at the double across the dunes. All the soldiers hated it. The regime was punishing and what was worse, most of the instructors had never even been to the Front and were held in contempt by many of the soldiers. All my patients used to complain about conditions at the camp.

Well, apparently there had been a problem at the end of August when a member of the Australian Imperial Force, known as the AIF, a Private Alexander Little, had verbally abused a non-commissioned officer after the water had been cut off during his shower. It seemed a minor offence, but he was taken to the punishment compound. Resentful, he resisted and aided by other Australians and some members of the New Zealand Expeditionary Force, known as the NZEF, he escaped. Four of the men who helped him escape were identified and court martialled for mutiny and sentenced to death. Three later had their sentences commuted because the AIF regulations barred the handing out of the death penalty to its soldiers. However one, Jack Braithwaite, an Australian serving with the NZEF, was considered to be a repeat offender and his sentence stood. He was shot by firing squad on 29th October 1917.

We were told very little about it at the time; I've learned about most of this since. The military hierarchy were very concerned and went to great lengths to hush it up in case the mutiny spread. However, relations between the soldiers and the authorities in the camp deteriorated after the 'Little' incident and they eventually came to a head on Sunday September 9th 1917. A New Zealander, a gunner called A.J. Healy, had by passed the patrols on the bridges crossing the Canche and crossed the estuary or river mouth at low tide to go to a fishing village on the other side. It was out of bounds to the men, but they all went anyway, crossing the estuary on foot like Healy. However, before Healy could return to camp, the tide came in and he couldn't get back across the estuary on foot. He knew he'd be missed and if he didn't want to be charged as a deserter he had no alternative but to return to camp across one of the bridges. Naturally he was arrested by the British Military Police, charged as a deserter anyway and put in a cell. When the New Zealand garrison heard of this they marched on the lock-up and a crowd gathered outside. They were in an ugly mood and wouldn't disperse even when they were told that the gunner had been released. It was obvious that the arrest of gunner Healy was just the excuse they were looking for to rebel. Apparently the atmosphere in the camp had been really tense for weeks. The arrival of the military police made matters worse and scuffles broke out between the men and the police. In the middle of all this a private called Reeve panicked and fired into the crowd. Unfortunately he killed a corporal called Wood who was a member of the 4th Battalion of The Gordon Highlanders. He also injured a French woman, an onlooker who was standing in the Rue de Huguet in Etaples. The mood was now really ugly and the police, fearing for their lives, just fled. News of the shooting spread and by 7.30 pm over a thousand men pursued the military police into the town, where they had gone to shelter. Once in Etaples town the mob raided the office of the Base Commandant. They pulled him out of his chair and carried him on their shoulders through the town, although they didn't harm him.

The following morning, in an attempt to keep the men out of the town, and prevent any more trouble, police pickets were placed on the bridges, but by 4.00 pm the men had broken through and were holding meetings in the town as well as in the camp. It was a very tense time. On Tuesday, the Base Commandant sent for reinforcements, as the demonstrations were gathering momentum and he was in danger of completely losing control. On Wednesday, the men broke out again, wilfully disobeying orders that confined them to camp, and marched on the town. Later that day, however, the reinforcements finally arrived. They were the Honourable Artillery Company or HAC, and were a detachment composed mainly of officers backed up by cavalry from the 15th Hussars Regiment and a section from the Machine Gun Corps. The threat worked. Only three hundred hard liners broke camp and they were arrested in Etaples. The incident closed and by Thursday peace had been restored and the reinforcements were dispersed, but it had been a very tense time. The authorities were terrified that rebellion would spread through the army as it had spread through the French army after Verdun.

It was nearly mid October before the 'Battle of Eetapps' finally ended and we were eventually allowed to leave the hospital compound. One afternoon, shortly after we regained our freedom, I went off into Etaples on a shopping expedition as I had run out of nearly everything whilst confined to quarters. I was alone as all my friends were on duty that day. I left early in the afternoon, but it was late afternoon and the light was fading when I started my return journey. I turned into the muddy road that linked Etaples to the camp, when suddenly a figure stepped out from between the sand hills that lined the edge of the road. He stood in front of me, looking around as if he was trying to find his bearings. I could see he was an officer, and even in the waning light he looked familiar, but I couldn't place him at first, I had met so many during the war. Slowly recognition dawned, but I thought I must be hallucinating or even worse had encountered a ghost. I uttered his name, but I didn't expect a response, however I got one. The officer abruptly turned on his heel to face me. There was no mistake, it was no ghost, I was not hallucinating, it was Guy! Oh joy! I dropped my parcels in a most unladylike manner and ran towards him. Slowly recognition dawned in his eyes and he ran to meet me and gathering me up in his arms, and swinging me round with delight. Within minutes he was kissing me and I was kissing him back. All decorum was abandoned, and there were no worries about fraternising. Looking back it was a most immodest way to behave, but I didn't care, the coincidence was too great to take in. Can you imagine how stunned I was? Eventually, he released me and held me at arm's length grinning broadly, then suddenly remembered where we were. He looked around furtively then took my hand and guided me to the side of the road where we sat and spoke, whilst sheltered in the lee of a sand dune. I talked ten to the dozen. I gabbled, I asked what on earth was he doing in Etaples. He told me he had been knocked out on the Salient, concussed by a shell blast, and he'd been sent to Etaples for a few weeks to recover as he'd had difficulty focusing and kept getting disoriented. I couldn't believe it. I looked at his tired, young, old, face. He looked so exhausted. I moved my hand to stroke his cheek and he grabbed it and kissed it, all the while staring at me intensely with those violet blue eyes. I looked back at him. Then he spoke in a strangled sort of way:

'Was it the same for you?'

I couldn't speak and just nodded. 'You have never been out of my thoughts since the wedding, not since that winter afternoon in the little chapel. At first I thought it was just the war, me, nerves, my state of mind, all sorts of things, because you read of this happening in novels, but not in real life. But you never left me, you were always in my thoughts, you had bewitched me and I knew it was something special.'

I laughed with delight, 'I thought the same as you, it was too sudden, too ridiculous and me a lady's maid. . .,' he put his finger on my lips, gently to quieten me.

'Out here, in all this,' he waved his arm round in an arc, 'Do you really think any of that matters anymore? You are a beautiful woman and a brave, well experienced part of a fighting force and worthy of anyone's respect. You certainly have my sister's and my brother in law's. Amy I love you, quite simply, I love you and after this agony I fully understand the meaning of that word for the first time in my life. I will never completely recover from the death of Garth; it was like losing a part of myself. I don't think that I'll ever feel whole again, but I've found you. Do you love me back, really? Is it possible? I'm a wreck you know, I shake, have nightmares, and a very unpredictable temper and I drink too much. . .'

This time I put my finger on his lips to hush him, and then I reached out and held him to me. I don't think that I have ever felt such a surge of emotion. We sat just holding each other and kissing for as long as we dared, then I had to make a move. I'd be missed at the hospital camp. Guy went to retrieve my parcels from where I'd dropped them, and when he came back he asked,

'Can I see you? Which hospital are you at?'

'Yes, of course, the 24th General, surgical ward. I am due to a day off next Monday. Will you still be here?'

'I'm fairly sure I will, I'll make sure I am. Where can I see you?'

'Can you get a vehicle of some kind?'

'Yes, I know one of the medical chaps, he was at school with me and he'll know how to get hold of something. I'll manage.'

'I'll meet you on the road to Hardelot, just where the pine woods begin.'

'Right, what time?'

'I'll leave after breakfast, about ten? Are you sure you can get out of camp?'

'I've been in the trenches for two and a half years I can get out of anywhere.' He smiled his sad smile. My heart contracted with love. I couldn't believe this was happening. He kissed me goodbye, then slipped back into the sand hills. He waved briefly before being swallowed up like a genie slipping back into his lamp. Metaphorically, I had rubbed the lamp so many times, and wished for the world, and now I had got it, Guy, here, in Etaples! Guy, who loved me as I loved him! I had to sit down for a minute to take it all in, then I realised the time and almost ran back to the hospital. The last thing I wanted was to get into trouble and be confined to barracks. I took my parcels back to my Alwyn hut and went in search of Frances. Should I tell her? How could I not? I couldn't keep this to myself. Would she believe me? I had to tell someone to make sure that it had actually happened that I hadn't imagined it. I found her alone in the mess hut and breathlessly recounted my meeting with Guy to her. She was dumbfounded, but delighted. She hugged me and couldn't stop smiling.

'This war, the strange things that happen, sometimes I think the whole of France is bewitched. It's wonderful, and he felt it too? That feeling you have described to me? A what, 'coup de foudre' the French call it, a thunderbolt, and he felt it too just like you? Amazing, no not amazing, you are gorgeous, just because you are trussed up in this attractive uniform surrounded by bandages and blood, doesn't change the fact that you are beautiful.'

'Don't Frances, I'll blush and you're being silly! But it seems that it hit him in the same way. I can't believe it. But Frances I'm going to make the best of it. It may be all I have for the rest of my life. He's going back into the Salient soon and I may never see him again.'

'Don't, don't, you mustn't say things like that. It's tempting providence. You have to have faith. You have to hope.'

We smiled ruefully at one another, wondering I'm sure just how much defence hope was in this murderous conflict, but that and faith in God was all we had.

17

I've never been as happy in my entire life as I was that week. Guy loved me. He wasn't a fantasy. He wasn't a figment of my imagination. He was my real life lover. He felt as I did. I kept pinching myself, it didn't feel real, but I was determined to make the most of every moment because I had no idea how long it may last. The day following our meeting I received a lovely letter from him. It was sent through the internal post and he poured out his feelings, much as he had in the chapel last December at Leaversham Hall.

My Darling Amy,

Are you real? Did I imagine meeting you last night on the road from Etaples? I don't know it seems too good to be true, and I wonder if I am hallucinating because of my concussion! What a strange and wonderful encounter! As I told you in the chapel that day last Christmas, the last few years have been barren ones for me. After Garth was killed it seemed as if half of me no longer existed and for a long time I was driven only by the urge to revenge his death. But I now realise that no matter how many Germans I kill, I cannot bring him back. His death was just the waste of a promising young life and if I survive, I will have to live my life for the both of us, and live it to the full.

During these arid years I have been half alive, just going through the motions. Life in the trenches, as I'm sure you know, is a round of boring routine, and unimaginable discomfort interspersed with periods of intense, treacherous activity. Every moment of every day your life is in danger even when doing the most mundane things like repairing the wire, and the strain wears you down. Sometimes I think I'm half mad.

Before we met at the wedding, Flick had written and told me how you had kindly contacted her immediately Bertie arrived at your hospital after the debacle of the Somme. She explained how compassionately you nursed him, and how selflessly you supported her when you must have been exhausted yourself. I was intrigued. I vaguely remembered you from Leaversham Hall in the years before the war, mainly because of that incident with Montague. I remembered you as being a pretty girl with dark eyes and unusual golden hair that looked auburn in certain lights, however I was not prepared for the impact that you made upon me at the wedding. When I walked into the hallway after the wedding service and caught sight of this stunning girl, dressed in the finest London fashion, standing by the fire place, I could not believe it was the Amy I knew before the war. You looked so lovely that it almost took my breath away, and then you looked up and held my gaze and my heart literally stopped beating. I have had very little to do with women, apart from some mild flirtations before the war, but I'm sure that what I felt was love at (almost!) first sight. It seemed to come from nowhere, but it overwhelmed me and has stayed with me ever since, and it has warmed my heart, and given me a reason to survive during these last weary months at Ypres.

I couldn't believe my luck when I caught you in the chapel later the following day and had the opportunity to talk to you away from prying eyes. I unburdened myself to you that afternoon in a way that I had been unable to with anyone else. My heart was so full and you listened so quietly and your responses were so sensitive and intelligent. As a nursing sister you knew what I had experienced. However, I had no right to take advantage of you and grab you in that clumsy fashion, but I'm glad I did. The memory of that kiss has kept my soul alive during the last few months.

I'm risking a lot, opening my heart to you like this. A beautiful young woman like you could have her choice of men. I am old before my time, burnt out and ill. I'm not much of a catch, but since our meeting last evening I have felt regenerated, alive, happy, and full of confidence. Please don't renege on our arrangements, I couldn't stand it. I have managed to wangle a vehicle and will meet you as arranged. I can't wait to see you again.

With love Guy

Please don't renege on our meeting! He had no idea how I felt; I don't think that he could understand that it was as intense for me as it was for him, and it was made all the more immediate by the urgency of war. I would make the very best of every moment with him; it was all I was living for. The patients in my hut were amazed by the transformation in me. I floated down the ward, my face wreathed in smiles. I no longer stamped about in frustration when the Beatrice stove wouldn't light; I spoke patiently to the orderlies, didn't nag the convalescing patients to keep their lockers tidy, and was a veritable angel! Nothing was too much trouble; they pulled my leg and said someone had cast a spell on me and so they had! There were one or two heart stopping moments when sister considered changing the off duty rota, but after due consideration, during which time I died several deaths, she left it unchanged, and I was reprieved. Life on the wards, although still hard, was calmer than it had been in the early days of the Battle of Ypres. Most of the patients on my ward were recovering surgical cases and they teased me about my happy state and guessed correctly that it was to do with my 'young man.' I pretended to be cross with them, but it didn't work!

I had told no one but Frances about my meeting, and on Sunday evening in our Alwyn hut, she helped me to prepare for my meeting with Guy. She had some liquid soap that she had acquired from somewhere, it was an untold luxury, but she let me use it to wash my hair, then she helped me to pin the front up. For some strange reason, call in intuition, I had bought that crepe de chine blouse in Boulogne, and it was perfect for my meeting with Guy. I wore it with my new cream linen skirt, because that was the entire mufti that I had with me! It was still warm enough to wear linen, so I would look quite respectable. Strictly speaking I should have gone out in uniform, but if I wore my uniform coat no one would know what I had on underneath. I was so grateful to be able to share my secret assignation with Frances. All the VADs helped each other out in any way that they could if there was the slightest possibility at all of one of us meeting a loved one. We would change shifts, lend clothes and jewellery, cover for them, indeed do anything we could to make their meeting a happy one, as happiness was such a rare commodity in the autumn of 1917. Frances was a dear and took my blouse and skirt to the laundry hut where she ironed them for me. I was in such a state of nerves that I couldn't think straight and do anything practical for myself. I was so grateful for her calming influence.

The following morning dawned bright and sunny. It was one of those nostalgic autumn days when you feel your heart will burst. I went to the mess hall to have some breakfast, but didn't succeed in eating anything but a slice of dry toast, and I had to choke that down. I left the hospital early, in case anyone tried to stop me or asked me to work an extra shift, and started on the road north to Hardelot alone. In my heart I couldn't believe that I was actually going to meet Guy. I was sure that something would happen to stop it. At first I walked briskly, and then slowed myself down, as it would mean I would arrive early, and I mustn't appear to be too keen, and then thought I was being ridiculous and speeded up again. I was a seething mass of nerves until I spied his vehicle parked up just where the pine woods started. He was leaning against the vehicle in the beautiful morning sunshine, and enjoying a cigarette. He hadn't heard me approaching so I could observe him for a few moments unseen. He looked so handsome in profile, and my heart went out to him, he must have sensed my presence as he suddenly turned, immediately discarded his cigarette, and rushed to greet me. I was gathered up into his arms and smothered with a kiss, and then he held me at arm's length, and smiled before taking my hand and tucking it under his arm, while we walked back to the vehicle. He opened the passenger door and helped me in then climbed into the driver's seat, and soon we were flying down the road to Hardelot. It was wonderful to have a motor vehicle and in no time at all we passed through Chateau Hardelot and turned left to Hardelot Plage. I had told Guy about the little hotel there and it seemed as safe a place as anywhere to spend our time together. I was so nervous, but after Guy had parked the car he went in to make sure that there were no other nurses or officers about. He knew how serious the consequences would be for me if we were discovered. We asked for a room with a small balcony, and requested that lunch be served up there. This meant that there would be little danger of anyone seeing us.

I felt strangely shy as I followed Guy and the porter up the creaky old stairs to our room. It was perfect, decorated in a lovely rustic French style with ages old mature pine furniture and an embroidered white lace counterpane and matching curtains. It looked heavenly to me after huts and hospital wards. We ate our meal in the warm autumn sunshine on the balcony and never stopped talking, and my shyness quickly evaporated. Guy reminded me of the time that he saved my honour from Ferdinand in Lady Felicity's bedroom, and we laughed at the memory. He said that visit home was the first time he had noticed me and he felt then that I didn't belong in service. I was too... well something, he didn't know what, but not a lady's maid. He had noticed Ferdinand watching me all day and trying to waylay me and decided that with his reputation, he better keep a close eye on him. He laughed gently and said that he hadn't realised then that he was saving me for himself. I blushed and he apologised for being insensitive, but I think that was when he first put into words what we both knew. We were not there just to share a good meal and bottle of wine.

For someone so inexperienced with men, I felt quite secure. I knew that it was unlikely that anyone would see us up there in our room, but I didn't even care, not really. I was with the one person in the world I wanted to be with and at that moment nothing else mattered. After the meal, Guy ordered coffee and two brandies, and we sat contentedly sipping our drinks then stood, leaning over the balcony admiring the view and whilst Guy smoked a cigar. The war could have been a million miles away. Suddenly Guy dropped his cigar, extinguished it with his foot and took me in his arms. He smelt of leather, tobacco and soap and it was lovely. Before I knew where I was we were in bed together. Although nothing had been said, we both knew that would be the culmination of the day. It was quite wonderful, being so intimate with someone I loved so very much. It is hard to stress just how innocent I was in such matters, but nursing had removed any feelings of embarrassment that I may once have had. I gave myself to him with complete abandon and with his guidance it was a magical experience. Afterwards we lay entwined together and talked, then made love again and talked some more. He told me of his life at school, his relationship with Garth, his family, everything. He made it clear that he intended to marry me after the war. I didn't argue or comment, although I felt his family might have something to say about that and I did ask him not to tell them about us at present. He argued, but finally agreed. I don't know why I didn't want him to tell them, maybe I was afraid they would reject me, I don't know, it was just intuition. All that concerned me at that moment was that he loved me, little Amy. I couldn't believe it; never in my wildest dreams did I ever consider that he would reciprocate my feelings. He also told me, tactfully, he had been very careful and I needn't worry. Oddly enough I hadn't given pregnancy a second thought. I really didn't care. In some ways I would have liked to be pregnant, to have something of his, in case. . . We stayed there talking and making love as long as we dared, then reluctantly we dressed and prepared to leave. Guy went downstairs alone first, to make sure that the coast was clear, but we were in luck. There were no other nurses or officers in evidence at all. He paid the bill whilst he was down there and then came back up to collect me.

We drove back to Etaples in contented silence. He held my hand and now and then he would lean over and kiss me. How he didn't crash I don't know. Eventually we reached our destination, and he stopped the engine. It was the moment we had both been dreading, we kissed goodbye and clung to each other in silent desolation. Eventually I couldn't stand it anymore. I pulled away from him, and opened the door. His face was a picture of misery, and I don't know where I found the courage to leave him. He kissed me one more time then after asking him to drive on and not look back I stepped out onto the road. I closed the door, blew him a kiss, which he returned and then the engine sprang into life and he disappeared in a haze of dust. I stood there on the empty road feeling lonely and bereft, yet joyful and exulted all at the same time, and I walked back to the camp in a daze of happiness and despair. The light was fading as I entered the hospital compound, and with it the old 'me' died completely. I was a new woman; no I was finally a woman, and independent woman and no longer a girl servant. The man I loved more than life itself had just left me and would be returning to the Salient within days. I knew the life span of officers who fought there and Guy had outlived his time already. But he would be with me now forever, I could still taste him, the smell of him was on my skin, in my being; I could feel his strong arms around me; he would never really leave me now, never and I thanked God with all my heart that he had at least allowed me that one day.

18

It was hard to settle to work the following day. I couldn't concentrate and wanted time alone to consider all that had happened in that lovely little room in Hardelot-Plage. Sister seemed to sense that my mind was not fully on my work and she plagued me all day. I was really relieved when it was time to go off duty, and I could be alone with my thoughts. Immediately I finished on the ward, I went to find Frances. and I found her in the mess. We made a cup of cocoa, which we took back to our Alwyn hut, and there, left to ourselves, we talked for hours, about Guy, about James, her fiancée, about our generation, the war generation. We wondered how any of us were going to put our lives back together when it was all over. Frances was such a comfort to me, my friends from London, Faye and Sophie, had not forgotten me and wrote regularly thankfully reassuring me that they and their loved ones were still safe. However, nursing in London was so different from nursing on Active Service that I felt after a while that I couldn't convey to them how I was feeling. My letters became chirrupy and cheerful with no substance. We would always be friends I was sure, but Frances and I had grown closer, because she was sharing the privations and dangers of Active Service and we understood each other fully.

I received a letter from Guy the following day. It was full of our wonderful day in Hardelot and his love for me. I had asked him for a photograph and he enclosed one that had been taken before the Somme. He was in uniform, but looked younger, still handsome, but almost baby faced. I thought that the war had added a terrible maturity to his face, which was now a part of who he was, the man I was deeply in love with. I wrote back and enclosed a photograph of myself that had been taken while I was in London. I didn't think it was very good, but it was all I had.

I realised it would not be long before Guy left Etaples. He would be sent back up the line almost immediately if they felt that he was sufficiently recovered, because they desperately needed every able bodied man at the Front. I was right, in under a week he was back with his regiment, which meant that there was no chance of me seeing him again until his next leave, and no one knew when that would be. He still wrote when he could, little missives hastily scribbled in a shell hole somewhere and covered in muddy smudges, and candle grease. Sometimes he found himself behind lines in a reasonable billet and he managed to write a lovely long letter.

The colonial troops, the New Zealanders and the Canadians, were taking most of the punishment during the Battle of Passchendaele. Haig had all but decimated the British troops on the Somme, but they were still involved in the battle either as front line troops or support, but not in the numbers that had been involved in the earlier big battles. Nevertheless, whether they were involved in a Push or not, anyone who was fighting in or around the Salient was fighting under atrocious conditions. Because of censorship Guy couldn't tell me much about the battle, but I gathered reading between the lines that the fighting was fierce and costly. After the dreadful summer weather the Salient had turned into a bog, and the conditions that autumn were even worse, if that were possible. The Salient had become nothing more than a huge swamp. I have learned since that more men drowned in the Third Battle of Ypres than were actually shot or blown up, although I don't know the actual figures. However, I will always remember the smell of Guy's damp, mud smudged letters. They emanated a peculiar smell of damp earth, blood, death and decay. It was a dreadful smell that will stay with me forever.

The first major attack for Passchendaele Ridge, now known as the First Battle of Passchendaele, took place on 12th October 1917, while Guy, thankfully, was still in the hospital at Etaples. The attack was launched by the New Zealanders, and they struggled forward through the mud and conducted themselves as well as could be expected. They fought with extreme courage, but it was an impossible task as the mud they were fighting in came up to their knees and sucked them under until they could hardly move at all. The enemy held the high ground all around the Salient and the soldiers were sniped at continually, and shelled day and night. They did gain some of their objectives though and on the basis of this flimsy success, Haig launched the Second Battle of Passchendaele on 26th October, this time the Canadians attacked, and Guy was back at the Front. I think he said that they gained five miles. I was never sure whether they captured the ridge or not, what I do know is that nearly 70,000 men were killed and 170,000 injured. By the autumn of 1917, the British Army was almost bled dry.

Thankfully the Americans had entered the war and began to be in evidence from early summer 1917. During the next few months American troops continued to arrive in France in substantial numbers and by March 1918 318,000 had arrived and they were the vanguard of some 1,300,000 that were to be deployed by August of that year, thank God. The British and Imperial troops were on their knees with exhaustion and couldn't have held out much longer.

I said to you before that I could never understand why Haig hadn't simply held the line until we had new, fresh, American troops ready to support any attack. I have always thought that he was desperate for the glory of victory and wanted to beat the Germans before the Americans arrived. I don't know, but he seemed to me to be a cold man with little consideration for his men. Why didn't he resign after the debacle on the Somme? How could he have the deaths of millions of men on his hands and still send thousands more to the same fate when it was avoidable? I accepted it then, because I knew nothing about military affairs and we were involved in a mammoth struggle for survival, but I've read the histories since and I'm not so sure. I suppose that compared to the Somme, the later casualties were lighter, but they were still unacceptably high during the Third Battle of Ypres.

Guy wrote and told me some funny anecdotes about the men, those wonderful brave, uncomplaining, irreplaceable men. He told me that one bright moonlit night they were squatting in a shell hole, and 'Jerry', as they referred to the Germans, had started shelling gas at them, so they put their gas masks on. Anyway just at that moment a runner appeared at the edge of the shell hole with a message. He didn't realise it, but he was silhouetted against the moonlight and made an easy target for Jerry. Guy shouted to him to come down, but he couldn't hear because of the gas mask, so Guy had no alternative but to grab him by the leg and pull him down. However, as he fell into the shell hole a bayonet that was leaning against the side went straight through his leg. Guy was horrified! He'd inadvertently wounded one of his own men! He said he was frightfully sorry, but the chap was grinning all over his face, pleased as Punch! He'd got a Blighty one, a wound that would not kill him, but get him home. Guy had to send him to the MO with a note to say that it wasn't a self inflicted wound; it had been inflicted by him! They didn't need the Germans while he was there to wound his own men!

He was always writing about his men. He really admired and cared about them. By 1917 they were becoming quite fatalistic about the war. He told me they used to say if you were a soldier in the line you shouldn't worry. Either you were alive or you were dead. If you were alive there was no need to worry. If you were dead you were unable to worry, therefore what was the use of worrying? They also joked about the length of the war; one joke that did the rounds involved two soldiers chatting. One said to the other:

'How long are you in for, Bill?'

'I signed on for seven years or Duration.'

'You're lucky! I'm Duration.'

By then they thought the war was going to last forever, certainly more than seven years! I think they had begun to think it would never end! Guy wrote that the classic response to any disastrous news, such as your rum ration hadn't come up the line or two companies of your battalion had gone west or your leave had been cancelled, was, 'Roll on Duration!' However, there were men who just found the war too much and their nervous systems simply collapsed under the strain. They called it 'shell shock', but one of the sisters who worked on a neurological ward told me that was a ridiculously simplistic term that completely failed to describe the dreadful state that some men were in. Once the mind had gone, it was hard to heal and she felt that mental collapse was worse than any physical disease. Earlier in the war she had worked in a casualty clearing station that was situated close to the front line. There she witnessed the full horror of what shell shock actually meant. The ward was no more than a tent with earth, or rather mud, as the floor. The men were kept in little cots surrounded by sandbags and when the shelling started they simply collapsed the cots to the ground so the men were shielded from flying shrapnel by the sandbags. One night the shelling was terribly heavy, and she told me that she had never been so terrified in her life. She found herself shaking uncontrollably, and she was a strong woman, the only thing that comforted her was that all the rest of the staff, including the doctors, were also shaking, but they could control their fear. However, the bombardment was just too much for some of the shell shocked men who were waiting to be evacuated from the front line, they simply couldn't take it, and completely lost control. They panicked and started to run amok in the dark tent, screaming and crashing into things with their hands covering their ears, trying to block out the din. When the shelling stopped the MOs gathered them together and calmed them down before giving them an injection. These were brave seasoned soldiers who couldn't take any more, and she said it was awful to watch that level of panic. She often wondered if the minds of those men ever fully recovered; if they didn't, did it mean that they were trapped in a time warp, in a loop where they kept re-living the nightmare of war until they died? It was too horrible to contemplate.

Whilst Guy sent me cheerful jokey letters and rarely complained, always insisting he was 'in the pink', as the soldiers put it, I knew he was just being courageous. All of us nurses knew how bad conditions were in the Salient that late autumn and winter. We saw the state of the patients when they were brought in and listened to their descriptions of the numbing cold, deadly mud and never ending rain. One patient told me it seemed as though God was sobbing at mankind's stupidity. I always remember a patient describing the attack that he had been involved in; it was so pitiful it made a deep impression on me. During the attack his battalion had made slow progress forward because they were sinking up to their knees in mud, they had been given a time limit to reach their objective at which point the barrage would be lifted to avoid hitting them. However, they were only half way to where they should have been when the shelling stopped, which meant that they were trapped by the mud with no covering fire. They couldn't move forwards and they couldn't move backwards and there was nowhere to shelter. The Germans simply picked them off one by one, like sitting ducks. My patient was lucky; he simply received a serious wound and was eventually retrieved from the battlefield and evacuated to the hospital, but the event had scarred him for life.

The patients also described the landscape of the Salient to us. After three years of war, every sign of life had disappeared on, not even a tree was left standing and the whole area was covered with rubbish, old tins, discarded weaponry, latrines, waste paper and the air was pervaded with the smell of dead, decaying bodies that were permanently ploughed up out of shallow graves by shell fire only to be buried again by the next round. It sounded like a petrified forest. All the soldiers were permanently filthy and covered in lice, the foetid stinking, poisonous mud clung to everyone and everything, and made movement almost impossible. Because it was so difficult to get supplies through to the trenches the soldiers were mainly on 'hard rations', which were dry biscuits, with no hot food to sustain them. Also they often had no fresh drinking water, and had to remain thirsty as to drink the foetid, poisoned water in the shell holes would have been fatal. Often they had no idea where they were as their so called 'objectives', a farm or a wood that appeared on a map at headquarters, had simply been destroyed by shelling and swallowed by the mud, so could hardly be identified.

Although the autumn of 1917 was one of the coldest and wettest on record, to me it will always be one of warmth and sunlight because of my lovely memories. In actual fact, I think that the day I spent with Guy in Hardelot had been the only warm, dry sunny day in the whole month, but that memory stayed with me, and coloured my view of the entire month. Although the rest of October was wet and cold, and we were run off our feet on the ward, I hardly noticed, because I was so happy. However, convoys were coming in almost daily, and the seriously wounded men had to be assessed and seen to very quickly. The seriously ill ones had to be operated on immediately, wounds needed to be dressed, the dead buried, and then the rest of that convoy would be evacuated to England and the work would start all over again with the next convoy. The work load really was impossible, but had to be dealt with and it stopped us having time to think. I mentally started to adopt the men's saying when overcome with work, 'Roll on Duration!'

October slipped into November and winter started to close in with a vengeance, and it soon became clear that it was going to be an exceptionally harsh one. I couldn't bear to think of Guy out there in the icy mud and snow. He seemed to spend most of his time in freezing cold, wet tents. His letters though, continued to be cheerful and full of love; I often wondered how he could remain so cheerful and positive under those conditions. He told me of little treats that got through, such as whisky, which was in very short supply, and he thanked me for the socks and scarves that I was furiously knitting and sending out to him. By the beginning of November the Flanders offensive and the fierce fighting around Passchendaele was drawing to a wearying close, but the soldiers still had to survive the everyday shelling, and sniping in that area, as well as the extreme cold.

Thankfully our Alwyn hut collapsed one November night into a pile of canvas and splinters and we were moved into winter quarters, where I was fortunate enough to share a room with Frances. I was so grateful that our hut had buckled under the strain of winter, as it was slightly warmer in quarters. As December progressed, however, literally everything froze. We had to sleep in our vests, because if we took them off and left them on the back of a chair overnight they froze solid and we couldn't get them back on. We had to squeeze every drop of water out of face flannels and sponges or they froze into blocks of ice, and the pipes that fed water to the hut kept freezing up so we couldn't get any water to wash ourselves properly. I was permanently filthy, but I suffered all the privations without a murmur, because no matter how bad it was for me, I knew it was a thousand times worse for Guy.

On the ward I looked like a tramp, and was working bundled up in layers of extra clothes and I never took my coat off. It was so cold that icicles formed on the inside of the windows of the ward huts. We stoked the stove as best we could and kept the men tolerably warm, but it was a tremendous effort. Just as in quarters the water on the wards kept freezing up and there never seemed to be any to wash the patients, make a cup of tea or mix the feeds.

19

As Christmas approached the convoys slowed down to a trickle, so the work load eased, and the loneliness and longing for Guy began to overcome me. I yearned to see him, if only for an hour or two. Then just when I thought things couldn't get any worse Frances got Christmas home leave and went back to England to stay with her family in Kent until the New Year. I was delighted for her, but missed my companion and it made Christmas seem even lonelier than ever. It was a strange bleak time for me, but I wasn't unhappy. I don't think that my senses have ever been as sharp or my emotions as intense as they were that winter of 1917. Felicity kept pressing me to go and stay with her and the family in Cornwall, but I couldn't go to visit her, because I had volunteered to do without home leave, I let those with family and loved ones in England take my leave allocation. My heart was in France and I didn't want to leave while Guy was still there. Her letters were all about the house and the renovations that were keeping Bertie busy. I was so pleased that he was well and they seemed so happy and content, but I felt guilty that I hadn't told her about my love for Guy. She passed on the news in his letters, and I had to be very careful not to slip up and mention something that he had told me and hadn't mentioned to her, but I hated the deception. I respected and cared for her, but I just couldn't risk his family knowing about our relationship at that point. I think I thought if they knew they would try to end it and my friendship with Felicity would be over and I couldn't have coped with that, they were all I had.

I kept hoping that Guy might get leave, but it seemed impossible. Although Passchendaele had officially ended there was still steady fighting in that area and there were rumours of another push. On 20th November a new offensive had began around Cambrai, where we used tanks for the first time to good effect, but it just seemed more of the same to us, we were war weary. My emotions were on a roller coaster, one minute I was happy and in love, the next minute desolate and defeated and all the time as Christmas approached I was overcome with an overwhelming feeling of nostalgia. It was a year since Felicity and Bertie's wedding and that was when I discovered my love for Guy. I now felt as though I had loved him all my life and couldn't imagine a time without him. As a way of coping with the nostalgia I made an anniversary card for Felicity and Bertie to celebrate their first year of marriage. I embroidered it with a panel of wild flowers and the date and year, 24th December, 1917 of their wedding. I also made a special card for Guy, which was embroidered with the date of our meeting in Hardelot and red roses. I seemed to spend all my spare time knitting and sewing, but it was second nature to me as I had been well trained whilst working as a lady's maid at Leaversham Hall and I found it therapeutic. I was knitting Guy a khaki sweater for Christmas and was terrified it wouldn't be ready in time. I knitted until my fingers ached and every stitch was filled with love. I managed to finish it a week before Christmas, and sent it off, praying he would receive it. Thankfully it arrived on Christmas Eve and he wrote back to say how much he cherished it. He wore it all through that bitterly cold winter, and said he felt as though it were a talisman, a good luck charm and while he wore it he was wrapped in my love and safe from harm.

The only way I could help feel close to Guy that Christmas was through my patients, I tried to treat each one as if it was him. The relationship between a nurse and her patients was a close one, but we were trained not to show emotion and to be professional and efficient at all times. However, there were moments when it was hard to be detached. I had tremendous sympathy and admiration for the suffering of some of the men and it was difficult not to get emotionally involved in their affairs. They were ill, alone, in a strange country away from loved ones and you were the only comfort they had. They wanted to tell you about their wives and children, things they normally would have been quite reticent about, and this closeness intensified at Christmas time. Obviously, any patient who was well enough to travel was sent home for the holidays, but we tried to make it as pleasant as we could for those who had to stay. The padre came in on Christmas morning and held a short service for the men and we sang carols then in the afternoon we had a tea party and each of the men was given a 'stocking' in which we put small presents, and some sweets.

The Red Cross supplied small gifts for every man, and I had bought some cotton and made seventeen handkerchiefs, each embroidered with 'France, Christmas 1917' on one corner. One of the other nurses had knitted woollen headbands to be worn under their tin hats to keep their ears warm, and another had made them a card each, so they had a pleasant surprise on Christmas morning. In the evening we attended a concert given by the convalescents who hadn't been sent home and it was great fun. They acted out sketches and sang Harry Lauder songs. He was enormously popular during the war, more so after his son had been killed in France, the men identified with him. I couldn't help thinking of that other Christmas in London before I left to go north for Felicity and Bertie's wedding, and I felt terribly nostalgic, but I enjoyed seeing the men's happiness.

I got through Christmas tolerably well, and was on night duty on New Year's Eve. At least I wasn't plunged into the dark despair the previous New Year, thank goodness, but I had a goal now, and something to live for. I spent most of the night whispering with the VAD who was on duty with me. She was engaged to a doctor, who was working in a casualty clearing station near the Front. She was hoping to marry him in the spring, and she shared her plans with me. I told her a little about Guy, and we just prayed that our men would survive the war. As we shared our dreams, the snow fell noiselessly outside and we felt alone in our little world, cocooned in the ghostly silence of the ward, which was in complete darkness apart from the shaded red light on the desk, which cast a warm halo of light around us. As in London, a year ago, I felt that we were not alone in the darkened hut, but were surrounded by the spirits of all the men who had passed through that hut during the past three years. My companion felt it too and it was quite eerie, but we were not afraid. I felt at one with them, those restless spirits of the young who had died before they had time to live. At midnight I did my rounds and whispered a Happy New Year to all the men, some were fast asleep, but most responded with a whispered greeting of hope for the future. One of them told me later that he had watched me by the lamp that night and said I looked like an angel of mercy capable of putting anything right, even ending the war. I just laughed, but fervently wished I'd had that power. New Year's Day dawned cold and fresh; what would 1918 bring I wondered? But I didn't dare contemplate the end of the war.

Frances returned from leave glowing with happiness. James had also got leave so she spent an idyllic week with him at home and they became engaged! She returned to France with a beautiful solitaire diamond ring that had belonged to his mother. She wore it round her neck on a chain under her uniform during the day and she never let it leave her person. I was so pleased for her, but slightly envious as well, because everything was so straightforward for them. She was generous in her happiness and kept squeezing my hand and reassuring me it would happen to me, but I wasn't convinced.

In the first months of the New Year, life went on as before, although I couldn't bear to go to Hardelot again. Instead, when I had time off, I went to Paris-Plage. January and February continued to be freezing cold. I lived for Guy's letters and the possibility of seeing him again. He was due for leave in March, but suddenly all leave was cancelled. On March 2nd, in Russia, the Bolsheviks surrendered to the Germans and signed the Treaty of Brest Litovsk. We were horrified; Russia was now out of the war and although she had been coping with a revolution, she had managed to keep large numbers of German troops occupied in the east and now, of course, the Germans had an entire army released from hostilities on the Eastern Front. They didn't waste any time transferring them to the Western Front to throw at us. On March 20th/21st what became known as The Great German Offensive began. A massive force attacked across the old Somme battlefield. The Fifth army were defending it, but they had just come out of the Salient and were depleted in numbers, tired and demoralised. They were heavily outnumbered and as evening fell it became clear that the Germans had broken through on a nineteen mile front. It was the first time that the British Army had been defeated in trench warfare for three and a half years. The Germans continued to press forward steadily and by April 4th they had advanced twenty miles over a fifty mile front. We began to be very afraid indeed.

20

During the big German push the hospital was bombed for the first time and I was absolutely terrified. It was always at night; the first sign was that the lights went out and then there were sudden bangs and flashes of light. We had no shelter and we had to try and protect the wounded men as best as we could. During that time we begged borrowed and stole sandbags and when the bombs started falling we took the men out of their beds and put them in little sandbag nests to try to protect them from shrapnel, just as my friend had in the casualty clearing station. The nurses sheltered under the table in the middle of the ward, which was little or no protection. Until you've been under fire you have no idea how frightening it is. The noise, the crashing, the flashing lights, the disorientating darkness and the lethal flying shrapnel were quite terrifying.

I remembered that summer afternoon in Kensington High Street and the relative tameness of that attack almost made me laugh! People had been hurt, buildings damaged and I had been very frightened, but compared with this it was nothing. My sense of outrage now seemed quite amusing in the face of the current barrage! We were lucky our hut never received a direct hit, but I dreaded the end of the raids, because we never knew what we would find. Once a hut near mine had been totally destroyed and both the VADs and all the patients had been killed. The VADs were friends of mine and it was heartbreaking to realise that I would never see them again. I began, in some small measure, to understand the men. They suffered this pounding day after day, often for years. It drove some of them mad, but I never understood how many just carried on stoically, and kept smiling. Where did their resilience come from?

It was a very frightening time, and we all began to realise the seriousness of the situation. We began to think the unthinkable that after four years of a war of bloody attrition, for the first time the British actually faced the real threat of defeat. It was truly horrifying, as it had never occurred to any of us that we may be defeated by the Germans. However, during those terrible weeks defeat became a reality as our beaten and crushed armies kept rolling back. Familiar names that had been in British hands since the beginning of the war were falling to the Germans, one after another, Peronne, Baupaume, Beaumont Hammel, all were gone and on March 27th Albert itself was taken. The shelling had even reached Paris. The retreating soldiers and medical staff all emphasised the same thing; there were so many of them and so few of us, and we were fighting for our lives as we faced one of the major offences in the history of warfare.

All through the end of March and beginning of April at Etaples we had the remnants of a fifty mile front retreating into the camp and the hospital, and we were overwhelmed. The Germans continued spasmodically to bomb the hospital, and what terrified me more than the bombs was losing my nerve and showing my colleagues what a coward I really was. Somehow you survived the first barrage, and felt quite relieved, but when it went on and on and you had to continue to hold your nerve it became quite exhausting. Apart from the overwhelming fear, we also had to cope with terminal exhaustion. Life was completely chaotic, as convoys of wounded were arriving almost daily, most of them were still in their filthy uniforms and had only received very basic treatment. Some had merely had a hole cut through their uniform and a field dressing placed on their wound. Many were stuck to their stretchers with congealed blood and we had to cut them free. The more serious ones had to be operated on immediately and the operating theatres were on the go day and night, the 'Fall In' sounded continuously and day staff took it in turns to help with the night convoys.

One day I walked into the permanent mess that my ward had metamorphosed into only to be told that the Germans were in the suburbs of Amiens. We all looked at each other with speechless horror, as we realised that there were only the advance units at Camiers between us and the front line. It seemed that it was only a matter of time before the Germans broke through and started marching down the road from Camiers. Then what? It was a situation none of us had ever contemplated. All across the Front casualty clearing stations were retreating in panic. Nurses and VADs had had to abandon all their possessions and just retreat, often when they reached us

141

all they had left was what they stood up in. We had to lend them uniforms, underwear, anything we could spare. In fact, the enemy was so close we were becoming nothing more than a casualty clearing station ourselves.

I had little time to think about Guy, although I fervently prayed that wherever he was he was safe. My ward was like an abattoir for over two weeks. Heaps of filthy uniforms littered the floor, together with soiled dressings and filthy stretchers. No sooner had the orderlies cleared it away than another convoy came in and pandemonium began again. I got very little sleep and managed to grab food as I worked. Often I really felt as though I couldn't go on, but it was the same for everyone, and you just couldn't give in. On 14th April Haig was so afraid that the Germans might break through in Flanders that he released his 'Backs to the Wall' speech. It was pinned up in the sisters' quarters and I read it as I staggered in for lunch. I may have disagreed with a lot that Haig had done during the war, but that rallying call appealed to my patriotism and made me determined that the Germans were not going to cross the Channel into my country and take away our freedom. I decided that no matter what happened I resolved to remain steadfast and fight hand to hand if necessary. It helped me find the strength that I needed to carry on, to find that last reserve of strength, and enabled the army to hold its line, and fight back.

TO ALL RANKS OF THE BRITISH ARMY IN FRANCE & FLANDERS

Three weeks ago to-day the enemy began his terrific attacks against us on a fifty-mile front. His objects are to separate us from the French, to take the Channel Ports and destroy the British Army.

In spite of throwing already 106 Divisions into the battle and enduring the most reckless sacrifice of human life, he has yet made little progress to his goals.

We owe this to the determined fighting and self-sacrifice of our troops. Words fail me to express the admiration which I feel for the splendid resistance offered by all ranks of our Army under the most trying circumstances.

Many amongst us now are tired. To those I would say that Victory will belong to the side which holds out the longest. The French Army is moving rapidly and in great force to our support.

There is no course open to us but to fight it out. Every position must be held to the last man: there must be no retirement. With our backs to the wall and believing in the justice of our cause each one of us must fight to the very end. The safety of our homes and the Freedom of mankind alike depend upon the conduct of each one of us at this critical moment.

D. Haig, F.M.

Thursday April 11th 1918
Commander-in-Chief
General Headquarters,
British Armies in France

I had disagreed many times with his strategies when they resulted in massive loss of life, but when I read Haig's 'Backs to the Wall' speech that spring afternoon, I knew that I would remain at my post until the last Tommy had left France. Even then I'd take up arms if necessary. I was rejuvenated and so were we all on Active Service.

An unrelenting roar of traffic filled the air day and night, as reinforcements and ammunition were being driven down the line, and wounded were being sent up the line. There was also the constant buzz of reconnaissance aircraft to cope with as they flew backwards and forwards over enemy lines, and the pounding of the guns never ceased. It was like Bedlam and the work was ceaseless. A never ending flow of wounded came up the line, and sometimes the noise, the tiredness, and the pressure of work seemed overwhelming, but now I had Guy in my heart and I felt that I could cope with anything. He was never far from my thoughts, and whenever I got a minute I scribbled a Field Post card, or note, and occasionally a letter, but there was so little time. I heard nothing in return, but thought little of it in the ensuing pandemonium. If I was struggling to find time to write to him, I realised with the whole army on red alert and fighting for their lives that he would have little or no time to himself.

Fortunately, the Germans slowed down their advance and then abandoned their strategy of one major thrust and formed a three prong attack. This change in tactics saved the allies, as one determined thrust would have broken our lines, but none of the three separate attacks were strong enough to succeed. They attacked south of the Somme in Flanders, in order to reach the Channel ports and cut off the British supply lines, and in the south targeting Paris. It was their last ditch attempt to win the war before they ran out of man power and the Americans came in to support the British and French with

143

fresh troops, and thank God it failed. The war has been criticised as unnecessary, but we who were there know that the Germans intended to subdue and overcome us, and during those weeks I learned how much I valued the independence of my country that they were so determined to take away. We had to defend ourselves against their aggression. It is easy to evaluate cause and effect now, because we have the security of knowing that we won, and I hated the destruction of youth that it involved. I was, and still am a critic of Haig's tactics, and was often angry at the waste of life, but it was a different thing when we were faced with losing everything that we treasured, our country, our freedom, and our way of life. I realised then what a German victory would mean and I didn't like it at all.

As the threat of a German victory receded, we were boosted by the support of the Americans and life became less stressful. I can remember the first time that I saw a group of American soldiers marching past the hospital. They amazed me because they looked so healthy and fit, and with their new uniforms all clean and freshly pressed they seemed touchingly virginal somehow, as they had not yet experienced the gruelling effects of war. When I compared them to our exhausted, war weary troops as I watched them march by I knew that victory and the end of the war were at last in sight. The Germans, because they abandoned their plan of one major thrust to break the British lines, had lost the advantage of their great offensive, and had no more young men to call up, but we had the help of the Americans, and now I felt that we could defeat them. A feeling of huge relief washed over me at that moment and the reprieve made me feel quite faint.

The work continued to be unrelenting, but towards the end of April it started to level off a little and that is when I started to worry. I had heard nothing from Guy since the end of March. I hadn't worried too much during the frenetic days of the Push, but now? Day after day I watched for post. Day after day nothing arrived, and as I continued to hear no word from him, I began to worry. In spite of my exhaustion I couldn't eat or sleep and I was near to collapse. Without Frances I think I would have gone under, as she was such a support. I was desolate, but had to admit that no news was good news. Then, at the beginning of May I received a letter from Felicity, who reported that Guy had been reported missing believed killed in the Salient. This was the news that I had expected for months, the news I dreaded. I read her letter over and over and over, but the reality would not sink in. I couldn't believe he was dead, I just knew he couldn't be dead. I tried to tell myself he was just missing, and would turn up, but I knew what the fighting conditions were around Ypres, and just because they hadn't found his body did not mean that he hadn't been blown to smithereens or consumed by the mud. It meant nothing. At first I was numb and simply worked on like an automaton, simply going through the motions, then the pain started, and the sense of loss was physical. It was a raw, crippling pain that caused me to gasp in its intensity. It was now May, summer was approaching and all the trees were bursting with blossom. The world was coming alive after the long tortuous winter and I couldn't bear to see it springing into life after that terrible winter had taken such a sacrifice. I wanted the world to stop and share in my grief, but the world had better things to do and kept on turning and I had to turn with it.

Somehow I survived, but I was only half alive, and barely conscious of my surroundings, then one morning towards the end of August I stepped out of the hut that housed my ward into the glare of the morning sun. I was very tired and not concentrating and I'm never exactly sure what happened, but it seems I tripped over the fencing that surrounded one of the larger shell holes outside our hut and fell into it head first. They think I landed on some shrapnel that had been thrown in there during the clean up. I was only discovered some time later when Frances came looking for me. I had sustained a fairly serious head wound, and was taken immediately to the operating theatre, where I was operated on as a matter of some urgency. I was told later that I had fractured my skull when I fell onto the shrapnel and this fracture had caused internal bleeding. If I had been left any longer, or not been near the main part of the hospital I would probably have died. As it was I was seriously ill, and my nursing career in France had come to an abrupt, unforeseen and somewhat ignominious end.

21

The first thing I remember clearly after my fall was waking up in a sunny bedroom decorated in pale blue flowery chintz, with no idea where I was. I was vaguely aware that I had spent a considerable amount of time being moved from hospital to hospital, whilst floating in and out of a drug fuelled consciousness. I vaguely remembered being in hospital in Etaples, then an agonising journey by train and boat when, in spite of strong pain relief, I felt that my head would explode. After that I had a hazy recollection of another hospital and another journey, which was not as painful. I also remember seeing Felicity, but I didn't know whether that was a dream or reality. Everything was hazy and I was clearly delusional for a time.

On awakening I looked around the cheerful room, but did not recognise it at all. I had no idea where I was. There was a nurse sitting by the side of the bed and as soon as she saw that I was conscious she stood up, leaned over, and smiled. I couldn't understand what was going on. Where was I? Who was she? I didn't recognise the uniform, and why was I in bed? I struggled to get up, but the nurse gently held me down and told me to hush. I gave up the struggle quite easily, as I was very weak. I tried to speak, but only an unrecognizable hoarse whisper emerged from my lips. The nurse held a drinking cup to my lips, and the water cleared my throat a little.

'Where am I? Who are you?'

With each utterance I continued to try to sit up, and the nurse continued to hold me down very gently. She smiled serenely and told me I was alright and must rest. I didn't want to rest! I wanted to know where I was! However, I was far too frail to protest, so I sipped a little more of the water she held to my lips, and then thankfully sank into a fitful doze. When I awoke the nurse had gone and had been replaced by Felicity. This time I thought that I was delirious. I just couldn't imagine what she was doing by my bedside.

'Felicity, I, where am I? What. . .?'

'It's alright Amy my dear, you're staying with us in Cornwall and you're quite safe now.'

'The war, France?'

'That's all over for you now. You've been very ill. You had a bad fall and injured your head, they hospitalised you over there then shipped you to a neurological unit on the south coast. You had designated your father as next of kin on your papers, and because he died last year they had to contact someone else. They found my letters amongst your things and wrote to see if I would visit you. Of course Bertie and I immediately drove to the unit to see you, and then tried to persuade them to let us bring you here. Once they were fairly sure that you were out of danger they discharged you into my care. They needed the space in the unit for more serious cases, and they knew that I had nursing experience and would care for you properly, so here you are'

'What exactly happened to me? '

'You tripped and fell into a shell hole just outside the hut where you were working, and caught your head on some shrapnel that had been cleared up after a raid and thrown into the bottom of the hole. You sustained a severe head injury, and it's taken you a long time to become fully conscious. You gave us all quite a shock, and we've been very worried about you.'

'Oh I'm so sorry I don't know what to say.'

She smiled down at me, whilst smoothing the bedclothes. 'Don't say anything, I was glad to help, and it's has given me something to concentrate on apart from the war. You can repay me by getting strong and well.'

'Oh I will, how long have I been here?'

'Well you were in hospital in France for about a month before it was safe to move you, then you were put on a hospital train and shipped to a neurological unit on the south coast where you spent six weeks or so until we collected you a few days ago. During that time you've slipped in and out of consciousness, but were also heavily sedated.'

I couldn't believe that I'd been out of the war for over two months. I had recollections of being ill, having a terrible headache and being moved about by rail and sea, but they were hazy recollections, like a dream. I vaguely remembered the hospital on the south coast, and seeing Felicity, but I couldn't place a time scale on anything that had happened.

'What is happening in the war? What month is it?'

'It is now October and the war is finally drawing to a close, thank goodness. The Germans are haemorrhaging men, and have no replacements, they can't last much longer.'

I felt an initial surge of relief, the war over, it hardly seemed possible, but then I remembered Guy. He was dead. He was killed during the big German push, so what did the end of the war matter, but maybe there had been some news of him, I had to ask. It was indiscreet, but I had to know.

'Has there been any word of Guy?'

Felicity gave me an unfathomable look and just shook her head gently.

'No Amy, no news, still missing believed killed, no body has been identified so there's still some hope, but we're almost resigned to losing him now. Anyway my dear, I think that's enough talking for one day, I don't want you to wear you out; you must rest and gather your strength. You are going to need it. I'll come to see you later.'

She placed her cool hand on my head, smiled down at me again and left the room. I just lay there thinking about the events of the last few months: the convoys of wounded in their mud encrusted, lice ridden uniforms, the terror of the bombing, the imminent fear of being captured, the news of Guy's death. It overwhelmed me and I was too weak to fight the memories. I felt so utterly exhausted that I allowed myself the indulgence of wallowing in self pity. I was completely worn out, both physically and mentally from my long years of unrelenting work and I was also weakened by the debilitating illness caused by my head wound. I thought of Guy, my wonderful Guy, and how fortunate I had been to know and love him, and how lucky I was that he had loved me in return. I closed my eyes and let the tears slip down my cheeks as I remembered him and prayed. Eventually I drifted off to sleep, but my dreams were not pleasant ones. I kept seeing piles of wounded, with limbs hanging off, screaming in agony just waiting for me to help them. But I couldn't; I was paralysed and I couldn't get out of bed. I was frantic; they needed help and I just kept ignoring them. Although my sleep was not peaceful, I must have slept for some time, because when I awoke, the nurse was back and she was trying to wake me to take some breakfast. I wasn't hungry, but she insisted that I eat something. I think it did me good to let my feelings out after keeping them bottled up for so long. At the time I did not realise how ill I was, it was only later that I realised how lucky I had been to survive such a severe head injury.

I lay in that warm, comfortable room for weeks with nothing to worry about but getting better, and for the first time in years I was not overwhelmed with work. The days passed slowly and peacefully, and one day seemed to merge into another as I lay cocooned from the world in my pretty blue bedroom. It was late autumn, but still warm enough for the windows to be left opened on fine days. I could hear the gardeners giving the lawns the final cuts of the season, and smelled the sweetness of the newly mown grass. The house was perched on a cliff top above the sea, so I could hear the sound of the waves breaking in the cove below, and smell the fresh salt air as it wafted in on the gentle breeze. It was like heaven after the smells of sepsis and decay that had assaulted my nostrils day after day for the last three years. I abandoned myself completely to my idle life and enjoyed my weeks of healing in this beautiful room surrounded by all life's little luxuries. It was so comfortable and pleasant, with the mellow autumn sunlight pouring in through the window, and the log fire burning brightly in the grate. Of course, the privacy gave me ample time to think about Guy and our wonderful time together in Hardelot only a year ago. Somehow I just couldn't believe he was no longer alive.

Felicity came in to see me every day. At first I didn't want to know anything about the war. I felt it was a voracious monster that would not be satisfied until it had consumed every man of military age on every continent in the world, Germans, Russians, Austrians, Turks, Hungarians, Italians, French, British and now Americans had fed its appetite in equal numbers; hardly any country was exempt and it seemed it would not stop until there were no young men left. The whole of Europe had been ground to dust under its feet and I was too weary to summon any curiosity about its progress. However, as I began to feel better, my curiosity got the better of me and I started to ask how things were progressing. Felicity then started to bring the papers in with her and read to me about the autumn campaigns. It was clear that the Germans were mortally wounded and were literally bleeding to death. They had no fresh troops left to replace the hundreds of thousands who had been slain and they couldn't rebuff the onslaught of the new, fresh American troops, who had come to France as raw recruits, but were now proving themselves to be an efficiently trained, and effective fighting force. Felicity and I were now quite sure that the war was finally drawing to a close. We felt no joy, but a certain relief

J.M. Owen

that it was nearly over and Germany would be defeated. It meant that our way of life was safe, but at what cost? The price had been too high to contemplate, but I had never forgotten my terror when I thought that we were going to be defeated in the spring and summer of 1918. What would life have been like under the Germans? I'm glad I never had to find out.

As I began to recover I got up for a few hours each day and sat in a rocking chair in the corner bay window. It looked out over the deep blue Cornish sea on one side and the beautiful wild moorland on the other side. I sat in the bay for hours rocking backwards and forwards, marvelling at the beauty of the ever changing sea. Some days, during the autumn storms, it was a threatening dark blue blanket that hurled itself wildly onto the rocks below, before exploding into snow white foam that sank silently back into the blue. On another day it would be as calm as a mill pond, an azure plain, almost turquoise blue in colour that crept gently forward to break with a silent sigh onto the beach below. October was drawing to a close, and we had been at war for over four long, weary, years, during which time my life and that of the rest of the country had changed out of all recognition. I remembered with deep sadness the third anniversary of the war when I attended the memorial service in the hospital at Étaples. I realised that my part in the struggle was now over, and had to admit I was relieved. I would not be well enough to return to France until the spring, by which time I was sure that the hostilities would have ceased.

During this time I began to consider my future, whilst Guy was alive there had been some hope of a future with him, but now I had no idea what I would do once the war ended. I had no one left, and I didn't really want to make nursing my profession, although I would certainly have to earn my own living. So it was that I sat and rocked, and ruminated, and enjoyed the lovely surroundings, and thanked God for the kindness of Felicity and Bertie.

I often wondered what had happened to my photograph of Guy and his letters, but didn't dare ask about them. I thought that they had probably got lost in the chaos in France, but I was deeply upset as they were all I had left of him, however I just had to accept that they had gone missing. Felicity came in to see me several times during the day, but she always made a point of having morning coffee in my room. One particular morning, she came in as was her habit, but she seemed ill at ease, as if she wanted to say something, but couldn't summon the courage to do it. She was carrying what looked like a handkerchief case, and eventually, after the maid had brought the coffee in, she stood up and looked out of the window then slowly turned to face me.

'Amy, I have waited for a suitable time to broach this subject, until I felt you were strong enough to talk about it and now I think that time has come. When we collected you from the neurological unit, they gave us your personal effects in a kit bag. I hope you didn't think that I was prying, but it was musty and smelled of the battlefield, so naturally I emptied it out so I could have your clothes washed and pressed. Of course I found the photograph and your letters from Guy, I immediately recognised the handwriting. Naturally, I didn't read them, but they led me to conclude that you were closer to him than I had originally thought. I have kept them safe for you and think it is time you had them back,' She then handed me the handkerchief case.

I took it from her with mixed emotions. I was overjoyed to have them back, but terribly embarrassed at my subterfuge. I felt ashamed that I hadn't confided in Felicity when she had been so kind, but I hadn't had the emotional strength or courage to broach the subject whilst I was recovering. With hindsight I think that is why she kept the letters, until she felt I was strong enough to deal with my emotions.

'I'm so sorry I didn't tell you Felicity, I was afraid the family would disapprove.'

My eyes filled with tears, the only people that I loved and cared for had trusted me and I felt that I had betrayed them by not being honest and open.

'Amy, Amy, whatever is the matter? I'm not cross or disapproving, no, no, on the contrary. Come dear, I'm sorry I upset you.' With this she knelt and took my hands in hers, 'Forgive me for withholding these from you for so long, but I knew when I gave them to you I would have to disclose that I knew that you were close and I was afraid that you might have become upset and had a relapse. I'm delighted Amy that my darling brother knew something about love before he died. He had such a short life and I'm glad it was you that he loved, because now we can love him together and talk about him. I miss him so much. It was hard enough when Garth died, but to lose both of them.' Her voice tailed off and she was silent for a moment, while she regained control then she asked me, 'Are you able to talk about it? I don't want to intrude, but I'd love to hear about him.'

Did I want to talk about him? He was all I wanted to talk about, so I told her about our meeting in the chapel after her wedding and then meeting him again in France and how we had become close and fallen in love. Naturally, I withheld the details of our wonderful afternoon in Hardelot, but I left nothing else out. Her reaction was not what I expected at all. She was delighted that he had known love in his last days and genuinely didn't object to the fact that it was with a former maid. She had loved her brothers very much, and she wanted nothing more than to talk about them, especially Guy, so we did just that, we talked about him for hours, and it eased the pain for both of us. The fact that Bertie had been spared was a source of wonder to her, when so many of her friends had lost their lovers, so she understood how devastated I was feeling, and was full of sympathy. She'd told Bertie her suspicions and apparently he had declared that Guy was a very lucky man.

It was such a relief that Felicity and Bertie knew, and wonderful to be able to talk about Guy freely and with affection. I apologised most sincerely for deceiving her, but she understood my fears, although it would never have occurred to her to have objected. I revealed to her how much I had loved him, and how we had hoped that we may have a future together, because he didn't seem to care about my background. However, it did occur to me that life was often very kind, I may have lost Guy, but I had the next best thing, a temporary home with his family.

A few days later Felicity came in looking very upset, and told me that her father had died of a heart attack the night before. I was shocked because he wasn't an old man, only in his sixties. We both came to the conclusion that his heart and his spirit broke when he was told that Guy was missing, believed killed. He simply lost the will to live without his glorious twin sons, and it was understandable. Not only had he lost his sons, Leaversham Hall no longer had a male heir to take it over, so his life's work was wasted. Lady Leaversham would inherit initially, because unusually the estate was not entailed, but she wouldn't be able to run the estate when she got much older. Felicity was her heir, but had made her home in Cornwall and had no desire to return to Cheshire. Her main concern now was her mother, who was living on her own at Leaversham Hall. It was now empty and most of it was closed up; it had become like a huge mausoleum. She wanted her mother to close the house up completely and come to live with her for the time being, and originally she seemed receptive to the idea, which was a relief. Felicity then planned to rent The Hall out on her mother's behalf. If she had a son, of course he would inherit The

Hall so she wanted to keep it in good order.

Only a week later Felicity came charging into my room clutching a newspaper, tears pouring down her cheeks, and declared, 'Amy, it's over, it's over at last,' I didn't understand for a moment and then realisation dawned. The war was over, it had finally ended. It seemed that the German High Command had signed an armistice at 11 o'clock on the previous day, 11th November. I stood up and rushed over and hugged her and we danced around the room crying with relief, then we stopped and looked at each other and remembered, all of them, those we loved and those we didn't even know, all of them, just for a moment, then we carried on rejoicing.

That evening Bertie held a small dinner party to celebrate the Armistice and I was invited. It was the first time I had ventured downstairs and it was an apt occasion. Since Felicity had learned of my relationship with Guy, she had started to treat me as part of the family, as she said if he had lived I would have been. I was very grateful for their acceptance of me. Christmas 1918 was fast approaching, the first Christmas of the peace. Lady Leaversham was coming down and Felicity was hoping to persuade her to move down permanently. I was now well enough to go downstairs each day, and Felicity and I had started to go for short walks together. On one of these walks she confided in me that her mother had inexplicably changed her mind about coming for Christmas, and told Felicity that she had no intention of going to live in Cornwall, and she was genuinely very concerned about her. She couldn't understand it as she was sure that she had been successful in persuading her mother to come and live with her. There was a lovely little dower house on the estate, where she would have been far more comfortable than in that huge empty house. Felicity was at a loss to understand her, but thought that maybe she couldn't bear to leave the house where she had loved her husband and brought up her family, but there was nothing she could do. Her mother had an independent income, and obviously Felicity couldn't force her to leave The Hall.

One day, as we were walking, I suggested that when I was well enough I should go to live a Leaversham Hall as a paid companion to her mother then I could make sure that she was well taken care of and report to Felicity. I had been thinking about the idea for some time. It would be an ideal arrangement, I had nowhere else to go and no means of earning a living and this way I could repay their incredible kindness to me. Felicity was thrilled, although she argued against it at first saying I wasn't strong enough, but I could see that she was relieved that her mother wouldn't be alone, and she would get regular bulletins as to her well being. She admitted that she had thought of it herself, but was wary of suggesting it in view of The Hall's association with Guy. I didn't say anything, but that was one of the other reasons why I wanted to go back. To remember and to forget, I needed time to grieve before I moved on with the rest of my life, and where else to grieve but amongst my memories.

22

And so it was that at the beginning of February I found myself on a train travelling north to Leaversham Hall. It felt very strange to be going back. So many ghosts awaited me there, so many memories, but I was still convinced that I needed to confront my past and deal with my war memories, before I could carry on with my life. Anyway, how could I refuse Felicity and Bertie after all their kindness to me? They were terribly worried about Lady Leaversham being alone in Cheshire. At least with me as her companion I was in a position to report to Cornwall and Felicity would know how her mother was and be reassured that at least there was someone looking after her.

Lady Leaversham had kept a small skeleton staff at The Hall to see to her immediate needs. There was the butler, Parkes, who had terrified me when I worked there as a lady's maid, and also when I had visited during my years as a VAD before I went to France, together with his wife. Mrs Foster, the former housekeeper had died of Spanish 'flu in May 1918, and the house was now completely shut up apart from Lady Leaversham's private apartments, and Felicity's old rooms that had been prepared for me as they were the closest to her mother's. One other area was used below stairs, which contained the living quarters of the butler and the servants' hall, but the vast majority of the huge Hall was completely closed up.

When I arrived at the station, there was a car waiting to meet me. Lord Leaversham had invested in a motor vehicle just before the war and one of the boys, David Wilkinson , a returning soldier who had learned to drive in the army, was acting as chauffeur. It occurred to me, somewhat ironically, that this was a slightly different reception from the last time I came home, when I had to hitch a lift on the farm cart. As it was now February, it was nearly dark when we reached The Hall at tea time. Wilkinson collected my bags from the boot of the car and rang the bell. It took some time for anyone to reply then we heard footsteps coming across the great hall and Parkes, the butler, opened the door, still dressed formally as the butler of a large house. He took my bag from Wilkinson , who bid us both goodnight and set off for the village. He still lived there with his mother, but occasionally slept in a room above the stables, which were now used as garages as all the beautiful horses had been sold.

Parkes greeted me in a most reverential manner, almost as one of the family, collected my bags, and motioned for me to follow him. It was quite a shock to see The Hall. All the furniture in the great hall was shrouded in dust sheets and our footsteps echoed loudly through the empty house as we crossed the hall and started to climb the staircase to the first floor. Parkes directed me to Felicity's old rooms and made sure that I was comfortable and had everything that I needed. He had even retrieved my clothes and belongings from Margaret and they were hanging in the wardrobes, and I was very grateful. Felicity had given me some clothes, but I only had a basic set and it was lovely to see my wedding outfit and the things that I had purchased in London, but it felt odd occupying rooms where I had once worked as a maid.

Parkes sent my supper up to my rooms, where I ate it alone. I was grateful to have time to adjust and settle in as I was still weak and the journey had tired me. He had arranged for me to meet Lady Leaversham at 10.00 am the following morning to discuss my duties. I was not looking forward to the meeting as I was sure that I couldn't return to the status of maid after working independently for so long, and I wasn't sure whether she would expect that.

At ten o'clock prompt I knocked on the door of Lady Leaversham's room, and she called to me to enter. I was shocked when I saw her, she was not an old woman, probably only in her sixties, but she looked at least a decade older. I remembered her as being a tall statuesque Edwardian beauty, but she looked as if she had shrivelled into an old woman. I need not have worried; she greeted me graciously, like one of the family. My duties were light, my salary was generous, and I had plenty of time to myself. She just wanted me to eat with her and read to her in the evenings after dinner. There were no rules other than we were situated in the East Wing and must keep to that part of the house. She stressed that the West Wing was closed up and must not be disturbed. I willingly agreed, although I had no intention of keeping my word. I wanted to explore the house, just one more time, for memory's sake and then I would be satisfied.

The following afternoon, about 4.00 pm, when Parkes and his wife had retired to the servants' quarters to prepare for dinner, and it was still fairly light, I decided to go exploring. I slipped out of quarters with my heart in my mouth, and crept towards the great hall. Once I was there I walked down the huge marble staircase, and looked out over the deserted hall. In the gloom, it looked like a graveyard for ghosts, with all the furniture covered in dust sheets, and I tried to remember how it had been furnished. Oh Tanya, how my heart ached. Even though I had been a servant in that world, it was my world, and I took pride in my position. I closed my eyes and tried to recall how The Hall had looked on the evening of the engagement ball. It wasn't difficult, I could almost hear the music, and smell the perfume of the blooms that decorated it. In my mind's eye I visualized the family forming a reception line at the entrance. Lord and Lady Leaversham headed the line, followed by Felicity and Bertie and then at the end of the line were the twins, blonde and tall and dashing in their new uniforms. Guy came first, because he was the heir, and Garth, the 'spare', stood at his side, but if they had changed positions no one would have noticed as they were so alike. Felicity looked beautiful that night in her cream satin dress that glinted with diamonds, and Bertie was so handsome, young, and virile with two good legs. His hair was prematurely grey now and his face was etched with lines although he was barely thirty, but importantly, he was still alive. And Guy, I watched him jealously that night, as the young ladies clustered around him, but realistically what could a servant girl hope for? Images of Guy at the engagement party led my thoughts in a different direction, to another celebration that had been held in The Hall. This time it was a more sober and informal affair, and Guy had aged from a dashing young twenty year old to a man old before his time. The celebration was Felicity's wedding reception held on that fateful Christmas Eve 1916. When Guy walked in, I was stood by the fireplace opposite the staircase, talking to that lovely couple who had lost their only son on the Somme. I opened my eyes briefly to glance at the fireplace now empty in the gloom then closed them again and tried to imagine the smell of the mulled wine, and the scent of the Christmas roses that pervaded The Hall that evening. I recalled exactly how I felt when I caught sight of him, my Guy, my darling, damaged, Guy, bloodied, but not bowed.

As I sat there reminiscing, the memories overwhelmed me, and the tears started to slip unheeded down my face, whilst my chest heaved with silent sobs. I needed to do this; I needed to cry, it was cathartic. However, suddenly, I had the feeling that I was not alone. I sat bolt upright and looked around, had Lady Leaversham discovered me sneaking around The Hall? I couldn't see anything, only sensed it, but it frightened me. The air in the hall suddenly felt cold, and I was sure that I was not alone, that unseen eyes were watching me, but whose? Mrs Parkes? It was possible, but she would have made herself known, as would Lady Leaversham, so who was it? Or what was it? I know that the servants used to gossip about The Hall being haunted, but I had never listened to such nonsense, however, tonight I wasn't so sure. Since the slaughter of the war I had experienced many unexplained presences, and sometimes felt that there must be a parallel world peopled by the ghosts of all those young men who had died before they had lived, and that sometimes they crossed over into our consciousness. I looked up to the gallery and swore I saw a slight movement, a shadow, no more. I was very frightened, and my initial reaction was to freeze, then slowly I started to climb to the top of the stairs, but of course there was no one there. It was nothing more than my imagination. I stopped for a moment to peer over the parapet into the hall, as I had the night of the ball as Amy the lady's maid.

It was now nearly dark so I walked slowly back down the stairs and across the hall and main corridor into the French salon. I wanted to continue with my reverie a little longer. How sad it looked, it was as if the house had died with the war. It had always been so full of life, with servants bustling to and fro, and guests sipping champagne, and gossiping with each other and the family. How could a thriving household be reduced to this shell in just over four years? It didn't seem possible. I wandered over to the French windows and imagined I saw Guy pacing up and down the terrace that terrible November of Garth's death. How I wished he were still alive and pacing up and down the terrace now. Oh how I longed for him! Ghosts, everywhere ghosts, my father and Tom in the garden, Guy and Garth, home from Eton playing cricket on the lawn. There seemed to be laughter, light, and joy everywhere. I think with hindsight that I was suffering from what modern psychologists term post traumatic stress syndrome, all the years of unremitting hard work, with the accompanying worry about first Tom, then Guy and the grief caused by their deaths, the loss of my father, together with the loss of my own identity and place in the world had left me vulnerable to a breakdown. Often when you are in the middle of a stressful situation you find the strength to carry on, but when you stop, you collapse, I think I had a sort of mini nervous breakdown, quietly amongst my memories, and steeping myself in the past in that rather self indulgent way somehow purged my spirit and healed me. I needed time to find myself after the war ended. Anyway, I wandered back across the corridor to the hall and began to climb the stairs when once again I had the sensation that I was not alone. It now completely dark and I had no lamp, and suddenly I felt very afraid. I ran up the remaining stairs then along the corridor to my rooms, where I shut and locked my door and determined that I would not go exploring again without a light of some kind. Parkes had turned on the lamps, so I went to sit in front of the fire to collect myself, I was shaking from my experience and it was some time before I plucked up the courage to go exploring again.

23

Over the weeks Lady Leaversham and I got to know each other quite well. I think she completely forgot that I had once worked there as a lady's maid, as she asked me about my experiences as a nurse in France, and we had some long discussions about the war. She treated me rather as if I was one of Felicity's old friends who had fallen on hard times. At that time I think we all rather suspended disbelief to survive. There were few visitors to The Hall now, as so many of the old families had lost their sons during the war, and having no one to inherit their estates had sold them, and retired elsewhere. However, what I didn't realise was that Lady Leaversham had given Parkes instructions to repel all visitors, and eventually the few that had continued calling stopped altogether. This meant that Lady Leaversham and I led quite a solitary life. On occasions I went into the village to see Margaret, but apart from those visits I hardly ever left the confines of The Hall. When I visited, Margaret and I would sit and talk about father, and life in the village as it had been before the war. At first I found it unsettling to see a new family in our cottage, but soon adjusted to the idea as I had no desire to live there myself. The village seemed to be full of strangers, and what I didn't realise at the time was that as Lady Leaversham no longer had any staff, she let the cottages to the tenant farmer's labourers, who I had never met before. There were still a few old families there though and I continued to visit them and other friends, especially those who were wounded in the war. I think talking about the hostilities was cathartic and helped us war veterans to adjust to our altered circumstances.

Felicity and Bertie kept writing and asking if they could visit, but Lady Leaversham also put them off. It was strange how reclusive she had become. I know originally she didn't even want me to go and live with her, but realised it was the only way Felicity would allow her to stay on at The Hall, so she had relented. She didn't seem to mind the solitude, and neither did I. We both tended to keep to our rooms, except when I went to her apartment to read to her or I accompanied her on a walk in the gardens. However one night I discovered a quite puzzling break in her routine. I had been down to the kitchens to ask Parkes for some cocoa to help me sleep, I could never get into the habit of ringing for servants, and I was returning to my rooms, when I heard the noise of a stick, tap, tapping along the floor of the main corridor. It sounded like Lady Leaversham's stick, and dying of curiosity I turned my oil lamp down and slipped into a side room. I peeped round the door and was astounded to see it was indeed Lady Leaversham, oil lamp in one hand and stick in the other, returning from the direction of the West Wing. I had no idea what she was doing up there at the dead of night on her own. If she wanted to explore and revisit old memories, why hadn't she asked me to accompany her? And even if she wanted to be alone, why had she gone exploring so late at night? I couldn't understand it, but instinctively I knew that I mustn't let her know that I'd seen her, so I waited while she passed and then picked up my cocoa and oil lamp and returned to my own room. I was mystified, but never found her wandering around at night again, so I simply put it out of my mind.

For a long time after the end of the war I experienced a terrible feeling of emptiness, and I had expected to enjoy the peace. I wrote to Frances about the way I felt and she said she was experiencing a dreadful feeling of anti-climax, even though her fiancée had survived and they had married, and were happy. We both came to the conclusion that it was a common reaction, and would pass with time. However, it left me with an uncontrollable feeling of restlessness and often in the evening I was so agitated that even though it was still bitterly cold, I had to go out into the garden and walk up and down the terrace trying to work off some of my nervous energy. I would remember and try to make sense of what had happened. It was over, but what had it really been about? What was worth such wanton destruction and huge loss of life? Was it for freedom, the freedom to carry on our way of life? I had to try to understand, but I couldn't - not really, and so it was that I walked up and down in front of the cold, dark, dead house, with only my thoughts for company. However, one evening I had been pacing the terrace for some time and was walking from the East Wing to the West Wing, when I noticed a light. It seemed to be moving along the windows in the far corner. It was only there for a matter of seconds, and then it faded and disappeared. I stopped dead with shock, a light, up there in the empty West Wing? I thought I must have imagined it, yet I was sure I had seen something. I walked back along the lawn, and entered the house through the servants' entrance and proceeded to the servants' hall to tell Mrs. Parkes what I had just seen, as it may have been intruders. She looked startled for a split second, then quickly recovered and said it was Parkes doing his rounds, he checked a different part of the house each evening. Well that did make sense even though it was rather late and as her answer had cured my curiosity, I just asked for my cocoa, and proceeded to my room.

As my health slowly improved, I began to find the solitude and inactivity rather boring, so I asked Lady Leaversham if I could use her library to continue to improve my general education together with my knowledge of history. It became important to me to understand why we went to war in 1914; I felt I could accept the loss if I could understand why it had been necessary, and so I started to spend the long gloomy afternoons studying in the library. Lady Leaversham had kindly instructed Parkes to open it up, and light a fire in there each day, so that I could work in comfort. I got lost in the books as I tried to make sense of history, and so it was, Tanya, that the days passed peacefully. I was still fairly contented to hide away there, and had no deep desire to go out into the post war world. I was aware that I would have to one day, but for the present I was happy to bury myself in The Hall.

Even if her mother discouraged her from visiting The Hall, Felicity never ceased to invite us to go down to Cornwall, but Lady Leaversham consistently refused. I couldn't understand her, she was becoming more and more reclusive, but nothing would move her. She would not leave Leaversham Hall under any circumstances. I tried and tried to persuade her, but she was adamant. She wanted to stay in her own home and nothing would persuade her to leave it. Felicity wrote to me asking if I knew why she was so determined to stay at home, because she was terribly hurt that her mother didn't want to spend time in Cornwall with her. I couldn't help her; I was no wiser than she was. Her attitude was baffling. She had always been close to Felicity and yet she seemed to be deliberately cutting her off. I did write to say that I thought that the grief caused by the loss of the twins had taken its toll, and she needed to be alone with their memories for a while. I didn't know how else to explain her behaviour. Why would someone want to lock themselves up in that mausoleum of a house alone, when they could be comfortable in Cornwall with their daughter's family? It was a mystery, but I had learned to my cost that grief had a strange affect on people, so I just accepted Lady Leaversham's behaviour without question and tried as best I could to comfort Felicity.

It seemed to me that it was inevitable that I would stay at The Hall for the foreseeable future, I had nowhere else to go and I felt that although her behaviour was somewhat baffling, I couldn't leave Lady Leaversham alone in that old house. On a Sunday evening I regularly attended Evensong with Margaret, and tried to persuade Lady Leaversham to come with me, but she always refused. I felt she would enjoy being among old acquaintances in the village, and enjoy what was always a moving experience. It was held in the small village church, and although the empty pews reminded us all of the many faces that were missing, the service helped us all to move on, and consider the future. Some young male members of the congregation were still in uniform as they hadn't yet been demobbed and of course several of them were recovering from wounds. But somehow gathering together there each week, made us, remnant survivors of the pre-war estate, grateful to be alive. We gave thanks each week that we'd survived and that Britain was now at peace and it was a positive experience that I felt Lady Leaversham may have benefited from.

After the service we all gathered in the small church hall for a cup of tea and a gossip. I chatted with old friends and was introduced to new ones. The talk often focused on the memorial that the village wanted to erect to the memory of the boys who had died during the war. They had started a collection and wanted me to ask Lady Leaversham if she would give a donation. I promised I would mention it and said that I was sure that she would give generously. She would want her boys to be remembered in a way that was fitting. It was happening all over the country, in towns and villages everywhere, large and small war memorials were being erected to the dead so that they would not be forgotten, and I was pleased that they would be remembered.

One Sunday evening after we had finished our tea in the church hall I walked Margaret back to her cottage as usual and made sure that she was settled in, before I set off back to The Hall across the fields. It was a cold, but beautiful, crisp, moonlit night; with a light hoar frost peppering the ground, which twinkled in the moonlight like so many tiny diamonds. My boots crunched on the brittle undergrowth underfoot as I strode purposefully towards The Hall, and I felt strangely at peace for the first time in many years. I marched along humming the hymns that we had sung, and felt quite light hearted. Then as I approached the back of The Hall I suddenly went cold and stopped in my tracks. The light was there again in the West Wing attics. It was in the same corner then moved along and down, just as it had a few weeks ago, when I saw it from the terrace.

It was only there for a moment, and then it disappeared completely. I stood for an instant trying to make sense of what I'd seen. Then I made a decision to find out just what was going on, and I continued purposefully towards The Hall. This time I wasn't going to say anything to Parkes. I was going to investigate myself, even though it was late. I let myself in by the servants' entrance and locked the door behind me. The Parkes's had left a gas light burning to light my return and a candle and matches to guide me to my room. I lit the candle and turned down the gas, but instead of going up the main staircase, which led to my apartments, I walked the full length of the corridor that ran through the old kitchens, storage larders and servant quarters of the house. It was a strange journey. The area below stairs had always been a bit spooky even when the house was bristling with servants, but empty it was very frightening and full of dark threatening shadows. However, I determined to go on. I knew that there was a staircase at the end of the main servants' corridor' that led up into the West Wing. That was where light was coming from, and I had to know what was up there, even though I was very scared. It was probably a reflection of the moonlight on the window panes; I was sure that there was a simple explanation, but I was curious and had to find out what it was, even though I was scaring myself to death. Eventually, I reached the bottom of the back servants' staircase, and started to climb up to the first floor. It was years since I'd used this staircase. We used it when we had guests in the bedrooms in the West Wing so we could access the rooms without being seen. I opened the door at the top very carefully and stepped out onto the landing. All was still and quiet. I tiptoed to the bedroom at the end, opened the door, and had a look round. It was all closed up and undisturbed, and it didn't look as though anyone had been in there for years. All the furniture was shrouded in dust sheets, including the bed so no one could be sleeping in it. I went out and had a look in the next bedroom, but that was the same, undisturbed with the covered pieces of furniture sitting quiet and still in the moonlight like so many shrouded corpses. These were the two rooms that faced the garden, and it didn't look as if anyone had been in them for years. I wasn't feeling quite so afraid now, curiosity was taking over. I stood still and listened hard, but all I could hear was silence, however I could smell something and I recognised it from the wards, it was a very faint trace of stale tobacco smoke. But who would be smoking up there? I crossed over and had a look in the two suites on the other side of the corridor, and the picture was much the same in there, the furniture was shrouded in dust sheets and the rooms were closed up, except I noticed that one of the dust sheets in the end bedroom had been slightly disturbed, as if someone had caught it as they passed and unknowingly pulled it along with them. I was baffled. There had been no one living in this part of the house for many years, probably since the war began, and there was a trace of stale tobacco smoke in there as well.

It was hardly a revelation, a trace of tobacco smoke and a slightly disturbed dust sheet, and I began to realise that it was really late, so I crept out of the bedroom and carefully closed the door behind me. I didn't know what I thought I would find, but I hadn't discovered anything, only smoke and mirrors, and there was a logical explanation for all of it. Parkes could easily have disturbed the dust sheet or even sat on the chair and had a secret smoke. I was letting my imagination get the better of me. It was probably nothing but moonlight that I saw, glinting off the windows or some other trick of the light. I'd seen it twice now so it must be the way the moonlight at night reflected off those particular windows in that corner of the West Wing. It was either that or the house was haunted. The thought of ghosts made me long for my own apartments and I felt silly and not a little embarrassed creeping around the house so late. What would Lady Leaversham think if she found out? It was no way to repay her many kindnesses, so I set off along the landing carefully shading my candle until I reached the great hall. All was quiet and still in there, as if its soul had died.

I crept carefully down the stairs and wasn't quite ready to return to my rooms. So I sat at the bottom, again remembering Felicity's wedding and my darling Guy. Was he dead? Of course he was. Only fools clung to the idea that loved ones, 'missing believed killed' were alive after a year of waiting. The problem with mechanised weapons was that they had the power to blow a man literally to pieces leaving no evidence that he ever existed, and that is probably what happened to Guy. Perhaps his ghost had returned to haunt the West Wing? Guy, oh Guy, even his ghost would be better than this aching void. I wondered if I would I ever be able to put him out of my mind, and live a normal life again, maybe meet someone else and fall in love. I couldn't imagine it happening, but I had to start concentrating more on the future, and stop dwelling so much on the past. As I sat there quietly thinking, I got that same strange feeling again that I was being watched. I quickly stood up and looked at the upstairs gallery. I was sure I detected a slight movement somewhere above me on the first floor balustrade, but again I couldn't be sure. I was suddenly very, very, tired. I couldn't allow myself this level of self indulgent grieving for too long, or I would become really unstable. I found I was shaking again, so much so that I thought I was going to drop my candle. I gave myself a stern talking to and pulled myself together, then walked up the staircase and onto my rooms. There was no one on the first floor corridor, I was quite alone, as I knew I would be. I walked along the corridor and let myself into my rooms and then quite suddenly and inexplicably I burst into tears. Was it with disappointment? Had I hoped to find something or someone in those deserted upstairs bedrooms? I didn't know. Anyway, whatever it was that I was hoping to find simply didn't exist anymore, so I indulged myself and wept quietly for a while before getting ready for bed. I soon fell asleep, but I had disturbing dreams.

I awoke with a headache, and felt ill all the next day. I decided that I would stop my midnight wanderings as they were pointless, they were upsetting me, and they would annoy Lady Leaversham if she found out about them. Having made my decision, I stuck to it, because it would be embarrassing if anyone ever heard me prowling about in the dead of night the night. As it was I don't think I'd been heard as no one said anything about my midnight ramblings, and I was true to my decision and didn't go exploring again, neither did I see the light in the West Wing again, so it was probably all just my imagination.

24

One thing that really puzzled me during this time was the fact that Lady Leaversham didn't want her son's names put on the village war memorial. She gave a generous donation towards its construction, but was adamant that their names should be left off it. I think the village committee felt quite slighted, but she would not change her mind. She said she wanted a private memorial in The Hall's chapel, and that would be sufficient, but when Felicity wrote to ask what kind of a memorial she was thinking of she remained silent on the matter. We were both confused by her refusal to commemorate the bravery of her sons, but we put it down to her age and growing eccentricity.

At the end of March Lady Leaversham and I received a letter from Felicity announcing that she was pregnant. We were all delighted. Lady Leaversham's eyes filled with tears at the news and she seemed lost in thought for a while. Eventually she looked at me and smiled, but she said something odd that didn't make any sense to me at the time. She said she had been expecting some news of this kind and it would really complicate matters. I thought she meant that now she would have to leave The Hall and go and visit her daughter and grandchild. Perhaps it was because Felicity's child would be the heir to Leaversham Hall, and it made her feel the cruel loss of her heirs, the twins, more acutely. She seemed to struggle with herself for a while, and I felt that she wanted to tell me something, but the moment passed, and all she told me to do was ring for Parkes. When he materialised she asked him to bring up a bottle of the finest vintage champagne and ask Mrs. Parkes to join us in drinking to the health of the new heir to the Leaversham and Ellerswood estates.

Some weeks after she wrote to us with her wonderful news, Felicity wrote again with a most surprising request. The government were now allowing relatives to visit and tour the battlefields in

Northern France and she wanted to go and find Garth's grave and see if she could find out anything about Guy, and she wanted me to accompany her. She felt that if she didn't do it now she never would. She certainly couldn't go when she was heavily pregnant and then when the baby was born it would be difficult for her to leave. She also wanted to see the battlefields before they were tidied up and sanitised. Because she knew that I loved Guy she felt that it would be a pilgrimage of love that we could both share. I must admit I had mixed feelings about the visit, but I would never have let her go without me. I owed everything that I was to her kindness and guidance. I also felt that it might do me good to get away from Leaversham Hall for a while and breathe some fresh air. My experiences when midnight wandering had shaken me a little and I felt that perhaps I had been living with ghosts for too long. Maybe a change of scenery was just what I needed. I also felt that if we spent some time together, Felicity and I could devise a way to persuade Lady Leaversham to leave The Hall and go and live in the Dower House in Cornwall near to Felicity and her expected grandchild.

When I approached Lady Leaversham about taking leave to visit France she was very supportive. She was quite sure that Mrs. Parkes could hold the fort for a week or two, and felt that the change would do me good. She didn't approve of Felicity's jaunt, but felt that if she did have to go, it was better that I was with her to take care of her. The main problem I had with visiting the battlefields was that I had no suitable clothing. I still had the clothes I bought while I was nursing, but I only had my uniform coat and no warm day clothes. Felicity had given me some sweaters and skirts before I left Cornwall, but I wore them every day and they were looking a little worn. The battlefields would be cold and wet and muddy. As usual Felicity had thought of everything. She instructed me to go to her dressmaker in Manchester and order whatever I needed. I was overcome at her generosity, but initially refused it until she pointed out that without suitable clothes I couldn't accompany her. I relented, and asked Lady Leaversham if I could have some time off to go into Manchester and she readily agreed.

I decided to go the following week, and caught the train to Piccadilly Station at Knutsford. I felt very strange being out and about again in the civilian world. I hadn't been in a major city since I left London to go on Active Service in France and that was nearly two years ago. Strangely I was quite surprised to find that the world had carried on without me, and things had changed quite significantly. For one thing there were far more motor vehicles on the road, everything seemed to be moving faster, and everyone seemed to be in a terrible rush. There were still a few uniforms to be seen, but they were beginning to disappear rapidly. The women's fashions had changed too, the skirts were much shorter and showed more ankles, and the hats were more utilitarian and more moulded to the head. A few daring girls had already had their hair cut short and shingled, but most women still wore it long.

It was a cold, fresh April day and as I walked to King Street, where the dressmaker was situated, I found I rather enjoyed being out in the world again. However, I felt very shabby and extremely old fashioned in my old VAD coat and Tam O'Shanter. I took my hat off and stuffed it in my bag. For the first time since the war I felt that I wanted to be a part of this new, modern world. Maybe I was beginning to heal a little. I found Felicity's dressmaker without any trouble and entered with some trepidation. I needn't have worried; they were expecting me and were very welcoming and helpful. She had written to them and explained what I would need for the journey to the battlefields and she had instructed them that I was to choose patterns for two suits and a warm coat. They sat me down with a welcome cup of coffee whilst they showed me swatches of beautiful cashmere and wool materials, in soft warm spring colours.

I was like a child set loose in a sweet shop. I chose a pale mauve and cream herringbone cashmere for one of the suits, and a lovely pale blue for the other one. I was measured and sized, and the dressmaker explained that they would create a dummy in my size on which they would fit the clothes, before I was summonsed for a final fitting. She showed me the latest pattern book, and I selected one pattern for both suits. It had a long jacket and straight skirt that showed my ankles. I was so excited. Once we had agreed on the suits, we turned our attention to the coat, I chose a heavier heather and green cashmere material for my coat and the dressmaker and I looked through some patterns that would suit the material. I chose a loose fitting, full length, kind of wrap around coat, which was much shorter than I was used to. I was in heaven Tanya.

Felicity had thought of everything. Besides the lovely suits, and the coat, she had ordered fine cashmere sweaters and two blouses to go with them. She told me that the clothes were a thank you for looking after her mother, and something to make up for the loss of

Guy. She was so very kind to me. The dressmaker's shop also had a list of items that we would need when touring the battlefields. It was compiled by Felicity and she had thought of everything, warm underwear, woollen stockings, and most surprisingly a divided skirt. I was quite shocked as I'd never seen one before. However, I had to admit it was a very sensible item for muddy trenches. She had also ordered a strong warm trench coat, wellington boots, stout boots, socks, warm sweaters, and a waterproof hat. It was quite a haul and I had never had so many clothes in my entire life. Once we had completed the selection, my old VAD uniform coat was brought for me to put on before I left the shop, and I'm ashamed to say that I felt a little embarrassed as it did look very worn and old fashioned.

I left the dressmakers and found a tea shop on St Anne's Square where I indulged myself and ordered tea and chocolate cake, just as I had in London during the war. I sat and thought of my friends, Sophie, Faye, Frances and all my other nursing colleagues. Most of them had kept in touch with me and we still wrote regularly, although my life had become quite dull. Miraculously, all their men had survived the war, and they were settling down to normal, happy civilian lives. I had chosen to sit in a window seat, and just sat and watched this new world as it walked by. I wasn't quite ready to enter it yet, but sometime soon I would have to, and I was beginning to think I wanted to, although I had no idea what I would do. At the moment, I stayed as companion to Lady Leaversham, as a way of saying thank you to Felicity and because I had loved Guy, but I didn't want to go back into service.

I wondered if I could perhaps take some exams, qualify as a teacher? I didn't know if that was possible, but it was a beginning. I made a list of things I could do whilst drinking my tea. I had a little money of my own so I decided to treat myself to a new hat to match my new clothes. I also purchased some pretty underwear and a new bag. I felt like a queen. When I returned Lady Leaversham wanted to know exactly what I had chosen and she seemed to thoroughly approve of my choice.

I returned to Manchester three weeks later for a final fitting, I could hardly wait and had been most impatient. The suits were beautiful, the material was so soft, and of course they fitted me perfectly. I looked at my reflection in the mirror and saw someone quite changed, a fully matured woman, quite unlike the girl who nursed during the war. I was still very slim, but more rounded and the assistants were very complimentary about my appearance, but then they were paid to be. However, without wanting to seem conceited I was pleased with what I saw in my reflection. I couldn't bear to take off the mauve and cream suit so I kept it on with one of the cream cashmere sweaters, and the all enveloping warm cashmere coat, whilst I went shopping. I arranged to have my uniform coat and the remaining clothes delivered to Leaversham Hall, and I left the dressmakers wearing my new outfit, and feeling wonderful. I had taken my new hat with me, and when I put it on the metamorphosis was complete, I was a modern, well dressed young woman. I returned to the tea shop in St Anne's Square and got some very interested looks, and I loved it. I had been far too worn down, overworked, strained, and grief stricken for too long to really think about the joys of life. Maybe I was starting to emerge from the traumas of the war at last, maybe I dared ask for something of life, something in return for all that I had endured.

Lady Leaversham was very complimentary about my new outfit when I returned that night. And when the parcels from the dressmaker's were delivered she wanted to see me open each one. I like to think she enjoyed it; perhaps it reminded her of her youth. She was horrified at the length of the skirts, but was most interested in the new styles. It was decided that I should get the train down to London and meet Felicity there rather than travel to Cornwall. We then planned to get the train from Victoria to the coast and cross on the ferry to Boulogne, just as I had when I went on Active Service. Felicity had learned to drive since the war, so we decided to base ourselves in Paris and travel to Amiens where we intended to hire a car which we hoped to drive to Amiens and then on to Albert and the Somme battlefield. We then intended to drive north and follow the trenches to Ypres, where we could visit Garth's grave.

I was quite concerned about leaving Lady Leaversham, but she seemed to be quite happy for me to go. I said goodbye to her after dinner, and retired early, as Wilkinson was driving me to the station early the next morning and I wanted to be up and ready when he arrived. I fell asleep immediately my head touched the pillow, but had disturbing dreams all night. First I dreamed about our coming visit to the battlefields, but in the dreams Felicity and I couldn't walk anywhere because the mud was like glue. Our boots kept sticking in it and preventing us from moving in any direction. We were so frustrated, because we'd travelled all that way and then couldn't explore. Then I dreamed about piles of corpses, which kept sitting up and laughing at us, cars that kept breaking down, and trenches that kept collapsing. I kept waking myself up, only to fall asleep and have even more bizarre dreams.

Sometimes I wasn't sure whether I was awake or asleep. Certainly that was so in one of my dreams. This time I was still in bed at The Hall when the door to my room opened and a figure holding a lamp entered. It was shading the lamp with its hand, so its face was in darkness; nevertheless I was sure it was man rather than a woman. Terrified I shut my eyes tight and pretended to be asleep. I felt the creature creep quietly over to my bed and stand there silently looking down at me. It couldn't have been there for more than a few seconds, when it turned to go. As I felt it turn, I opened my eyes for a moment and caught the side view of its face. Well I say face, it was lit from underneath by the oil lamp, which rather threw it into shadow, but even so I could tell it was completely featureless, as though it had been made of a sort of wax that had melted and reformed without any definition of feature. It looked horrific in the half light and I couldn't stop myself from taking a sharp breath. I'm sure the figure heard, for it seemed to falter for a second, and I felt, rather than saw, it turn and look at me again, but by then I had quickly closed my eyes, and resumed my sleeping pose. It must have been satisfied that I was asleep, because it then left the room. Once the creature had gone I lay there in the darkness, half asleep, wondering if I'd dreamed it, or if it had really happened. Convinced it was just a dream I eventually drifted back to sleep and more frustrating dreams.

When I awoke the following morning I was convinced that the coming visit to the battlefields of Northern France had triggered my dormant memory and caused me to dream about the trenches, the bodies, and the disfigured phantom who visited my room. Even so that dream disturbed me more than the others, because there was something oddly familiar about the apparition, and I couldn't think what it was. Anyhow, in the excitement the following morning I forgot all about it, and it wasn't until we were in France that the memory returned to haunt me.

Felicity and I had arranged to stay in a hotel close to Victoria Station. Bertie had driven her up to London, but was accompanying us no further, as his leg was still too bad for him to cope with the mud, and shell holes of the battlefields. At first he had insisted in accompanying Felicity to France as he was far from happy about her 'jaunt', as he referred to it, but she told me that it wasn't difficult to dissuade him from coming, because he was still severely traumatised by his experience on the Somme, and although he was deeply concerned about the welfare of his wife, he didn't really want to return to the scene of that battle, so Felicity got her wish to travel alone with only me as a chaperone. Although Bertie was concerned about her visit, he fully understood why she wanted to go; he knew better than anyone how distressed she had been by the death of her twin brothers.

I caught a taxi from Euston and met them at the hotel. They both looked extremely well and very happy, particularly Felicity, who was blooming. Pregnancy obviously suited her. I was relieved to see that she was wearing a similar suit to mine and had a warm tweed coat in tow. I was always afraid of looking like a provincial housekeeper next to her. She was always dressed so immaculately, even her nurse's uniform looked smarter than anyone else's, but I needn't have worried, my outfits were quite suitable. We had tea together, and talked about our coming trip and all our plans. Bertie harboured grave doubts about our ability to manage alone, and warned us time and again to be very, very careful, but he had accepted that we were going and succumbed with good grace, as he said, he knew better than to argue with two wartime nurses.

We caught the boat train the following morning, and a very concerned Bertie saw us off, convinced he'd never see Felicity again. The crossing was quite smooth and we were in Boulogne by late afternoon. We stayed in the same dowdy little Hotel Louvre, where I and my fellow VADs were housed before we moved to Etaples. Once we had checked in, we went for a wander round the town before dinner, and I found it looked much the same, although it was quieter as it was no longer teaming with nurses and officers. I showed Felicity the shop where I had bought my crepe de chine blouse with the crystal buttons, and felt momentarily very sad.

We dined out and got to bed early then the following morning caught the main Boulogne to Paris train. It followed the same route along the coast that we had travelled as nurses. When we reached Etaples I hung out of the window trying to get a glimpse of the hospital. I could see that the huts were still there, but most of the marquee hospitals seemed to have been dismantled, and the whole thing was reduced in size to a mere shadow of its former self. I felt very nostalgic looking out over those dunes and remembering the emotionally charged and intense years I spent nursing there. Felicity busied herself with a magazine and pretended not to notice how affected I was, and I was grateful. I couldn't have spoken about how

I felt seeing it all again. After living through that war, our emotions would never seem as vivid and alive as they did then.

25

Felicity had prepared well for the trip. Bertie had advised what to take and helped her compile her list. He emphasised how bad the mud was and that the mud and general filth would ruin any good clothes we had. I was a bit put out at first, I had only had the opportunity to wear my lovely suits in Boulogne and Paris and I so wanted to wear my new clothes and show off a bit, but Felicity had more sense than me and insisted that they had to be left behind in Paris. Consequently we travelled to Amiens wearing thick sweaters, divided skirts, heavy boots and trench coats. Bertie had advised us well as the old battlefields were in a terrible state and any good clothes would soon have been ruined. They were also very cold and inhospitable and we were glad of our extra layers. We didn't have any definite plan, other than we would head for the Somme battlefield via Amiens and Albert. Looking back we were very naive, goodness knows, just turning up like that so soon after the war. It was years before tours of the battlefields were efficiently organised, and everything was still in a terrible mess. I don't know what we expected to achieve, an understanding, a desire to see how it really was for the men that we loved? I don't really know, but I know that I never, ever regretted going before the battlefields had been cleared and tidied up a little. We saw them in their raw state, almost as they were when the fighting stopped, and the men returned home. It helped us to understand just a small fraction what they had experienced, even if it was only the dreadful conditions and the discomfort that they had to endure, which was indescribable.

We picked up a vehicle in Paris and drove to Amiens. I was very impressed with Felicity's handling of the car, although there was quite of lot of gear grinding, and bumping going on. The road wasn't marvellous, but it was only lightly rutted until we reached Amiens, when it deteriorated considerably. The name, Amiens, still had the power to instil terror in me; Amiens, the place where the allies had only just managed to stop the Germans from breaking through in 1918. I hadn't forgotten the chaos at Etaples as wave upon wave of doctors, sisters and their patients poured into the hospital as one by one their casualty stations were overrun by the rapidly advancing German Army. How we accommodated them I'll never know. Apart from dealing with the chaos we had to face the possibility that for the first time since the beginning of the war, there was a real possibility that the Allies may be defeated.

I never thought then that I would be returning to visit Amiens in peace time and the reality was quite a shock. This was where the war damage really began in earnest. It had been smashed to pieces by enemy shellfire and whole areas had been completely reduced to nothing more than rubble, however, by some miracle, civilians were beginning to return home to start to rebuild their city. Signs of life where everywhere, houses were being rebuilt, roads repaired, and shops and cafes were open for business again. We managed to find a small cafe and had a plain but substantial meal of soup, bread and cheese, and red wine, before we continued our journey to Albert and the Somme battlefield.

Once we left Amiens the road really started to deteriorate badly, as there had been fierce fighting in the area. The army had made some repairs and filled in the worst of the shell damage, but Felicity had to swerve all the time to avoid shell holes and war debris. I don't know how she did it. All the way down to Albert, we encountered groups of Tommies who had volunteered to stay on and help to clear the battlefields, and they exchanged good hearted banter with us in true army style. Many French and Allied soldiers had volunteered to stay on in the army in France when the hostilities ceased, to help with the clean-up operation, which was a daunting task. The structural damage was immense, and there were four years of unburied bodies still lying in the mud all over the battlefields. No one could even start to estimate how many there were, but it ran into thousands and they all had to be identified and given a Christian burial. There was also the massive problem of war debris, with unexploded shells and bombs lying hidden in the mud, each one had to be carefully defused and made safe. The devastation was so extensive at Verdun that the French didn't even attempt to clear the area where the worst of the fighting had taken place, they had simply declared the whole area a burial ground and constructed a moving and dramatic war monument to the dead.

As we progressed slowly along the road we drove past ruined villages, some of them little more than a pile of bricks and rubble. They were unidentifiable apart from the crudely painted boards, which were propped up in front of the piles with their names crudely painted on them. Names that in 1918 put the fear of God into the whole hospital at Etaples, as one by one they fell to the Germans, places such as Baupaume, Clery Villers, Bretonneaux, Grisvesnes, and Hedauville. I couldn't believe that these piles of rubble had been of such strategic importance during that painful struggle. What would have happened if the Germans hadn't extended their supply lines to exhaustion and been brought to a halt on the outskirts of Amiens? Fortunately we never found out as they had abandoned the attack that was focussed on Paris and turned their attention north towards Ypres, and we in Etaples, and soldiers all across the Front, breathed a collective sigh of relief, only to start worrying again when the Germans threw their might against Ypres and the Channel ports.

The devastation grew gradually worse as we approached Albert, but O Tanya, nothing had prepared us for Albert. I can't describe to you the scene of devastation that greeted us, there was hardly a building left standing, the roads were littered with broken carts, trucks, burnt out cars, and skeletons of horses. It was simply awful. There was a row of army huts situated near the ruined Basilica where the golden Virgin and child had hung, suspended horizontally after the Battle of the Somme. During the war the Tommies used to say that when the Virgin fell, Albert would fall, and she did the day the Germans took it in 1918. It was just another of those strange mystical stories that the war spawned, the Angels of Mons was another.

Just as in Amiens, some of the former residents had returned to Albert, and could be seen rummaging through the rubble and debris trying to salvage building materials so that they could start to re-construct their town and their lives. It must have broken their hearts to return home to such a scene. As we had no definite plan in mind, we decided to approach the officers in the army huts near the Basilica, and ask their advice. The huts had been constructed to house the Tommies who were involved in the clearing up operation, and we hoped they may be able to help us. We thought that they may know where we could get information about the identity of bodies that had been unearthed in the clean-up operation. When they found out we had been nursing sisters, they greeted us like long lost friends and we were immediately invited in for a cup of tea and a warm by their fire. They were intrigued to know what we were doing there, and obviously thought we were slightly mad. Although they admitted that relatives of missing soldiers were beginning to turn up every day looking for their sons, husbands or lovers. Others simply wanted to visit the grave of a dead soldier. They told us that the clean-up operation was an almost impossible task, and there were so many bodies being unearthed and reburied that they didn't have much confidence that our pilgrimage to find Guy would reveal any new evidence, but they welcomed us anyway and we enjoyed our tea.

Whilst we were there, like Bertie, they warned us to be very, very careful. Although the army had reluctantly started to allow civilians to visit the battlefields and cemeteries, they were still very concerned about their safely because of the large number of unexploded shells and other weaponry that was still lying about. They warned us emphatically on no account to touch anything, especially if it resembled a shell. They had cleared most of the towns, the roads and the areas close to the roads, but they could give no guarantees, and really stressed the danger. I think that both of us thought that once the Germans had gone the danger was over, but it was not so. We finished our tea and thanked the Tommies then as we started to leave the hut to return to our vehicle, I heard my name being called out.

'Sister, Sister Amy, stop!' I couldn't quite believe my ears and for one moment felt as though I was back in the hospital at Etaples. Felicity and I both stopped and turned, only to see a wildly gesticulating officer running towards us. I recognised him at once as Christopher Quayle, a young man who I had nursed in Etaples back in 1917. He had been quite ill with a stubborn leg wound that wouldn't heal, as he was too ill to move, he stayed with us for some months and we got to know each other very well. I thought his leg was so badly damaged that he had been invalided out of the army, but looking at the way he was running over the rubble towards us, it seemed as if he had made a full recovery apart from a slight limp which I noticed later. He was quite out of breath when he finally he reached us, and couldn't speak for several moments as he stood trying to regulate his breathing.

'Sister, sister, I thought it was you, but I couldn't believe my eyes, what on earth are you doing here? One of the Tommies told me that a nursing sister called Amy was sitting in one of our huts, but I couldn't believe it was you. What are you doing here now that the war is over? It's so good to see you, it really is, I never had a proper chance to thank you for all you did for me at Etaples you were so kind and patient.'

He went on and on, hardly pausing to catch his breath until smiling I interrupted. 'I can't believe it either Captain Quayle, it's wonderful to see you so fit and actually running on that bothersome leg, but I thought you had been invalided out of the army,'

'No, I thought I was going to be, but then the war ended and I was fit enough to be considered as a volunteer for the clean-up operation and it's something I wanted to do. I needed to come back, you know, lay a few ghosts.'

'Well we both understand that, don't we Felicity? That's why we're here ourselves, to find out what we can about Lady Felicity's brother.'

'Well maybe I can help you. You helped me, saved my sanity during those black days when my leg wouldn't mend. I felt so low, it was terrible, and you talked me out of them and turned me round.'

He was so genuine that I felt really embarrassed, but simply told him I did what any nurse would have done, but he wouldn't accept that. However, I was delighted to see him and it was helpful to find a friendly face in this alien landscape that knew the ropes as it were. He was horrified when we told him that we intended to go wandering about the battlefield alone and insisted on accompanying us to the old Somme battleground. When we told him that we then intended to travel along the old Front to Ypres he became even more agitated, and insisted that we could not travel up there alone. However, he thought that there was a chance that he could escort us. He was due to go north in the next few days in a staff car and offered to try and wangle us a lift. We were delighted at this bit of unexpected luck. We had only had a vague plan about travelling to the coast and his offer was a Godsend. In the meantime he was going to see if we could stay in one of the army huts. We talked for a little longer then Quayle directed us to a cafe where we could get hot food before he left us to see if he could find somewhere for us to stay and make arrangements to accompany us to Ypres.

He returned about an hour later to tell us that one of the army huts was free and he had made arrangements for us to sleep there that night and then the following morning he was going to drive us to the old Somme battlefield. He was fairly sure that we could accompany him in his staff car to Ypres, but had to check that it would be safe. After we'd finished eating Quayle directed us to the army hut where we were to be staying. We then went for a wander about Albert before settling down for the night. I found it strange sleeping in an army hut again; all the smells were so familiar to me, the unseasoned wood, the paraffin of the Beatrice stove, and the smoke from the wood stove. It was like returning home, and Felicity was quite comfortable too. However, the one smell we couldn't accustom ourselves to was that of rotting corpses. It was a sweet, fetid smell that pervaded every part of Albert and the battlefields. The soldiers didn't seem to notice it, but it made us heave with nausea at first, eventually though we became accustomed to it, but it was vile.

Quayle collected us the following morning. It was a cold, dull April day and it kept trying to rain. He drove us in an armoured car, which was just as well as the road was very difficult to traverse and virtually impassable in parts. It was pitted with shell holes, and although attempts had been made to repair it, was difficult to negotiate. I think Felicity was relieved to relinquish her place behind the wheel to a more experienced driver in a sturdier vehicle. The whole of the old Somme battlefield covered over fifty square miles of total, unimaginable devastation and the true nature of that devastation became clear to us as we moved further out of Albert. It stunned Felicity and I into silence. Quayle was really helpful as he pointed out the different areas where fierce fighting had taken place, and he explained what had happened there. Having him with us as a guide made it all come alive somehow, when we reached a sector that he considered to be fairly safe he stopped the car so that we could get out and have a closer look. We were on high ground and had come equipped with binoculars, so we had a good viewpoint. It was freezing cold as we climbed out of the shelter of the car, and the sleet lashed at our faces as we stood and surveyed the scene before us. We felt overawed and somewhat humbled at the sight, and could only wonder at the courage and endurance of the men who had lived and fought over that terrain for four interminable years. Before us stretched a cold, colourless, seemingly flat landscape, which was wreathed in mist and sleet. It was a horrible place bereft of any sign of life apart from small groups of volunteer soldiers moving about like so many worker ants in the middle distance. Quayle told us that they were out on burial patrol conducting the gruesome, but necessary business of unearthing the remains of dead soldiers for identification and burial, and marking and clearing unexploded shells and bombs.

The featureless landscape was interspersed with clumps of matted tree trunks, standing gaunt against the sky. Their stunted trunks, splintered by shellfire, looked like broken teeth. Crumbling, half flooded trench lines scarred the battlefield, each one fronted with rolls and rolls of rusting barbed wire supported at intervals by stakes. It was like a sinister forest of tangled briar stems, and had trapped and held legions of soldiers like defenceless insects while they were then picked off by German snipers. The whole area was covered with water-logged shell holes, some of them the size of lakes, and it seemed that the whole battlefield was littered with all kinds of war debris. There were piles of old cartridge clips, abandoned shell cases, every kind of rusting tin can you could imagine, old boots, rotting great coats, abandoned gun carriages, it was unimaginable. And an indescribable, sickening, acrid smell of death and decay hung over everything. It was much stronger out here than it was in Albert, and we found it hard to stomach.

The other characteristic of the Somme was the mud. There was mud, mud, mud, everywhere, but it wasn't like any mud that I had ever encountered before, it was a thick, fetid, clay mud that clung to our boots and our trench coats. We seemed to sink into it, and every step became a greater effort as it weighed us down, and I thought what a totally, life sapping environment it was. Guided by Quayle, we started to move out into the battlefield. I don't think we had any conception of how dangerous a place it was, there were still unexploded shells and grenades lying all over the place, many of them hidden in the mud. Quayle guided us to an area that had been carefully cleared, and was considered to be 'safe'. However, he told us very sternly to be very careful even here and not to disturb anything, because it could easily be dangerous.

We felt rather foolish, and a terrible nuisance. The sheer scale of the devastation we were witnessing overwhelmed us and in silence we simply followed Quayle's directions. We just wanted to see what a trench was like, to experience in some small way what our men had experienced. He led us to a communication trench and gestured to us to clamber down a makeshift ladder into it. We stumbled down, Felicity went first, and landed on filthy duckboards, which squelched down into the fetid water and mud beneath. My trench coat was already covered in mud, as was Felicity's, and I blessed her for her foresight in bringing suitable clothing. It was horrible in the trench. The water and mud seeped up over our ankles, it was bone chillingly cold and the smell was sickening, it was a mixture of death, decay, earth, mud and squalor and it choked you and made it difficult to breathe. I felt claustrophobic and slightly panicky. We were trapped between two walls of mud shored up with wooden struts and sand bags, and couldn't see anything but sky above. There were fire steps and periscopes and we both stood on the fire steps and looked out over the battlefield onto No Man's Land, and wondered how it must have felt expecting the enemy to attack at any time, or worse still being ordered over the top into an almost certain death. At least we were safe, there were no Germans out there shelling us or trying to snipe at us, but it was still an awesome experience. One of the things that really struck me was the fact that there was no colour anywhere, everything was dull grey or brown, there was no green, no sign of life, no birdsong or smell of flowers, there was absolutely nothing of beauty, just this feeling of being buried alive and the fetid smell. As I clambered down from the fire step something resembling a cat ran over my boots, and I looked down at the most enormous, mud covered rat that I have ever seen. I couldn't help myself, and screamed out loud, the noise caused a stream of rats to leave their hiding place and run down the trench, just as Felicity and Quayle came round the corner, like me she screamed, but Quayle hardly flinched. He was quite immune to the repulsive things. They were huge and hideous, bloated with the meat of corpses. If this was a trench that had been cleaned up a bit, I couldn't imagine what it was like before, it looked appalling to us. How did men live here? We looked into a dug out and saw the bunks where the officers had bunked down. It had a rough table in the centre, which was covered in candle grease and ring stains, six makeshift chairs, and two tier bunks, with rusting springs lined the walls We wandered about quietly, and all I could think of was Guy and what he had endured and how he'd endured it. I think Felicity was thinking of him too and Bertie and Garth and she was looking distinctly pale so I gestured to Quayle that we would like to leave and he obliged me. Felicity vomited as soon as she cleared the ladder and we helped her back to the car, where she just slumped down on the running board and put her head between her knees. I gave her a shot of brandy from the flask I'd brought with me and took a pull myself. Quayle had wandered off to have a smoke where it wouldn't bother Felicity. We were glad to be alone. We couldn't speak, but our eyes said it all. There were no words could possibly describe how we felt.

Quayle eventually returned to the car and we made our way back to Albert in the silence, as none of us felt like talking. I've often thought that we must have been mad to have gone back, especially with Felicity in her state, yet I never regretted it, and was glad that I went back before it had all been cleaned up and sanitised. It helped me understand just a little. On our return, Quayle told us that the army were making up daily lists of newly discovered bodies that had been identified and we went over to one of the huts that was acting as an office. The officer in charge there consulted his recent lists, but could find no reference to Guy. Anyway we were fairly sure that Guy was in the Ypres sector when he went missing, but thought we could lose nothing by checking all the lists. We thanked him and didn't know whether to be relieved or not. It was difficult not knowing, but better having his death confirmed; at least we still had some hope.

Quayle had arranged for us to dine in the officers' mess that night, where we dined on a hearty meal of bully beef hash, washed down with a bottle of rough red wine, and then made our way back to our hut. We were absolutely filthy; we washed our hands and faces, but were resigned to the fact that there would be no baths for some time to come.

It took a day or two for Quayle to finalise the arrangements to travel up the Front to Ypres, so he arranged for a Tommy to take us around the battlefield. We mainly saw more of the same, some areas were clearer than others, but it was all dreadful, although we soon became immune to rats, the smell, the remains of corpses, and the general sense of death and decay.

Eventually Quayle managed to obtain the necessary permission needed for us to travel with him and arranged to collect us from our hut the following day. It would have been impossible for us to drive up to Ypres alone, so we were grateful for his guidance and help. We had a fairly easy ride in the solid armoured car, and the driver knew how to avoid the pot holes. On the journey we witnessed more of the devastation of the Somme area. The driver told us that when the Germans were advancing across the old Somme battlefield in March and April 1918 against the exhausted and depleted Fifth Army. It was the atrocious condition of the battlefield that slowed them down and gave the British a reprieve. They just couldn't move men and ammunition quickly enough across that desecrated land in order to consolidate their gains. It was quite ironic really that a battlefield that claimed the lives of so many Allied soldiers, actually aided them in the end.

We drove up through Arras, and stopped at Loos, where I visited Tom's grave and thought of father. We also stopped at Vimy Ridge, where the Canadians fought so bravely then drove on through Lens, La Bassee, Neuve Chappelle, Armentieres, Messines, names that resounded with us, yet like the towns we identified on our way to Amiens, they were mostly just piles of rubble. But the battles fought there had claimed the lives of millions of men, and would never be forgotten. It took us several hours to get to Ypres and I was beginning to adjust to the devastated landscape, however if we thought that the Somme was bad, nothing had prepared us for Ypres. Initially Quayle took us to a farm behind the lines that did bed and breakfast and we left our kit there and had a meal with him and our driver before we entered Ypres. The fighting around the Ypres Salient had lasted over the full four years of the war and the town had been literally smashed to pieces. The beautiful old Wool Hall was nothing more than a ruin and the cathedral was totally destroyed, everywhere we looked we saw piles of bricks and stones and smoking bonfires. As in Albert, huts had been constructed to house the soldiers who were undertaking the impossible task of clearing the battlefield.

However, it wasn't the town that had the greatest affect on us, although the state of it had shocked us to the core. We had no experience of ruins on that scale; it was the surrounding area that made the biggest impact on us. King Leopold had ordered the dykes to be opened in the early days of the war and the shelling had broken the drainage system so the ground just couldn't absorb any water, also the ground was fought over for four long years, and churned up by shellfire. It had become nothing more than a swamp, a petrified forest, a stinking, putrid, featureless landscape. Apparently General Kiggell, when he saw the approaches to the battlefield for the first time burst into tears and said 'My God, did we really send men to fight in that?' Only to be told that it got much worse further up the line. I couldn't believe it could be any worse, but we would never be allowed any further into the battlefield. It was simply too dangerous, we could easily have slipped off the duckboards and drowned. All I could think of was Guy, writing his cheerful letters whilst living in this hell hole. It was too painful to contemplate.

At least on the Somme you could follow the outline of trenches, but the Ypres battlefield was a muddy morass, where the trees had been reduced to splintered stumps. It was nothing more than a series of boggy lakes of shell holes linked by duckboards in a sea of liquid, glutinous, evil smelling mud. We drove out along the Menin Road with Quayle, but we couldn't venture onto the battlefield. It was far,

far too dangerous. He told us that it had dried up slightly since the end of the fighting and the smell was not as bad, but even in April 1919 I would not like to have fallen into that evil smelling mud. At the hospital at Etaples, the soldiers told us many stories of men who fell off the duckboards and were sucked under by the mud. Even when their comrades tried to save them they were pulled under, but they always made light of it, they never gave us an inkling of just how treacherous the mud was. It would be a struggle merely to survive the conditions here without the added complication of the enemy ranged on three sides of the Salient, all trying to kill you.

The debris here was worse than on the Somme battlefield. There were still the remains of rotting horse carcases lying about, although the worst ones had been removed, but it was the removal of human remains that was the priority and there were burial parties working all over the battlefield. The debris of war, mementoes of death that we saw on the Somme littered the landscape. I was becoming accustomed to the stench of death, but it here it was accompanied by the smell of burning as large bonfires were constructed to burn rubbish, the remains of animals and broken carts. The waste was dreadful. All we both could think about was that Guy had lived and fought in this God forsaken place for months on end in the freezing winter. I felt close to him here, so close, and I loved him more for what he had endured. We both did. I was worried about Felicity coping with all the emotion and the physical hardship of tramping around and climbing on and off lorries in her condition, but she was wonderful and didn't complain at all. I think she felt like me, that we simply couldn't complain when men had fought in this for years without a murmur.

We stayed in Ypres for two nights, where we attended a service in the ruined cathedral. It was a most moving experience, as usual Guy was uppermost on my mind, I felt that somehow, I had shared a little of what he had endured and it threw my uncomfortable conditions at the hospital into sharp relief. That was four star accommodation compared with this. As Garth had been killed in the first year of the war he had been buried out here and had a grave and headstone. We travelled to Zandvoorde to visit it, take photographs for Lady Leaversham and leave a wreath. Felicity said she was almost glad that he had been killed at the beginning of the war, whilst the fighting was clean and mobile and had not deteriorated into a trench war of attrition.

We made enquiries about Guy, but no one had unearthed any new evidence, so we felt we had to finally accept that he had been killed in the fighting. The whole trip had been a harrowing experience, but I was glad that I had decided to accompany Felicity. I thought that I had experienced war in the hospital at Etaples, but it was playing with war compared with this and it completed a picture for me. What an accursed generation we were and we would have to live with the blight for the rest of our lives in one way or another.

26

Felicity and I were both quite changed by our experience of the battlefields. It made us realise why the men didn't talk about the conditions in the trenches or the war generally, never mind the brutality of the fighting. Until you had seen the battlefields and stood in a trench, even a sanitised one, you simply could not understand how awful it was. I think the reason that they didn't talk about it was because they were unable to convey the horror and so they locked it away inside of them. If they said the mud was bad, well what experience had we had of mud on that scale? Mud sounded trite, fighting in a bit of mud would be inconvenient but not tragic. How could civilians envisage liquid mud, putrid with the rotting flesh of corpses that was like sinking sand that sucked you in until you drowned? They couldn't, so the soldiers, afraid of being misunderstood, said nothing and bonded together in their silence. Even we nurses on Active Service, who knew more than most, had no real understanding of what they were enduring.

We drove back from Ypres with Quayle in silence, which was broken only when we asked him pertinent questions about where he had served, what fighting he had experienced and so on, he answered dutifully, but made light of his experiences like most of the soldiers. The reality was buried deep within him and that is where it stayed for most of them. It was over ten years before the first war novel was published and the civilian population learned a little about the horror of the war. However, before the veteran soldiers and civilians could begin to deal properly with the after affects of the First World War, an even more terrible war was upon us. So it really remained for the later generations in the eighties and nineties to realise and understand the impact, the sacrifice and the horror of the First World War and the Tommies had to fight their demons alone and in silence. There was no counselling for post traumatic stress syndrome for them. I think your generation, Tanya, has a far greater understanding and appreciation of the suffering endured in both wars by the soldiers on both sides than either my generation or the proceeding generation ever did. Maybe we were too close to it, I don't know.

Tanya broke her silence, 'You endured and accepted it, we have lived in peace and prosperity, and to us the things that all of the young people did in both wars is unimaginable. The loss of so many young lives, the bombing of cities, the privations, we are awe struck that you survived it all. We owe you a terrific debt of gratitude that can never be repaid and we have the added advantage of education and hindsight. We know how it was and to us it was inconceivable. So we honour them'

The women smiled their understanding at one another and Amy continued with her narrative. Tanya was a good listener and rarely interrupted or asked questions, she was content to just listen to this fascinating story.

'Quayle dropped us back in Albert, where we said our goodbyes. We thanked him profoundly for his help, and we kept in touch with him for years afterwards by exchanging a card at Christmas. He eventually left the army in 1920, put the war behind him and started his own furniture business and prospered I'm pleased to say.

When we arrived back in Albert, we were very tired, but decided to collect our car and press on to Paris. During our days touring the battlefields, we said very little to each other, we were just trying to absorb everything, and also felt that we owed the dead some respect. We could never forget that those battlefields were really enormous graveyards. The work of the Imperial War grave commission had only just started and none of us had any idea how enormous the memorials would be that one day would dominate the landscape of that area. I did go back later and was amazed at the wonderful work that had been done in constructing the graveyards and memorials, but that my dear is another story.

Once we left Albert, we travelled up through Amiens to Paris, and we talked incessantly all the way. We talked about Garth, Bertie, dear friends who were now dead, my brother Tom, Guy, everyone and everything. It was amazingly cathartic. When we arrived back in Paris, muddy, smelly and unkempt, we drew some strange looks as we walked through the smart foyer of our hotel. We were so thankful to climb out of those filthy clothes and wash away the mud and death of the battlefields. We ordered a meal through room service and then slept the sleep of the dead. We were physically and mentally exhausted. Once we had recovered, our conversation returned to the living, and we left the dead on the battlefields. We spoke many times of that momentous journey over the coming years, and I'm sure that Felicity discussed it with Bertie when they were alone and intimate. I only ever discussed it with one other person, but that is for later. I related a sanitised version to Lady Leaversham on my return, but she could never have understood and I didn't want her too. It would have hurt her too much to have known what Guy endured.

The following evening over dinner, Felicity and I discussed Lady Leaversham. She was terribly hurt that her mother insisted in remaining in that mausoleum of a house now that the war was over and it was fairly obvious that both her sons were dead. She wanted me to try and persuade her to close the house up and move to Cornwall. I did stress that I had little influence with her mother, but would do what I could. I then told Felicity about the extraordinary experiences that I had had in the house, the feeling that I was being watched, the strange light in the West Wing, finding her mother creeping around late at night and the odd apparition in my bedroom on the night before I left for France. She listened carefully, but did not mock me. She said that the house was so large that it had always been a bit spooky when it wasn't full of guests. As children she and the twins loved scaring each other to death with ghostly stories about imagined apparitions, so she wasn't surprised that I had experienced occasional feelings of being watched. However, she thought it odd that I had seen a light in the West Wing. She laughed and said I was like Jane Eyre wandering about Thornfield Hall, experiencing odd sensations and not knowing that there was an unknown lunatic in the attics. I commented, somewhat wryly, that the similarity hadn't escaped me, but we both knew that there were no lunatics at Leaversham Hall, except perhaps me.

I confided in Felicity that several times during the months after I left Cornwall I thought I was having a breakdown. She was very sympathetic. She said Bertie had had similar experiences and gone through stages when he thought he was becoming unhinged. He had terrible nightmares about the Somme, about seeing his friends fall and die from gunshot wounds or worse be blown to bits by shells. In the years immediately following the battle, he often woke up in the middle of the night, screaming, drenched in sweat, but the nightmares were less frequent now. He still sank into dark despair, black dog days, he called them, when she had to try and help him to work his way back to normality. He thought at times that he was losing his reason. She too dreamed about the hospital and the terrible wounds she had to tend. She was sure that it was a common symptom experienced by all sensitive people who took part in the war. She was as equally sure that we would all eventually return to normality as the memories receded and life got back to normal. She smiled and patted her tummy and commented that she was sure that this little scamp would help the healing process. I fully agreed.

However, she was intrigued about the light. She, like me, considered the fact that it might have been the moonlight playing tricks, but it was odd. From what I had told her she thought that the light seemed to be coming from one of the West Wing bedrooms. I explained to her that I had gone up there and explored, but found nothing more than a disturbed dust sheet and a strange aroma of tobacco. She thought for a moment and then asked if I'd had the courage to explore the valet's rooms. I didn't know what she was talking about. I didn't know that there were any valet's rooms above the West Wing bedrooms, but then logically I wouldn't, as Felicity commented I would have had no reason to enter them as they would have been the responsibility of the male staff. They were rooms right at the end of the attics, but they could only be reached from the bedrooms below. They were for the valets of gentlemen guests. They would sleep there to be near their masters. They were reached from staircases between the West Wing bedrooms and adjoining bathrooms and had been constructed so that the valets could see to their gentlemen's needs without trailing through the house. It also meant that they were on hand and available during through the night if they were needed. However, those attic rooms were never used for anything else and were separated from the rest of the attics. There was door at the end of the main attic, but it looked as if was part of the gable wall and was generally kept locked when the rooms were unoccupied. The butler looked after them and the male servants cleaned them and changed the linen, so there was no reason why I would know they were there. I only had a vague notion of the sleeping arrangements of the visiting male servants. The two sexes were vigorously segregated and if you were caught in the gentlemen's area it was a sacking offence, so I felt it was safer just to ignore it. I asked Felicity if the valet's rooms were haunted and she laughed and said she had no idea. I then forgot about the attic rooms and we talked about her coming baby and the preparations she was making. I did envy her. If only Guy had lived. . . but he hadn't and all the men of his generation had died with him so the likelihood of me finding anyone else to marry was very slim, but I would have loved to have children. Felicity saw the wistfulness in my eyes and placed her hand over mine on the table and gave it a sympathetic squeeze.

'You are becoming maudlin living with ghosts in that closed up old house, perhaps I have been selfish asking you to look after mother for so long. You've been buried alive up there.'

'No,' I replied quite firmly, 'It has been right for me; I needed to spend time with my ghosts while I tried to heal and I'm happy to stay until we can persuade your mother to leave.'

'Thank you Amy, I owe you quite a debt of gratitude, again, but you must come and stay when the baby is born. It will give you a break, if only a change of scenery.'

'My dear, wild horses wouldn't keep me away!'

We left Paris the following day and caught the train back to Boulogne. I took a last nostalgic look at the remains of the hospital at Etaples as we passed through. However, that was in the past now, I had to put it behind me and move on with my life. I was still relatively young, but what was I going to do with it? It was almost as if Felicity had read my thoughts, tentatively she asked me if I had considered returning to nursing. I emphatically shook my head. I nursed to help the war effort and to share the burden of the fighting men, but without that incentive it held no interest for me. She then asked if I had considered an academic life, university perhaps. I just laughed, that's when the differences between us were highlighted, Felicity had never had to consider money when she made decisions about her future, whereas, I had to earn my own living. I pointed out to her, as gently as I could, that I couldn't possibly afford it. She said that she and Bertie had discussed my future, I had helped them and they felt that they owed me a debt of gratitude. I couldn't see why, except I think she was thinking of what Guy would want for me if he'd lived. She was aware too that it was unlikely, although not impossible; that I would meet a husband and that meant I would have to earn my living until I retired. She felt that with a university education I would have the chance of a better job. I was terribly touched and thrilled to bits. Of course, I initially made a show of rejecting her offer, but I have to admit that it was a like a gift from heaven for me. I told her I would consider it only if I could pay them back. She smiled and agreed.

We talked some more about what I subject I should read and how

I would go about applying. There were special schemes for returning service men so there may be help for nurses too. She said she would enquire for me. It was so unexpected, me Amy Scott, ladies maid, at university. It was unbelievable! Felicity felt that I should apply to Oxford, as that was where the twins went. I didn't care, the thought of university made my head spin. Again we stayed in the same shabby hotel in Boulogne from which I launched my nursing career on Active Service. Each step put the war further behind me and with the unexpected, yet generous offer from Felicity I felt that I could at last start to look forward to a new life.

The rest of our journey was uneventful and a nervous, but terribly relieved Bertie met us in London. There Felicity and I reluctantly parted, and I continued my journey back to Leaversham Hall.

27

When I arrived back at The Hall, it was late evening, so I went straight to my room to bathe and change. Parkes had informed me that her ladyship wanted me to dine in her rooms, so once I was ready I joined her there. She wanted to know about everything that I had seen, so I told her the sanitised version. She asked about Garth's grave and I gave her all the details that I could. Felicity had taken a camera and she was going to send the photographs once they were developed. This gave Lady Leaversham a sense of peace. She was too old and frail to visit his grave herself, but if she could see a photograph of the headstone and that was the next best thing. We talked for a long time and all I could think of was that tall, elegant, lady who I had been so much in awe of in the years before the war. She had run Leaversham Hall so efficiently and been a gracious and welcoming hostess. That was her world and she could not possibly have foreseen what was to come, but the war had broken her. She seemed to have shrunk physically, and she had aged prematurely, but there was still an indomitable light in her eyes. However, it seemed cruel that fate had dealt her such a blow. The loss of her beautiful twin boys, her husband and her entire way of life in less than six years, it was too much for anyone to withstand, but there were so many like her. So many mothers who had lost their husbands and sons as a result of the war, yet they had to find the courage to carry on somehow. I estimated that Lady Leaversham would only be in her late fifties or early sixties, but she seemed much older than that.

After dinner I went back to my apartments, but I couldn't settle. I had experienced so much in the last few days that my head was whirling. I was also so excited at Felicity and Bertie's generous offer to fund me through university. The thought that I may be able to go to a real university to study was something that was beyond my wildest of wild dreams. I had been studying on my own for several months now, learning about the world, history, reading the classics and generally educating myself, and I loved it, but a formal education was something that I had never even dreamed about. I was so excited and so restless I couldn't settle to anything.

My mind kept returning to the conversation that Felicity and I had about the valet's apartments that she had told me about above the bedrooms in the West Wing. Was it too late to go exploring? Did I dare? It was probably only nine o'clock, but it was dark. I could take an oil lamp and Lady Leaversham and Parkes and his wife would have retired, so I was fairly sure of being undetected, whereas during the day you never knew where Parkes was. I made a decision, I was going to go and explore. I picked up the oil lamp that was kept in my apartments in case of power failures. I lit it and with my heart racing, I set off for the West Wing. Felicity had been right in her description of the empty house. It was spooky and the oil lamp gave out a small arc of light which threw the shrouded furniture into sharp relief. Each piece seemed to loom out of the darkness and grow in stature as the light from my oil lamp fell on them. Shadows played all around me and I was, frankly, terrified. Yet I was driven by an all consuming curiosity. What on earth I thought I would find in the valet's rooms I had no idea. I don't think I expected to find anything really. I'm sure I thought that the light that I had seen was nothing more than a reflection, or moonlight, nothing more, but I was restless and inquisitive and this propelled me on in spite of my fear.

When I finally reached the West Wing I walked to the end bedroom, the one facing the terrace. I knew these rooms well and had no difficulty in locating the bathroom. I tip toed through the bedroom to the passage which connected the bedroom and bathroom. It was only narrow and quite dark. I looked to my left and sure enough there it was, just as Felicity had described it, a door. If you hadn't known it was there you would have missed it as it seemed to form part of the panelling, which covered the wall. I tried the door, which I expected to be locked, and to my surprise the door knob turned, so I gently eased it open. It opened outwards into the passage, and revealed a small staircase. I was so afraid I could hardly breathe. I crept quietly up the stairs and found myself on a small landing facing two doors. There was also another small staircase parallel to the one that I had just climbed up, which obviously led down to the bedroom at the back of the West Wing. I could smell tobacco again. Nearly faint with fear I walked to the door on my left hand side and turned the knob, the door opened and revealed a scene that is seared into my memory for ever. It was a smallish room set out like a sitting room with a sofa and chairs. The room was in darkness apart from one corner which held a desk. This was lit by an oil lamp, and there was a man crouched over the desk writing, however, I couldn't see his face as he had his back to me. I was so shocked I nearly dropped my oil lamp. I must have caught my breath or uttered a sound, because he turned round to see who was there, and I found myself looking at the melted face that had leaned over me, in my bedroom on the night before I left for France. I fought an urge to scream, but managed to control myself. I was a nurse. I had seen wounded faces before, far worse than this one, but it was finding someone hiding in the attics at The Hall that shocked me. Who was he? My legs had turned to jelly and my hands were trembling, as I fought to regain control of myself. So many thoughts rushed through my head I couldn't think clearly so I just blurted out,

'Who are you?' He turned and struggled to stand, and I knew immediately who he was, I would have known that figure anywhere, but there was a problem, he was supposed to be dead.

He then spoke my name, 'Amy, oh no, no – I never intended that. . you . . .

It was Guy, it was his voice. I didn't know how he came to be in this attic, or whether he was real or an apparition and I didn't care. It was Guy. I put down the lamp and ran towards him; he hesitated for a second then caught me in his arms. It was him, I breathed in his lovely warm smell of tobacco and leather, and felt his strong yet gentle touch, and then he was kissing me and I was kissing him and crying and kissing him, and hugging him, and crying again. It was complete madness, but I didn't care, Guy was here, alive, it was a miracle. Finally he let me go and held me at arm's length, but averted his head. I put my hand out to turn his face back to me, but he just shook it off and kept his head averted. I persisted and tried to turn it round. He resisted, I persisted and eventually he turned to face me, but covered his face with his hands. I could only just reach them, and I gently took them away. I didn't know what to expect when his face was revealed to me, but I knew it was crucial that I did not flinch. What I saw on one side was his young, old, handsome face, and I was overwhelmed with love and gratitude, but that was only one side of his face. The other had been badly wounded, and was nothing but scar tissue. It looked as if someone had melted one side of his face below the eye. He had been hit in the face by shrapnel I found out later, and as the wound healed his features had merged into an indistinguishable mass of scar tissue below his eye. I cannot deny that initially I was shocked. It was a mess, but it didn't alter my feelings for him in any way. It just made me love him more, but it was a love tinged with pity for the suffering he must have endured.

I guided him to the sofa and gently eased him down. It was then that I noticed that he was limping badly on the same side as his face was wounded. He must have caught the blast on that side. I looked him in the eyes and asked him very quietly what had happened and how had he come to be living in the attics at Leaversham Hall. He looked down and told me in a choked voice that he had been involved in heavy fighting around Ypres (I felt a shudder go down my spine after what I'd just seen of that terrible place). It was the desperate last ditch stand to stop the Germans breaking through in April when Haig had sent out his 'backs to the wall' message. One minute he was involved in hand to hand fighting, and the next thing he knew he awoke in a hospital bed in a German convent. He had no idea who he was or what had happened to him. He was suffering from amnesia. He was badly wounded and learned by feeling down his body that his left leg was bandaged, and his face was swathed in dressings. His arm was affected too, but that was just a surface wound.

He said his time in the convent hospital was so strange, as he had no idea who he was, and just had to exist in the present. He said he was very lucky, the nuns looked after him well, and had a decent supply of morphine and other drugs, which were in short supply at that time in Germany, so he didn't suffer too much pain. The loss of his memory was far more distressing to him than any physical injury, they started to heal, but his memory didn't return.

There were other facial wounds on his ward, and terrible damage was revealed as the dressings were removed. It made him terribly afraid, but when they took his bandages off, the other men assured him that he was not badly deformed. However, he was not terribly comforted, as he knew that they all lied to one another about the severity of their facial wounds. There were no mirrors available on the ward or indeed in any of the bathrooms or recreational rooms that the men used. The nuns were aware of how difficult it was going to be for the men to cope with their deformities, and had removed them all. They allowed them access to a mirror only when they felt that they were strong enough to cope. Whilst he was on the ward he said it wasn't too bad. The nuns eventually allowed him access to a mirror, and whilst he was shocked, he realised that he was a lot better off than some of the men, who had lost half their faces. As his general health improved he was moved into the POW camp, which had grown up alongside the convent hospital, once the men were well enough they were transferred there as their beds were needed for more serious cases.

However, it was when he was moved there that he realised how badly wounded he was, and how it was going to impact on his future life. The other men kept were staring at him with a mixture of horror and pity. He hated it, and he felt as if he were part of a freak show, and more and more sought the company of the other men with facial wounds. They all tended to congregate in a specific area, and live there together apart from the main camp. It wasn't that the men were unkind in any way; they were just incapable of hiding their shock when they encountered fellow soldiers, who, in effect, had lost their faces. There was a German speaking padre in the camp, a wonderful man Guy said, and he got hold of a mirror then with tact and sensitivity he sat each man down and talked with them about their deformities, giving them confidence to face reality, and making them realise that they were still men, still human beings deserving of love. He prayed with them, and listened to their fears, and generally supported them through a very difficult time. Guy told me he just plunged into a black despair, which wouldn't lift, and he felt as if his life was over, whatever life that was, because he still hadn't recovered his memory, although he was beginning to experience flashbacks. The padre also talked to him about his past, tried to coax him to remember anything at all. There were clues in the way he talked, the fact that he was obviously an educated man, and it all helped. Then a minor miracle occurred, he had told his neighbour in the hospital that he knew a man from Liverpool called Edward Kingsley. His memory had been oddly selective right from the beginning; he could remember inconsequential details, but not the important things. Anyway, the neighbour remembered what Guy had said, and when he was discharged he asked the army to contact this Edward Kingsley and see if he could reveal Guy's identity.

In the December after the war ended Guy found himself in a convalescent home in southern England and Edward came to see him. He was in a bad way himself as his fiancé had died of a virulent disease whilst he was in France, and he was trying to come to terms with his loss. As soon as Edward walked into the day room he recognised

Guy, in spite of his injuries. It was a tremendous help just to have his identity confirmed, and Edward was very kind and continued to visit him and talk to him about his past and his family, and slowly Guy's memory started to return. Once the army had confirmed Guy's identity they contacted Lady Leaversham to inform her that her son had survived, but had been imprisoned in Germany, and lost his memory. Guy wrote to her immediately, and begged her not to tell anyone else that he was alive, as he couldn't face seeing anyone, especially me. He was afraid that I would reject him. She did as he asked, but in order to provide him with a home and privacy she had to remain at Leaversham Hall and that explained why she cancelled her arrangements to come to Cornwall for Christmas in 1919, and why she wouldn't leave Leaversham Hall or invite any guests to stay, even her own daughter. She was terrified that Guy's existence would be revealed. I was an inconvenience, but one she knew she had to tolerate, and as I seemed unaware that there was anyone in the West Wing, she relaxed and accepted my presence with good grace. However, she didn't realise that my curiosity had been aroused and that I had an idea that there was someone else in the house.

All the time we were talking Guy was searching my face for evidence of revulsion or rejection, which he did not find, because I did not feel it. I was ecstatic, it was a miracle and after the first initial shock, I didn't even see his wounded face, I just saw Guy, my Guy, alive. He broke off talking once or twice and turned away from me saying, 'It's no good, it can't work, leave here tomorrow and forget that I ever existed.' My training as a nurse came in useful here. I knew all the highs and lows, feelings of worthlessness, frustration that wounded men feel. They think they are less of a man, unworthy of a woman's love. Oh no Tanya, Guy was not getting rid of me so easily, I won't say we didn't struggle over the coming months and he told me over and over again to go and leave him, but he didn't mean it and I knew he didn't mean it. I stayed with him that night in the attic. He was so afraid that his leg wound and face would make him repulsive to me. He was a foolish man, and later as he relaxed and accepted my love, I would laugh with him as he limped about the bedroom, but that was much later on.

We lay in bed talking for hours, just talking. It was simply magical having him there, alive, and he slowly began to accept that I was not going to leave him, and still loved him. I kept hugging him, just to make sure he was real. Our love was just as potent as ever, a complete joy. He still wasn't ready to face the outside world, so we decided that I wouldn't tell Lady Leaversham, or Bertie or Felicity that he was still alive. This did not sit easy with me as they had been so kind and supportive to me, and I knew what joy it would be to Felicity to find out he was still alive, but I had to take his wishes into consideration. Oh Tanya I felt as though I had died and gone to heaven, I couldn't believe how lucky I was. I still spent time with Lady Leaversham, and saw to my duties, and she did comment that I was looking very well, because I couldn't hide my happiness. However, at night I retired to my own rooms, then as soon as I was sure that the household had settled down for the night, and Lady Leaversham had paid her daily visit to Guy, I went up to the little attic room and spent the evening, and the night with him, then sneaked back downstairs early, before Parkes was about and returned to my own rooms. It took time, but I did convince Guy that nothing had changed and he slowly began to relax with me. I did try to persuade him to let me tell Felicity, but he said he needed time. However, events overtook us.

28

Guy and I talked about everything under the sun during those magical few months together. I had only had a few snatched days with him previous to this, so it was wonderful to talk, and really get to know him. I was intrigued to know whether he had seen me in The Hall before I discovered his hiding place. He said that obviously Parkes and his wife were aware that he was alive and living in the old valet's quarters, but they had been sworn to secrecy. His worse moment was when his mother told him that I was going to live there as her companion. He had never told her about our relationship, and as far as he knew, neither had Felicity. He was furious with his mother, and banned me, but she explained to him that Felicity would only agree to her staying at Leaversham Hall if I went to stay as a paid companion to look after her. Otherwise she would have insisted that Lady Leaversham went to live in Cornwall with her. He reluctantly agreed, as he needed his haven of peace to hide in alone in order to deal with the trauma of his war experience. He was in no fit state to face people, even his beloved sister. Apart from his physical wounds, his facial injuries and his fear of being stared at, he was suffering from severe neurasthenia or I suppose we would call it post traumatic stress syndrome. That was why he chose to live in the West Wing, far away from the main living area. He had all the usual nightmares that many returning soldiers suffered from, and often woke up screaming and drenched in sweat. During the day he imagined that he saw piles of corpses on the terrace outside and the slightest bang would start him shaking uncontrollably. He couldn't go into society and function in any normal way, so he felt it was better that people should continue to believe he was dead that way he could lead a life of quiet contemplation and study.

I'm not sure how long he would have continued to live that life of enforced isolation. He needed medical assistance, but I think his mind would eventually have healed as his body healed and ultimately he would have needed the stimulation of company. He had a deep love for his mother, and told me that she had been a tower of strength, and quite wonderful in her acceptance of his requests. She was just delighted to learn that one son had survived the war and was alive and back where he belonged, but she had to bear the full burden of his ill health, and she was no longer young, but she had been a tremendous support to him. If he wanted his survival to be kept secret, if he wanted to hide away in the attics, so be it. She would acquiesce to any of his requests as she was so grateful that he had survived at all.

I told him about my despair the night I arrived, when I had explored The Hall, all closed up and silent. I told him how I sat on the stairs and tried to imagine The Hall as it had been on the night of Felicity's engagement ball. He smiled. He told me he knew I was in the house, and that he had crept down from his attic, hoping to catch a glimpse of me. He took good care not to be seen and had eventually discovered me sitting on the stairs in The Hall. He stood on the balcony above, shielded by one of the draught curtains and observed me below on the stairs crying. He said he didn't know how he had stopped himself from revealing his presence to me. However, his desire to come down and comfort me was eclipsed by his terrible fear that I would reject him and he just couldn't face that. He stood watching me for a while then he realised that I had sensed that there was someone there. He quietly moved away and fled back to his attics where he lay on his bed sweating and shaking. He couldn't believe the ridiculous position he had found himself in, skulking around his own home like a fugitive and hiding his presence from the one person in the world he wanted to be with. He knew his appearance frightened people, and felt that he had turned into nothing more than an ugly gargoyle, and he didn't know what to do. In fact Tanya, his facial injuries were quite terrible, I can't deny that, but the strange thing is that I never saw them, not really, I just saw the man I loved and the facial wounds became irrelevant. But he didn't know that was going to be my reaction when I saw them and he simply couldn't face my rejection, so it was easier to hide.

Guy admitted to watching me on many other occasions, and he tended to observe me when I was outside, because it was safer to watch from the windows of the West Wing, rather than risk discovery moving around the house. So when I was pacing the terrace in my agitation that cold February evening, it was his shaded oil lamp that I saw in the West Wing. The one thing that he underestimated was that although the light thrown from the oil lamp was quite dim inside The Hall it would light up the window from the outside and alert me to his presence there. He realised that I had seen a movement or a light, when he heard me rustling around in the West Wing bedrooms below the valet's room later that evening, and he was really afraid that I would find his hiding place. I told him that I smelt his tobacco, and he admitted that he hadn't realised that the smell could give him away. He loved his pipe and the tobacco he smoked had a distinctive smell, and he couldn't bear to give it up, but never really considered that it would reveal his whereabouts. I recognised it that night, of course, but thought it was a trick of my imagination, or wishful thinking. He said he was sure I'd check the valet's rooms, but of course, didn't realise that I knew nothing of their existence. When he told me that he had been watching me when I was really distressed, I was irrationally annoyed with him for remaining hidden, when I needed him so much. How could he watch me suffering, heartbroken because he was dead or I thought he was dead, when in fact he was living in the same house? He was too cruel. However, in reality, of course I understood his motives. I understood them only too well. We were both trying to come to terms in our own way, with the consequences of four dreadful years of war. The irony was that we were struggling alone, and unhappy only yards away from each other.

He also told me that he got used to my presence in the house, and although he couldn't talk to me, knowing I was near soothed him. Consequently, he panicked when I left the house for any reason. Usually, as I've said, I only left to go to church on a Sunday or to visit Margaret, but he kept a silent vigil at the window till I returned safely. He was distraught at the thought of me going to France and leaving The Hall for several weeks. He thought I may never return, and he may never see me again, so he broke his own rules the night before I left, and crept down into my room. He just wanted to be near me for what may have been one last time, and to see me at close quarters, before I left for France, possibly forever. I was so touched Tanya when he told me how he had watched over me, even if it was only for a few seconds. However, he knew he'd disturbed me as he was leaving my room, and he realised that I had seen him. He was sure that his appearance had frightened me, and it only strengthened his resolve to remain hidden from me. My rejection would have destroyed what tenuous hold he had on life and happiness. So the night before I went to France with Felicity he was the apparition that I thought I saw in my room, although I was half asleep and thought I had dreamt it.

I asked him if his mother was aware of his stalking of me. He objected strongly to the word stalking and I laughed, but he told me that she had no idea that he was interested in me, so would not have suspected that he was watching me. He didn't tell her anything because he was afraid of her sending me away, and she may have done that if she thought that my presence was causing him anxiety. Although, as he commented, my presence in The Hall was causing him exquisite pain, but it was also giving him a reason to exist, however, he was very careful that she should not suspect anything. His mother would go to his room every evening when I had retired and just talk to him, and her company had been a wonderful comfort. She would also sneak up during the daytime if I was resting. Parkes knew he was there, of course, as did his wife, but he was completely loyal and would never have betrayed Guy's presence in the house. It was a strange situation, but Tanya the men who survived the war were all damaged in some way, even those with no visible scars. I daren't think what agonies of mind he endured alone up there in his attic, but his state of mind must have been terrible when you think that he wanted the world to believe he was dead rather than face it. He also had to come to terms with the death of his twin, Garth.

When we lay together at night I told him about my trip to the battlefields and what I had observed. I didn't know whether he would want to remember the war, but he found it quite cathartic. He told me little anecdotes about his men. He had loved them, their strength and endurance. He tried to explain to me the unique relationship that is created by men thrown together in war, men who have to rely totally on their comrades, put their life in their hands. It was a potent relationship. We talked about the conditions in the trenches and on the battlefield. He asked me about the hospital and my patients, and we talked and talked, but after that time I don't think we ever referred to the war again. It was always there between us as an invisible bond, but we never talked about it in such sustained detail as we did in his little attic room during those special months.

We also discussed our future. Guy wanted us to marry and live a quiet life. I was in full agreement, but wondered if I would ever be able to pry him out of his attic. Every time I broached the subject he would find some reason to stay there a little longer. He was also still prone to periods of terrible depression, and he still suffered from nightmares, although I was now with him to comfort him when he woke. And so the five of us, Lady Leaversham, Parkes and his wife, and Guy and I lived together in The Hall, and played an elaborate game of hide and seek for several months.

I had to pretend to Lady Leaversham that I knew nothing of Guy's existence and she kept up the pretence that he was dead. It was very difficult, and I was terrified of slipping up and saying something that would give me away, but luckily I never did. However, discovering Guy's existence made me realise why she didn't want her sons' names to appear on the war memorial. She couldn't allow Garth's name to go on and not Guy's, but she couldn't allow the name of a man who was still alive to go on a memorial to the dead. Her refusal and the reason she gave, that she wanted her own memorial, caused some ill feeling in the village, but there was little else that she could do. And so we played out our elaborate farce, but looking back it was inevitable that something would happen to alter the status quo, and so it did.

29

One summer's evening I had been into the village to see Margaret. We had become very close since my father's death and she was the only link that I had to him now. It had been a very hot summer's day and the ground seemed to have soaked up the heat and radiated it back into the night. The air was full of the smells of newly mown grass, wild flowers and the warmth of summer. I felt more alive than I had ever felt in my life before, so happy, so in love, so peaceful, it was wonderful. The dark days of the war were slowly receding. I still had an occasional nightmare, but my life was now more about the future, about living and no longer focused exclusively on death, decay and destruction. I hadn't believed that I would ever feel like this again during the war.

I decided to walk back up the main front drive of The Hall rather than come the back way across the fields. I don't know why, it was just a whim. The drive, as I've described before, wound round and you couldn't actually see the house until you turned the last bend and it came into view, it was a clever trick of the garden designers. I was in my own little dream world of the future, of country cottages and Guy and children, when I became aware of the smell of smoke, a pungent cloying smell of smoke quite unlike that of garden bonfires. I couldn't understand what it was, but I realised that it was coming from the direction of The Hall and I could see wisps of smoke rising above the trees, alarmed I broke into a run, but it's a long drive and I quickly became breathless and had to keep stopping. Eventually I turned the last corner and the house came into view. I froze as I saw the spectacle that greeted my eyes. The whole of the far end of the East Wing was ablaze, flames were starting to shoot into the sky, and smoke was billowing out of the top windows.

Men were starting to arrive from the village and they were trying to quench the flames with buckets of water, but it was an impossible task. I ran up to the nearest one, a chap called Wood, to ask what was happening. He said that men had gone into the house to look for Lady Leaversham, the butler, Parkes, and his wife.

'But,' I thought with horror, 'no one would be looking for Guy, because no one knew he was there!' I ran up the remainder of the drive and quickly assessed the situation. How was I going to get to Guy quickly and help him to get out of the attic? The fire was at the far end of the house, so he probably wasn't even aware that there was a fire. There was no such thing in those days as fire alarms. Even if he realised that the house was on fire he would be terrified of leaving his sanctuary and facing the world. I had to make a quick decision. The men of the village would be looking for Lady Leaversham, it was down to me to rescue Guy, but how, how? I ran round the side of the house and entered the servants' quarters. Parkes and his wife were nowhere to be seen, but I couldn't worry about them. I didn't know how quickly fire spread so I didn't know how much time I had to get to Guy and get him out. He was still not terribly agile because of his injured leg, so it was not going to be easy for him to manage the stairs, but worse than that how would he react to danger, would his shell shock return? Would he freeze, and refuse to leave his sanctuary? All these thoughts were whirling in my brain as I ran around to the servant's entry.

I had decided that the safest way to the West Wing would be along the servants' corridor, the one that ran the length of the house. The fire seemed to be contained in the East Wing for the time being anyway, so I had time on my side. I don't know where I got my strength from that day. I flew along the servants' corridor' until I reached the staircase at the end that led to the bedrooms in the West Wing. It was the same staircase that I had used when I was investigating the West Wing bedrooms the night I'd noticed a light in one of the windows. As I flew up the staircase and onto the landing, wisps of smoke were already wreathing their way down the corridor, and making me cough. I had to hurry, because there was no exit from the servants' corridor' at the western end and we had to go back down the corridor towards the fire in the East Wing and there was every danger that we could be cut off. That was still the safest option though, because there was little flammable material in the way of furniture and material to feed the fire down there. I rushed into the bedroom and up the little stair case to the attic. When I burst in Guy was standing at the window, aware that something was wrong as he could see the men rushing around outside, and he could smell the smoke, but he had no idea that the house was on fire, or that he was in extreme danger. He quickly grasped the gravity of the situation, but I could tell he was terrified and struggling to control his nerves. In some ways I think he would have preferred to stay in his sanctuary and die rather than face the world outside, but I was not going to give him time to consider any option but escape.

I grabbed his stick and he lent on me for balance. He moved painfully slowly, but I had to be patient. We managed to struggle down the little stair case to the West Wing bedroom, but I was alarmed to see that it was rapidly filling with smoke. I had no way of knowing how quickly the fire had spread and no one knew we were in there, so I had to move swiftly. Guy moved as rapidly as he could across the bedroom, and I left him to struggle unaided whilst I went into the bathroom and pulled two large Turkish towels out of the linen cupboard and soaked them in water. I ran out carrying the towels and caught him up on the landing, which was now rapidly filling with smoke. We both started to choke as we headed for the servants' staircase. Our progress down the stairs was painfully slow, and we had to descend two levels to the servants' corridor. We finally reached it and Guy did his best to hurry, but he struggled. I could see by his face that he was in a great deal of pain and he kept telling me to rush ahead and save myself. What a fool he was, there was no me without him. We struggled along for what seemed like hours; he leaned on me, and with his stick managed to keep going. The smoke was starting to seep into the corridor from the fire in the rooms above, and as we progressed the smoke became thicker and thicker. Guy and I had wrapped ourselves in the soaked bath sheets and they afforded some protection from the smoke.

We passed the mid staircase that led up from the kitchens to the dining rooms and entertaining salons, and I briefly considered going up to the ground floor, and trying to escape through the front entrance hall, but if the fire had got hold above us it would be racing through there and we could get trapped. Also it would be full of men salvaging the paintings and valuables, and Guy might find it too difficult to face them. He was in bad shape now; the tension had brought back the nervous tick in his cheek. He was reliving the war I knew, and he looked haunted, but was struggling hard to control his fear, and I knew how hard that was. As we reached the servants' hall the heat was becoming unbearable, and we could hardly breathe. Hot ash and sparks were falling down on us as parts of the ceiling were starting to burn. I thanked God I had the foresight to grab the towels as they gave us some protection. We struggled through, I went ahead and held onto Guy's hand, we were coughing and were blinded by the thick black smoke and some small burning embers were falling into the corridor behind us. I just prayed to God that the corridor in front wasn't blocked with falling beams or masonry. As we passed the servants' hall there was a terrific crash, and part of the ceiling behind us collapsed. It would have blocked our exit if it had fallen one minute earlier. I shuddered and we soldiered on. We were half suffocated now, but the end was in sight. We struggled to the exit, and Guy had to fight to push the door open. It had swollen in the heat, so he had to give it a massive shove, eventually it burst open and we fell out into the servants' courtyard. We were out of the blazing house, but by no means safe. Masonry was crashing down behind us and even outside the air was still thick with smoke. Making one last huge effort we struggled out of the court yard and onto the front lawn. What a sight greeted us Tanya! We moved to the shelter of the rhododendron bushes that framed part of the gardens and collapsed in their shadow. We were exhausted and just lay there gasping for breath as we watched the inferno blaze. One of the men noticed us and came over to ask if anyone else was inside. I just shook my head. He sent one of the women over with a drink, and then we were left alone, whilst everyone struggled to save what they could. The lawn was strewn with packing cases, valuable paintings, antique furniture, and wall hangings which had already been rescued.

How we got out I'll never know it must have been pure adrenalin. The fire had spread along the house from east to west and the West Wing was now starting to blaze. All along the house flames leapt into the sky and smoke billowed out of the windows. It was a terrible scene. Men were still handing paintings and valuables out through the French windows that led onto the terrace. Others were trying to stem the fire with water, but it was impossible. Guy and I just lay there, wrapped in our singed towels, speechless. He was exhausted and was lying with his eyes shut. He had returned to some hell where I could not follow, so I just held him, hoping he would calm a little. When he seemed quieter and I had recovered a little I walked back towards the house. I needed a drink and so did Guy and I wanted to know what had happened to his mother and the Parkes. The local fire brigade had eventually arrived, but the fire had really taken hold, and they were virtually powerless. I asked one of them about Lady Leaversham, he looked at me keenly assessing my capacity for coping with tragic news, so I knew before he told me. She had been sleeping in her sitting room and had been overcome by the smoke. They found her on her chaise longue, where she had suffocated in her sleep, but he was sure she had not suffered. He questioned me about the others in the house. I told him about Parkes. Bless him he had tried valiantly to save the old lady, but he was old, and the smoke was too thick. He was suffering from smoke inhalation and burns and had been taken to the infirmary. He apparently kept trying to tell them that someone was trapped in the West Wing attics, Guy, the son of the house, but the village men said he was killed in the war; both the sons were, so the butler must be suffering from lack of oxygen and hallucinating. Sadly we found out later that the struggle had been too much for his heart and he died. I felt so saddened he was a wonderful faithful old man, but somehow it seemed right that Lady Leavesham and Parkes had died with the house that had been so much a part of their lives. When the life died out in the house after the war, they just existed there, relics of a grander era. Apparently Mrs Parkes had gone to visit her sister in the village so thankfully she was safe.

I located some brandy in one of the packing cases on the front lawn, and struggled back to Guy who was now sitting up, still wrapped in his towel, which was a blessing as it hid his face. He was just sitting there and watching as the fire destroyed his beautiful home. The towel protected his identity, but I had to think quickly what to do. How would he face the inquisitive intrusion of strangers if they realised who he was? I had to protect him. He had some notion of helping with the rescue work, but I dissuaded him, he just wasn't well enough, and the effort he had made trying to escape had exhausted him. We simply sat and watched the beautiful house as it was ravaged by the fire. God bless the village men for their courage. They had tried to save Lady Leaversham and managed to retrieve many beautiful paintings, and items of silver, porcelain and glassware, from the burning house. Later Guy rewarded them generously for their help and assistance.

Eventually I persuaded Guy to leave the scene and decided to take him to Margaret's house until we could decide what to do. He could just about manage to walk that far. As we left the house behind us, the fire was beginning to burn itself out. Margaret was wonderful, when she eventually got over the shock of seeing a dead man walk into her cottage, especially one with such an obvious facial wound.

Although she was dying of curiosity she didn't ask any questions until we had settled Guy into her bed. Then I poured a small brandy for both of us and related the whole story to her. She was stunned, but very pleased to learn that at least one twin had survived the war. I eventually joined Guy, and fell fast asleep, and neither of us woke up for ten hours.

When I did wake it took me several seconds to work out where I was. Then I remembered what had happened. The Hall, the fire would have claimed it by now. I looked over at Guy, but he was still sound asleep, so I quietly got out of bed and went downstairs. I asked Margaret to send for the doctor and then went back upstairs to wake Guy. He was much calmer than I expected, and seemed oddly relieved. Maybe with the death of The Hall he had buried some painful memories of Garth. He hadn't asked about his mother yet, so I didn't volunteer the information that she had died in the fire. I fetched a bowl of water and we both tried to wash some of the smoke away. The doctor, a very shocked doctor, came some minutes later. He was overjoyed to find that Guy had survived the war, even though he had sustained such terrible injuries. He gave him a thorough overhaul and checked his leg, which needed some attention and then he examined me. Apart from suffering from the effects of smoke inhalation we were both surprisingly well. I was bothered about Guy's mental state, but the doctor seemed quite confident that he would cope.

It was strange, I thought Guy would be devastated by the loss of his inheritance, but it never really seemed to trouble him, in fact he seemed rather relieved. He told me later that The Hall now had too many tragic associations and belonged to a different era. If it had survived he would have felt duty bound to live there and try and to run the estate, but now he was free of that responsibility.

Later that morning we returned to view the house. The sight that greeted us was heart breaking. The house had completely disappeared, the roof had caved in and all that remained were some supporting walls and smoking ruins. Guy set about organising the salvage operation, he seemed immune to the shocked looks he got from the men, firstly because they had heard he was dead, and secondly because of his dramatically changed appearance, which was a good thing. He worked hard and arranged for the goods that had been salvaged to be collected, catalogued and stored by a removal firm. I was relieved to see him acting so normally.

Whilst looking at the smoking ruins Guy finally found the

courage to ask about his mother. I told him as gently as I could that she had died in the fire. He was deeply upset. She had been his rock and saviour, but he, like me was glad she had been spared the sight of her beloved Hall in this state. As Felicity was the known heir, she had been contacted at once and was on her way up from Cornwall with Bertie. We couldn't continue to stay in Margaret's little cottage, so we opened up the old Dower House, which was still partly furnished. We instructed the removal firm to select glassware, crockery, pans, bedding, rugs, carpets and small pieces of furniture to make it habitable, and some of the ladies from the village came to help us set up home. Fortunately, it was nearly ready when Felicity and Bertie arrived.

The reunion between brother and sister was joyous to behold. When they arrived, I went out to meet them to explain that Guy was still alive, but had a bad facial wound. I told them why Lady Leaversham had kept his survival a secret, and why she wouldn't leave The Hall. Felicity was, not unnaturally, astounded, but also overjoyed. She rushed past me into the Dower House and grabbed Guy. She didn't seem to notice his facial disfigurement, she was so delighted to find out that he had survived, so she simply hugged him to her, until he protested and wriggled free. The four of us stayed in the Dower House, catching up on the past events, until The Hall and its contents were secure, then we all went back to Cornwall to stay on Bertie's estate.'

30

Amy and Tanya had been strolling round the garden for over an hour while Amy related her story. It was getting cold, so eventually they retired to the conservatory while she finished her narrative. Tanya was totally engrossed in Amy's story and didn't want to stop her flow, but with the reunion of Guy and Felicity, Amy had come to the end of her story and became silent. Tanya was quite amazed.

'What an eventful life you have had,' was all she could say, 'I find it quite unbelievable that you could have survived all that pressure when you were so young, and yet you talk about it all so calmly now.'

Amy sighed and looked at her hands, which were clasped in her lap. 'It was all so long ago, Tanya. I will never forget the people who fought in that war, but once I found Guy again, I wanted to forget it and enjoy some happiness.'

'What happened next?'

'Oh well Guy arranged to have the ruins of The Hall made safe, and he kept the land. He then purchased a small estate near Bertie and Felicity in Cornwall. There was a lovely house on the estate that looked out over the sea, it was perfect. We married a month after the fire, and moved into the Cornish house. We also bought a small house in Oxford, and I studied for my degree, while Guy completed a Ph.D. I was so happy. We commuted between the two houses until I had completed my studies, and then I became pregnant and gave birth to a wonderful son who we named Garth, after his uncle. Two years later I had a daughter and we called her Rebecca, which was one of Guy's mother's names.

Guy and I lived a quiet life together in Cornwall. We spent a lot of time with Bertie and Felicity and their daughter Sophie, and twins boys, Alexander and Piers.' Tanya smiled at the reference to the twins and Amy smiled back, 'I know, we couldn't believe it ourselves, but they are delightful boys, almost identical and so like their Uncles Guy and Garth. It's almost as though they are a compensation for the loss of Garth in the war. They are running the Cornish estate now, Bertie died two years ago and Felicity followed him six months later. They were inseparable, so it seemed natural that they would die close to each other, but they'd had a very happy life.

Whilst we spent a lot of time with both of them, we didn't socialise much elsewhere. Guy was always conscious of the way he looked and was more comfortable with his family and his books than in society, and we were very happy until his death last year. So Tanya, Felicity and I were fortunate indeed that the men we loved survived that terrible war and we were able to have happy and fulfilled lives with them, lives that were denied to so many others. After Guy's death I continued to live in the Cornish house until it became too much for me. Garth is now living on the old Leaversham estate and renovating The Hall. He's going to turn it into a conference centre and Rebecca is helping him. When I was choosing a retirement home, I wanted to be near them, so it made sense to select one in Cheshire, near to The Hall so that they can visit me easily. You are bound to meet them and I'm sure you'll all get on famously. They are settled here now, in the land of their ancestors, so I think I made a wise choice.

I like to hear about Garth's plans for renovating The Hall, but I have no desire to visit it again. I think it's best to let my ghosts rest in peace, although judging by my nightmare last night I don't think they will let me rest. You know my dear one thing I have learned is that war casts long shadows that are hard to escape.'